THE SHORTEST PATH HOME
IS THROUGH THE HEART

THE SHORTEST PATH HOME IS THROUGH THE HEART

Lynda Schultz

CHAPEL HILL
PRESS, INC.

This is a work of fiction. Names, characters, places, and incidents either are the product of the author's imagination or are used fictitiously, and any resemblance to actual persons, living or dead, business establishments, events or locales is entirely coincidental.

Copyright© 2008 by Lynda Schultz

All rights reserved. No part of this book may be used, reproduced or transmitted in any form or by any means, electronic or mechanical, including photograph, recording, or any information storage or retrieval system, without the express, written permission of the author, except where permitted by law.

ISBN: 978-1-59715-046-0

Printed in the United States of America

Published by
The Chapel Hill Press, Inc.
1829 East Franklin Street
Chapel Hill, NC 27514

ABOUT THE COVER

A childhood spent in the jungles of South America, the cultural centers of Europe, and the mountains of Southern China, have all combined to shape the creative vision of Simon Bull who has since become one of the world's most compelling living artists. His work is collected by royalty, presidents, celebrities, and museums as well as a growing number of private collectors who find their lives enriched by the color and emotion of his work.

For more information on Simon Bull's work, go to: harmonyfineart.com

To Simon: Heartfelt thanks to you for your generosity in designing the cover of this book and for the special gifts you bring to the world.

Lynda Schultz

FOREWORD

In my dreams, it was always the same. "Run, Annie Lizbeth, run!" I would cry. And run we did, swift as the wind through the dense forests that threatened to engulf us. If we could just run fast enough, long enough, surely we could escape the shadowy figure that followed in close pursuit.

The dream always ended the same. Annie Lizbeth and I, holding tightly to one another's hand, found our way to the edge of the clearing, our hearts pounding with fear, afraid to look back in case the shadowy figure had caught up with us. But the shadowy figure never crossed the clearing, because there stood Granny and Daddy, a sure and steady fortress against the dream intruder.

That dream haunted me through my childhood, and into my adulthood. It was only when I understood what the shadowy figure represented, did the dream end. Annie Lizbeth and I were running from our past, and the shadowy figure chasing us was the mother that abandoned us, leaving Daddy and Granny to pick up the pieces of our shattered beginnings.

At the tender age of six months, Mattie Rose and Annie Lizbeth Radley are left behind by their mother who prefers to seek greener, unencumbered pastures. Nine years later, these bright and high-spirited twins are ready to enter fifth grade, and conquer new challenges.

Supported by the love of their wise and practical grandmother, and their hard-working, loyal father, the twins' tenth year proves to be a time of fun, typical childhood foolishness, and also, a time of awakening to the realities of a more complicated world.

This is the poignant story of childhood innocence, resilience, the drive to overcome hardship, and the acceptance of bitter truth. It is the story of family and the unbreakable bonds of sisterly love.

Lynda Schultz

ACKNOWLEDGMENTS

TO JOSH: *My touchstone, and to whom this book is dedicated.*

TO HOWARD: *When you look up the word "tenacity" in the dictionary, your picture will be beside it.*

TO BRENDA: *My love, respect and admiration for you transcends time and space.*

TO LOUISE: *They say when one door closes, another opens, and there you stood. Little did you know I would send you draft after draft of chapters to review and critique. Words can never express my gratitude for your love, support, and encouragement during the writing of this book.*

TO PATRICIA: *They say if you have one true friend at the end of your life you were rich. That being said, you, dear one, are priceless.*

TO CHARLOTTE: *Who encouraged me to follow my path and write this book.*

TO MARY DARYL: *Friends to the end. You are a lifelong treasure.*

TO MUS: *If ever there was an earth angel, it is you.*

TO GRANNY: *Your spirit lives on in my heart, and your light guides my way.*

TO DADDY: *You left us much too soon and are sorely missed.*

TO THE CHAPEL HILL PRESS: *A special thanks to the publishing staff that took this project from spark to publication.*

HARRIETT'S GIFT

In our front yard stood several imposing oak trees, many of which had set down roots several generations before us.

Among these mighty oaks stood one in particular that towered majestically above all the rest. We called it "Granny's tree." Its branches grew in meandering ways, its leafy foliage providing shelter from the blistering summer sun. It possessed a silent, reverent spirit all its own.

Annie Lizbeth and I both agreed that if Granny were to be born again, she would come back as an oak tree. She possessed a masculine energy that was mighty, strong, enduring, and steadfast. We depended on these qualities in Granny, and later, came to respect and revere them.

How our granny came to be was a story of which Annie Lizbeth and I never tired of hearing. We would sit captivated as she recalled for us the wondrous, yet sometimes tragic journey of her mother's life. In order to understand Granny, you had to know from where she came. This is the story of Harriett's gift.

Harriett Crenshaw was the only, overly protected child of Henry and Mary Crenshaw.

As was the custom of the era, Harriett attended and completed all eight years of education offered to girls in the late 1800s. She received the basics in reading, writing, and arithmetic, a subject in which she excelled.

There was only one schoolhouse in rural Durham, North Carolina; a white, wood-framed, one-room dwelling located right at the edge of Main Street. The only transportation to and from school was attached to your body. Most folks call them your legs and feet.

Mrs. Lois Ann Johnson was the official schoolmarm, who oversaw the day-to-day administrative duties of the school.

Miss Hilda Mae Framingham was the school's only teacher. She ran a tight ship when it came to her classroom. Boys and girls were kept on opposite sides of the room, and if there were any classroom infractions, they were quickly addressed by a wooden yardstick Miss Framingham kept in plain sight for all the students to see.

At fourteen, Harriett received her eighth-grade diploma. Her formal education now complete, she worked alongside her mother, Mary, in a small dressmaking business.

Shortly after Harriett's birth, her father Henry converted the upstairs attic into a sewing room so that Mary could work from home and still tend to Harriett. Over the years, Mary taught Harriett the finer points of dressmaking, and by age seventeen, Harriett had become quite an accomplished seamstress. She delighted in designing wedding dresses and veils for local brides-to-be.

Harriett also helped her father Henry with light bookkeeping duties at his shoemaker's shop located right in the middle of the town square. Henry Crenshaw was a decent and hard-working man who worked long hours to support his family.

Harriett was good with numbers, and kept detailed records of Henry's end-of-week receipts, listing those who paid and those who owed for the shoes her father made or repaired. She was of great help to her mother and father, and they valued her dedication to both family businesses.

One Friday afternoon, Harriett saw a flyer posted in Jesse McGraw's General Store while running errands for her mother. The poster boasted that a community wide get-together was going to be held at Town Hall on the third Saturday of May in 1885. The civic leaders thought a community social would be the perfect venue to encourage country folks to leave their farms and meet some of their city-dwelling neighbors. The attendees of the "meet and greet" would enjoy an afternoon of socializing, fiddling, and square dancing. There would be a pot luck dessert table, courtesy of the ladies attending the social.

The social's organizers, Mrs. Bessie McCoy, Mrs. Sadie Penfield, and Mrs. Mavis Matthews, spent weeks personally visiting each of county's outlying farms, handing out the same hand-printed flyer Harriett had seen posted in Jesse McGraw's General Store.

Durham, North Carolina, was a small southern town, primarily known for its flue-cured tobacco. Most farm families worked long, hard hours on isolated tracts of land that bordered the county line.

What little bit of free time they had was spent sitting in church on Sunday morning listening to one of Preacher Jackson's fire and brimstone sermons. A Saturday afternoon community social sounded mighty inviting to many of them, providing a welcome break from the monotony of their day-to-day lives spent in back-breaking tobacco fields.

At seventeen, Harriett felt she was old enough to attend the community social unchaperoned by her parents. Henry and Mary were reluctant to allow her to go unattended at first, but knew that Harriett was a proper and responsible young woman. They granted her permission, with one exception; she had to go with a group of girlfriends. Harriet wasted no time in assembling some of her favorite companions to accompany her to the social. Since the flyer said the ladies would provide refreshments, Harriett and her mother baked a chess pie for the event.

Willie McCoy, Horace Penfield, and Robert Matthews were "volunteered" by their wives to arrive early on the day of the social. A huge turnout was expected, and every ounce of their collective masculine strength would be needed to pick up and place multiple tables along the back wall of the massive Town Hall gathering room where the desserts and liquid refreshments could be displayed and served to guests.

The three men carried table after table, perspiration pouring off their brows; their sweaty shirts sticking to their backs, until one continuous row of tables extended across the entire back wall of the Town Hall. The tables were draped in freshly starched and ironed white cotton tablecloths providing a neutral backdrop for the colorful array of homemade cakes, pies, and puddings that would soon cover it. Multiple pitchers of sweet iced tea and lemonade were placed at both ends of the serving table so that thirsty guests could help themselves.

When Harriett and her friends arrived at the main entrance of Town Hall, they were dressed in all their finery, heady with excitement. The Town Hall was mobbed with people, some of whom Harriett recognized and others she did not.

In the Hall, women clumped together in groups as they laughed about their children's antics, gossiped about who had on a new dress at church last Sunday, and complained about how much housework they had waiting for them at home after the social. The men clustered too, their conversations focusing on the year's tobacco crop, land taxes, and the cost of hiring farm hands and day laborers during harvest season.

The civic leaders took their places on the podium and extended a big welcome to everyone in the room. Special acknowledgements of appreciation were given to Mrs. Willie McCoy, Mrs. Horace Penfield, and Mrs. Robert Matthews for their efforts in organizing such a spectacular community event.

Harriett, whose attention had been on the speakers was surprised when she turned around and found her friends had disappeared from sight, swallowed up in the growing swells of happy, chattering people.

Harriett was holding her chess pie, draped with a red checked cloth napkin tightly in both hands, pressed close to her chest to prevent it from being crushed by the sea of people that stood between her and Mrs. McCoy's refreshment table at the back of the gathering hall.

"Now how am I going to get my chess pie through that crowd and back to Mrs. McCoy's table in one piece?" she pondered.

Slowly, as she began making her way through the crowd, Harriett held the chess pie in one hand, and used her other hand to lightly tap folks on the shoulder, as she politely asked, "Excuse me. Excuse me, please. Can I please get through?"

Harriett felt swallowed up by the surging tide of people in the room as she waded through them on her way back to Mrs. McCoy's dessert table. With her eyes focused squarely on the refreshment table, already groaning from the vast array of confectionery treats that were displayed upon it, Harriett accidentally bumped into someone and found herself face-to-face with a man she had never seen before.

Ralph Kelsey was a giant of a man, standing six feet five, his body rippled with muscles he accumulated during his years as a North Carolina tobacco farmer. He was of Scot-Irish descent; his ruddy complexion a gift from his heritage, and leathery, no doubt, from his days of working in the unforgiving Southern sun.

His deeply tanned skin complimented his deep, cobalt-blue eyes. His nose was long and narrow and above his thin upper lip was a small faded scar. His shaggy brown hair, streaked from the summer sun, had never seen the inside of a barber's shop. He wore it combed straight back, and the wispy ends of his hair flipped slightly upward as they nestled against the back of his neck.

Before Harriett could utter the words, "Excuse me," the tall man with deep blue eyes slowly surveyed every inch of the young woman that stood before him.

Harriett was embarrassed and unsure of what to say. No man had ever looked at her in that way before, and she felt ill at ease.

The petite young woman with narrow hips and slender shoulders standing before him was already blossoming into full womanhood. Her brunette hair hung loosely about her shoulders as the light from the window reflected the auburn highlights that ran through it. Her creamy-white, flawless skin was that of a city girl, untouched by the harsh rays of summer sun, or roughened from working the land. Harriett's eyes were the color of dark chocolate and fringed with long curling black lashes. Her lips were full and berry pink.

Harriett quickly mumbled, "I'm sorry if I bumped you; it was an accident, I assure you."

In an effort to make a graceful exit from an awkward situation, Harriett forgot that she was wearing a brand new pair of patent leather pumps her father had made just for this occasion. Henry had warned Harriett that the soles of the shoes were slick as ice. He had encouraged her to walk off some of the newness of the shoes on the dirt and gravel road in front of their house, but Harriett had not listened, fearing her new shoes might get scuffed and marred.

In her hurried attempt to make a quick getaway from the man with the piercing blue eyes, Harriett spun around quickly. The slick soles her father had warned her about lost contact with the floor, and before she realized it, she had lost her balance. As Harriett would later tell her girlfriends, divine intervention stepped in, and she and her chess pie were rescued from disaster by the steady, strong arms of Ralph Kelsey.

Ralph held Harriett in his arms a few seconds before lifting her back to her feet. As she composed herself and inspected her pie for damage, he inhaled the heady aroma of lilac cologne that lingered in her freshly washed hair.

He then escorted her and the chess pie through the throngs of people that filled the Town Hall to the safety of Mrs. Bessie McCoy's refreshment table.

Mrs. McCoy, shocked to see young Harriett with a male companion, most particularly one of Ralph Kelsey's reputation, looked first at Harriett, and then at Ralph, as she gingerly took the pie from Harriett and placed it on the table.

"My, my, Harriett, who do we have here?" a sarcastic Mrs. Bessie McCoy inquired, knowing perfectly well it was Ralph Kelsey.

Harriett face flushed with color, as she suddenly realized she did not know the name of the person standing beside her. "Why, I don't know, Mrs. McCoy. We haven't had time to introduce ourselves."

Before Harriett could turn her head back in Ralph's direction, his cobalt-blue eyes took on a menacing glare as he shot a warning look at Mrs. McCoy. Knowing that Ralph Kelsey was not a man with whom she wanted to reckon, Bessie McCoy quickly excused herself by saying, "Harriett, dear, I hope you don't consider me rude but I must attend to the other guests," as she hurriedly made her way to the other end of the table.

The room was flooded with people, and the fiddlers were beginning to warm up their instruments. Harriett could barely hear herself think when the tall man with blue eyes tapped her on the shoulder and asked if she wanted to find a quieter place to talk. Harriett's heart skipped a beat as she said yes, and quickened even more when he offered her one of his rough, chapped hands to guide her down the steps of Town Hall to the street below.

Before they began their stroll down Main Street, Ralph looked down at Harriett and said, "With all that ruckus inside, I don't think we've had the opportunity to exchange names." A smile inched across his face, as he jokingly said, "I'll tell you mine if you'll tell me yours."

Harriett, whose youth and inexperience were no match for the cunning charms of Ralph Kelsey, looked into his dark eyes and said, "My name is Harriett Crenshaw, and I am very pleased to make your acquaintance."

With their eyes still locked together, Ralph looked at Harriett and said, "The pleasure is all mine Miss Crenshaw, so let me introduce myself. My name is Ralph Kelsey."

They continued making casual conversation until they found their way down the street to a wooden bench located in front of the general store. Ralph towered over the petite Harriett, creating in her a feeling of security. He walked with an air of confidence, his shoulders squared and his head held high. As they sat on the bench and talked, Harriett learned that Ralph's family had been tobacco farmers for generations, and like his father and his father before him, Ralph worked the land.

Now twenty-four, Ralph told Harriett that his father had died two years ago, leaving him sole heir to the family's 100-acre tobacco farm. With the exception of Pearlene, the family's domestic, who went home after preparing supper every evening, he lived alone on the farm. Sure, he had farm hands and day laborers around, but they had lives and homes of their own, where they too, retreated at day's end.

Ralph was curious about Harriett's life. She told him her father was the town's shoemaker and her mother, a dressmaker. She told Ralph how she had learned to sew from her mother, a skill that came in handy when her mother needed help finishing last minute customer orders.

Ralph was attentive to Harriett's every word. His easygoing manner made conversation easy, something that did not come natural to her. She spoke of her love of school, and how she had mastered the basics of reading, writing, and arithmetic. She was particularly proud of her arithmetic skills because they came in handy when her father needed help in keeping his business receipts and expenses in order.

Outside of her father, Harriett had never spent this much time with a man before. As the afternoon drifted by, Ralph asked Harriett if she was thirsty. Shyly, she said no, but was secretly delighted when Ralph went inside the general store and brought out an icy cold lemonade for them to share. Harriett was smitten.

The sun was going down, and Harriett knew she had better get back to the Town Hall before her father arrived to pick her up. When they stood up from the bench to leave, Ralph bent down, his sun-chapped lips quickly brushing hers. It was Harriett's first kiss, and she felt as if an electrical current was going through her body as Ralph's lips touched hers. When they arrived back at Town Hall Ralph asked Harriett if he could see her again. Barely able to breathe she managed to whisper the word, "Yes."

Now Ralph was smitten, but for other reasons. He wanted the female companionship of someone like Harriett at the end of his long working days in the field. He wanted to come through the door and find someone other than Pearlene, standing at the stove fixing supper. He wanted someone on whom he could depend to help him work the farm. Most of all, Ralph wanted someone young and strong to bear him sons so that he could replace the farm hands and day laborers with his own offspring. Harriett fit the bill in every respect.

At first, Harriett began seeing Ralph secretly, lying to her parents about her comings and goings, knowing they would not approve of the unlikely match. Fearful of being caught, Harriett confined their dates to afternoon visits to Ralph's farm.

One lazy afternoon in early spring, while sitting under a blossoming dogwood tree outside one of the barns Ralph used to flue-cure his tobacco, a farmhand walked by and recognized Harriett from the Town Hall social. She and Ralph were sitting close, giggling, and holding hands. It took no time for word to spread like wildfire throughout the town that Harriett Crenshaw and Ralph Kelsey were courting.

That same afternoon, Agnes Porter, town gossip and self-appointed supervisor of community morality, conveniently dropped by Henry's shoe shop to have the soles of her black patent leather Sunday shoes repaired. Agnes told Henry, a mild-mannered man by nature, that she felt it was her moral obligation to share with him some things Ralph Kelsey had been saying about Harriett.

She scanned the shop with her narrowed brown eyes to make sure no one was within ear shot of what she was about to say. "Now, Henry, I'm not here to upset you," Agnes said in a low tone. "But my husband Wilbur heard it from his brother Nate, who heard it from one of the men that drinks and gambles with Ralph Kelsey up at his place every Saturday night, that Ralph has been saying some improper things about Harriett." Agnes continued her private rant by telling Henry that Ralph was bragging to the boys over a game of poker that Harriett was going to be his child bride. She said he also boasted that, given time, he would have no need to pay for day laborers and unreliable farm hands because Harriett had all the necessary equipment he needed to produce his own farmhands.

Henry's blood was reaching the boiling point when Agnes concluded by saying, "And would you believe it? Wilbur said that Nate's friend said that he, Ralph, and all his drinking buddies broke out into a huge roar of laughter at the mention of Harriett's 'equipment' as they raised their shot glasses in a toast to Harriett's fertility."

As Agnes Porter prepared to leave the shop, she told Henry that she was sorry she had to be the one to share such despicable news, but she knew he and Mary would want to know that Ralph Kelsey had less than honorable intentions where Harriett was concerned. The typical mild-mannered Henry was furious at the suggestion that his daughter was being courted for the sole purpose of producing offspring for Ralph Kelsey.

Over supper that night, Henry confronted Harriett, demanding to know if she was secretly seeing Ralph Kelsey. When she defiantly answered "Yes," he begged her to listen to reason, to think about her life and the opportunities that awaited her, opportunities she would never realize with Ralph Kelsey. Harriett, refusing to hear anything negative her father had to say about Ralph, bolted from the table, ran into her room where she locked her door and refused to come out.

Harriett's parents watched, in dizzying slow motion, as Ralph became the domineering influence in Harriett's young life. She dissolved all ties with family and friends who spoke ill of him. She barely spoke to Henry and Mary, preferring to spend her nonworking hours in her room, often taking her meals there. Harriett's parents did everything in their power to keep them apart, but their resistance to the relationship only stoked the fire that burned in Harriett's heart and her determination to be with Ralph.

One night, when Harriett made a rare appearance at the family's supper table, already tense with emotion, a heated exchange began between Henry and Harriett. Henry told Harriett he found her window unlocked again, and accused her of sneaking in and out to meet Ralph. A defiant Harriett, upset and frustrated, screamed at her father that Ralph had given her a choice. She could choose to marry him, or live a spinster's life with them.

When Harriett turned eighteen, and was of legal age, Ralph asked for her hand in marriage. Her parents opposed the idea right away. Harriett was far too young and inexperienced to marry a man like Ralph Kelsey, and they feared for her future. However, fearing the loss of their only child's love and affection, Henry and Mary Crenshaw resigned themselves to the marriage of Harriett and Ralph. The summer wedding took place in the small, white-framed, country church Harriett had attended since childhood.

In a white lace wedding gown, hand-stitched by her mother, Harriett stood beside Ralph. She carried a bouquet of white lilacs and orange blossoms as symbols of her youthful innocence and purity and wore a few of the flowers in her upswept hair.

The minister began the ceremony by saying, "We are assembled today in the presence of God and the face of these witnesses to celebrate the joining of Harriett Crenshaw and Ralph Kelsey into the bonds and unity of marriage."

Mary Crenshaw, bitterly resenting what was taking place before her, leaned over and whispered in Henry's ear, "I bet this is the first time Ralph Kelsey has ever been in the presence of God or any other Holy person for that matter!"

As Harriett and Ralph exchanged marriage vows, the minister asked for the ring to be placed on the bride's finger. It was his mother's wedding band that he found stashed in a box of his father's leftover belongings. The ring was not given to Harriett out of love, sentiment, or tradition; it was given to her because it cost Ralph nothing. As Ralph slipped a thin gold band, whose luster had long since worn away, on the fourth finger of Harriett's left hand, the minister repeated, "Harriett, Ralph offers this ring to you as a symbol of the vows he has just spoken. What meaning will it have for you as you wear it?"

Harriett spoke softly, and with tears running down her face stated, "As I wear this ring, it will remind me that you and I will be together for a long time. I will remember that when you are struggling, I will struggle with you, and that when you rejoice, I will rejoice with you."

The words that Harriett spoke from her loving heart would turn on her in the years to come. Yes, she and Ralph would be together for a long time, and, yes, as she would come to learn, when he struggled, she would struggle more; and sadly, their time of "rejoicing" would quickly sour and become a lifetime of remorse.

When the minister pronounced them husband and wife, Harriett's mother sobbed quietly into her freshly pressed linen handkerchief. "Harriett, my precious Harriett," she grieved silently. "You have just surrendered your independence, your name, your destiny, and now your will over to Ralph Kelsey. May God be with you."

"Uh, Ralph," stumbled the minister, "I think you have forgotten something important. You may now kiss your bride."

As Ralph looked into Harriett's radiantly happy face, he quickly kissed her pursed lips and thought smugly to himself, "From this day forward, you belong to me." And from that day forward, she did.

There was no time for a honeymoon; it was summer, a time when planting the tobacco took priority over everything. Harriett's life as a "city girl," living in modestly comfortable surroundings, ended at the age of eighteen when she said "I do" to Ralph Kelsey. She was now a farmer's wife whose life was totally dictated by the growing and harvesting seasons of the flue-cured tobacco Ralph's fields produced. Even with Pearlene's help, Harriett's typical day lasted 10–12 hours, except in harvest season. When the time came for the tobacco to be harvested for market, Harriett's days stretched into 12–14 hours.

When Ralph was short of workers, you could find Harriett working side by side with the day laborers under the unbearably hot and humid North Carolina summer sun, sometimes just weeks short of delivering a child.

The life Harriett envisioned with Ralph dissolved into nothing more than a tedious succession of endless days and nights that were frequently interrupted by outbursts of drunken anger and rage. The days blurred into months and the months into years.

The toast Ralph and his drinking buddies made to Harriett's fertility prior to their marriage was not in vain. During their twenty-three years of marriage, Harriett bore Ralph seven hearty and robust sons. Her oldest, Ralph

Jr., was twenty-two. Her youngest, Marcus, was twelve. Harriett was now past forty, and thought her family was complete but, Mother Nature had other plans. At forty-one, Harriett found herself pregnant with her eighth child. That child would turn out to be our granny, Ruby Mae. Harriett was stunned at the discovery, since twelve years had passed since the birth of Marcus, but since she and Ralph still shared a bed, one could not rule out the possibility.

At first, she kept the pregnancy a secret, fearful of Ralph's reaction when he learned another child, twelve years younger than his last, had been conceived. As her belly expanded, Harriett knew it was only a matter of time before the life growing inside her would reveal her secret. As Harriett entered her fourth month of pregnancy, her swollen belly was beginning to show. She had made every attempt in the early months to conceal her condition by layering pinafores over her dresses during the day, and wearing cotton slips underneath her full-length, billowy nightgowns at night.

One night while in bed, Harriett was half-asleep when Ralph pressed up against her back and slipped his arm around her waist. As he pulled her closer, he whispered, "Harriett, you're getting a little thick around the middle. Perhaps you need to cut back on some of those biscuits you've been eating."

Harriett, in an effort to shift Ralph's attention from her expanding waistline, shoved his arm away and huffed, "It's nothing more than a woman's natural aging process. Now go to sleep Ralph and leave me be." Ralph sulked for a while, but eventually drifted off to sleep.

Harriett brooded for two more weeks about how to announce the arrival of the new baby. She did not want to be alone with Ralph when she shared the news, fearing his explosive temper. Harriett devised a plan to announce her pregnancy. The supper table was the only place where she could gather Ralph and the boys for any length of time. "They say the way to a man's heart is through his stomach," Harriett recited to herself for reassurance. Perhaps with a good meal warming his belly after a hard day in the field, Ralph's heart might also warm up to the news that our granny was safe and warm tucked in hers.

One clear, cold Wednesday morning in February, after Ralph and the boys had left early that day to plow the fields in anticipation of spring planting, Harriett sent Pearlene out to the chicken coop to catch a plump young hen for that night's supper. Pearlene came back with a three-pounder. Working side-by-side, Harriett and Pearlene plucked the feathers from the hen, washed and soaked it, then put it in a big stew pot on the back of the old wood stove where it simmered in water with various root vegetables to add flavor to the broth. When the meat began to fall off the bone, they took the chicken out of the pot and allowed it to cool. They would later shred it and stir it back into the dumplings right before serving time.

Pearlene made the dumplings, because no magician existed that could transform flour, salt, and water into the plump, square, lighter-than-air pillow dumplings she rolled and cut by hand and slowly simmered in the rich chicken broth. The simmering pot of chicken and dumplings was kept company by a roasting pan filled with chunks of candied yams, all sticky and fragrant with cinnamon, brown sugar, and butter. Harriett and Pearlene had picked a mess of turnip greens from the garden earlier that day and cooked them until they were tender, seasoned with smoky, fleshy ham hocks.

Two cast-iron skillets of freshly-made buttermilk cornbread were kept warm in the oven. Their crusty brown tops were slathered with freshly churned butter, and would soon be used for sopping up the turnip greens' pot likker. To finish off the meal, Harriett baked two chess pies, Ralph's favorites, that sat cooling on the window ledge.

As she rang the supper bell, signaling the boys and Ralph to come in from the field, Harriett's heart quickened as she felt the life inside her beginning to move. She rubbed her belly, offering comfort to the little one she carried knowing there would be no turning back. Tonight, when she served the chess pie and coffee, she would make her announcement.

A big wooden barrel was located in the back yard near the kitchen door. Every afternoon, Pearlene filled the barrel with fresh water she pumped from the well. Wasting nothing, bits of leftover lye soap were stacked in an old tin cup and placed on top of the barrel. The soap was used for "washing up" before the men entered the house for supper. Nearby was a drying towel made from cloth cut from an old flour sack.

Tobacco farming was hard work. Tobacco farming in the hot and humid North Carolina climate made it even more difficult. Supper was the one meal the male folk really looked forward to because it signaled an end to the day's labor.

After washing up, Ralph and his seven sons, ravenous from the day's work, entered the weathered farmhouse and the simply furnished kitchen. Kerosene lamps cast a warm glow throughout the room. After they took their seats around the big wooden table that sat in the middle of the kitchen, they did what they did every night…bowed their heads while Harriett led them in prayer and gave thanks for the food they were about to receive. When she concluded the prayer with "Amen," the boys lifted their heads and turned their attention to Pearlene who was dishing up the plates of food she and Harriett had so painstakingly prepared.

Ralph and his sons devoured the food set before them. When the last piece of cornbread was gone, and they could eat no more, the men left the kitchen to go outside for their nightly smoke. All of Harriett's sons, including twelve-year-old Marcus, smoked hand-rolled cigarettes made from the tobacco they cured.

Pearlene and Harriett were left to do the "women's work." After the dishes were cleared from the table, washed and put away, the kitchen swept and tidied, Pearlene prepared to say goodnight to Miss Harriett and leave for the day.

Harriett considered Pearlene to be part of the family. As her way of saying "thank you" for all the effort Pearlene had put into tonight's supper, she quickly filled an old peach basket with leftovers. Ever mindful of Ralph's stinginess, she looked out the back kitchen window to make sure he was in the back yard smoking before signaling to Pearlene that it was safe to leave. Pearlene, grateful for the food, gave Miss Harriett a quick kiss on her cheek and snuck quietly out the front door.

Harriett prepared a pot of fresh coffee to serve with the chess pies. The smell of wood smoke and boiling coffee mingling with the leftover aromas from supper infused the kitchen with scents comforting and familiar. For a few precious minutes, alone in her kitchen, Harriett felt safe and secure.

Harriett rang the supper bell again, this time signaling to the men that dessert was about to be served. As she set about pouring cups of steaming black coffee and cutting slices of pie, Ralph and the boys rambled in, each one pausing at the back door to take the last drag from their cigarette before throwing it on the ground and entering the kitchen.

With everyone seated around the table, Harriett, without fanfare or drama, simply looked around the table, pausing for a second or two to make eye contact with each of her beloved seven sons. She purposely avoided looking at Ralph, fearing she would "chicken out" from the confession she was about to make. Taking a deep breath and slowly exhaling, Harriett stated without emotion, "By early summer, I am going to have another child."

The boys sat speechless as they slowly took in their mother's words. When Harriett finally had the courage to look at Ralph, all she could see was seething rage in his dark blue cobalt eyes. Ralph could feel the adrenaline rushing through his body as his brain started to comprehend Harriett's words. His rage continued to grow as he reflected back on the night he had pulled her close to him, only to be pushed away and lied to about the secret she was carrying.

When Ralph's rage found its voice, he began shouting at the top of his lungs.

"You lying hussy. You may have been hiding the fire but what'll you do with the smoke?"

Ralph had sweat pouring down his beet red face and Harriett could see his fists were clenched as his continued his tirade.

"You knew I didn't want another mouth to feed. You knew I didn't want no more young'uns, and here you are trapping me into another one. I ought to throw you out of the house right now and let you fend for yourself."

Harriett was trembling with fear, but found enough strength inside herself to look Ralph straight in his eyes and say, "Ralph, you and I both know I did not do this alone. I did not plan for this to happen, I did not trick you. It was Mother Nature that tricked us!"

Tears were now streaming down her face but the tone of her voice grew stronger. "There is nothing you can do to me to stop me from having this child. God has willed it, Ralph, and you will just have to accept it." Ralph, whose body was still shaking with rage, raised his arm to strike her.

Without a word, Ralph Jr., Harriett's oldest son, grabbed his arm and confronted Ralph. "Pa, there's one of you and seven of us. We are not going to let you do anything to hurt our mama, so you best get out of here and cool off before we all do something we'll regret later." Ralph stormed out of the house, almost tearing the back screen door off the hinges as he left.

Ralph Jr., for the first time in his life, had finally stood up to the tyrannical Ralph, and in doing so, gained newfound respect for himself as his own man. His six brothers were also willing, for the first time, to confront their father that fateful Wednesday night. They, too, found an inner strength that in years past had been suppressed by Ralph's intimidating personality.

Ralph's rage over Harriett's pregnancy consumed him. Leaving the farmhouse, he made his way into the backwoods where he kept his still, and filled an old gallon jug to the top with some of his homemade white lightening. He made himself a makeshift bed near the furnace in one of his flue-curing barns, and there he stayed, drunk and passed out, for three days.

Harriett and her sons had lived through years of Ralph's terrorizing outbursts of violent behavior. They knew it would only be a matter of time before he came back, more belligerent than when he left.

The confrontation between Ralph and Harriett over her pregnancy only served to strengthen the mother-son bonds that existed between Harriett and her boys. With Ralph away, they enjoyed an ease and openness with her that did not exit when Ralph was present. They saw the joy that Harriett held in her heart for the child she was carrying; and her joy was theirs as well.

On Saturday morning, Harriett got up bright and early to prepare breakfast for her boys. Harvest time would soon be upon them, and there was work that needed to be done to prepare the tobacco for market.

Coming off his three-day binge, Ralph stumbled back to the farmhouse reeking of moonshine whiskey and the stench of not bathing for three days. The minute Ralph entered the backdoor of the farmhouse, he was overwhelmed by the smell of home cooking. A huge platter of crispy smoked bacon was already sitting on the sideboard, fresh eggs were cooking sunny side up in Harriett's favorite cast-iron skillet, and a pan of plump buttermilk biscuits was sitting on the warming plate of the wood-stove oven. As a special treat, Harriett had blended equal parts of molasses and butter in a pottery bowl for the boys to slather on the flaky biscuits with the lightly browned tops.

Ralph's belly rumbled and reminded him that he had not eaten solid food in three days. He was suddenly ravenous, and without so much of a glance at his seven sons sitting at the table, awaiting the breakfast Harriett was making for them, he demanded that Harriett dish him up some breakfast and serve him first.

At first she protested, but she could see the after effects of the moonshine whiskey taking hold in Ralph's body. His normally deeply-tanned skin had turned pale and clammy, and sweat was beading on his furrowed brow, occasionally running in small streams down his heavily-creased face. His hands were shaking uncontrollably. She prepared Ralph a plate of food that he devoured in minutes. "Ralph, you need to go easy on second helpings, because you haven't had anything in your stomach for three days but moonshine," she warned. His hands were shaking so bad he could hardly get his coffee cup to his mouth.

"Shut up, woman, and get me my second helpings since I'm the one who puts food on the table in the first place!" he sarcastically retorted. Ralph Jr., clenching his fists under the table, bit his bottom lip to keep himself from saying something that would set Ralph's agitation into motion.

Harriett, without saying a word, prepared Ralph a second, and then a third plate of food. She knew he was going to be violently ill when all that food finally made its way to his stomach, after drinking moonshine for three days. When he finished eating, Harriett summoned Ralph Jr. to take his Pa out to the wood barrel and wash as much of the stink off of him as he could.

Later that day, while working in the fields, the heat and humidity proved more than Ralph's abused body could bear. The food on which he had gorged took revenge against him, and left him begging for mercy as waves of nausea swept over him as he lay helpless and alone in his makeshift bed in the tobacco barn.

For the next five months Ralph worked the tobacco fields, took his meals in the house, but spent his nights in the tobacco barn, his self-imposed exile designed to serve as punishment to Harriett as her belly, and the life inside her, grew bigger and bigger.

On June 9, 1910, Harriett gave birth to her only daughter and named her Ruby Mae Kelsey. Pearlene, who had helped Harriett deliver each of her seven sons, stayed with Harriett through the long and difficult labor. When Pearlene finally placed the tiny little bundle in Harriett's arms, tears welled up in her eyes as she realized her miracle wish had finally come true. The seal Harriett had kept on her heart for nine months was now broken, and like a natural spring whose water flows freely from sources deep beneath, she allowed herself to be flooded with all the soft, warm, and joyful feelings of maternal love.

Harriett delighted at looking into her newborn daughter's delicate little face, whose cobalt-blue eyes were the exact color of Ralph's. She lightly stroked the soft little tuff of sandy brown hair covering the top of her head. She examined her long slender fingers and lightly tickled her ten toes. When Harriett was confident that her daughter had made a safe arrival into the world, she handed her to Pearlene and slept, exhausted, until she was awakened to the sounds of a baby crying seeking nourishment and comfort from her mother's breast.

When Ralph saw Ruby Mae for the first time, he did not fail to show his disappointment and utter disgust when the boy, to whom he thought he was entitled, turned out to be a girl. "You made her, you raise her," he hissed at Harriett as she sat rocking her newborn daughter to sleep.

As he left the room, Harriett whispered softly to herself, "Yes, Ralph, I will raise her. I will raise her to be all the things I should have been had I not married you. She will be strong, sturdy and sure of herself, and I pray I raise her to make better choices in her life than I did in mine."

Ruby Mae lived an isolated childhood on the Kelsey tobacco farm. Her mother and Pearlene were her best friends, teachers, and playmates. She hardly knew her brothers because Ralph was their taskmaster, and he worked them from dawn to dusk tending the acres of tobacco he grew. By the time she turned eight, her youngest brother was twenty, her oldest thirty.

Every year, from the age of five, Ruby Mae and her mother planted an acorn in the front yard of the farmhouse to mark the occasion of her birthday. At the planting of each acorn, Ruby Mae anxiously awaited any sign of growth. Years five, six, and seven produced nothing, but on year eight, Ruby Mae was overjoyed when the acorn's baby seedling popped up from the ground and sprouted its first set of leaves.

As the roots grew down into the soil, they secured for themselves a fruitful place in which to grow. When the stalk was six inches high, a second flush of leaves grew. With stable roots to support its growth, the oak tree's stalk thickened. In the years that followed, the stalk was replaced with a trunk layered with grayish bark that formed shingle-like plates. The trunk continued to grow thicker to support its widening branches. The leaves flourished in spring and provided shade from the summer heat. In late summer and early autumn, acorns, the fruit of the oak tree, fell in great quantities on the ground, providing food for the squirrels to sustain themselves through winter.

Our granny, Ruby Mae, whose life lay undiscovered before her, was not so different from the oak tree she had planted as a child. As a seedling, Harriett had nurtured and given her life. As her young life took root, Harriett's love was the rich soil that allowed her to grow strong and flourish. As the years passed, Ruby Mae's roots deepened and anchored her to the ground. She had become a mighty oak.

As her childhood years slipped by, Ruby Mae watched as her brothers left, one by one, the confines of the farm to live life on their own terms. This left her to care for an increasingly frail Harriett, and an aging, sarcastic, bitter Ralph.

Ruby Mae was twenty-one when her beloved mother Harriett died. She was laid to rest in the small family burial plot located behind the tiny, white clapboard frame church she had attended since she was a child. It was the same church in which she had been married, and where she reared her children in the foundations of the Christian faith.

Headstones were rare in this rural area, so Ruby Mae had Ralph Jr. carve Harriett's name on a sturdy cedar plank and mark her grave with it. The bowers of tall arching trees were covered in soft, fluffy flowers. These graceful trees lent an ethereal beauty and peacefulness to Harriett's final resting place. "Rest well, Mama. God knows you've earned it," Ruby Mae whispered softly, as tears of grief streamed down her face.

Ralph died five years later of farmer's lung disease. Unlike their beloved mother Harriett, Ruby Mae and her seven brothers held no funeral service for him. They chose instead to have him buried at the opposite end of the graveyard from where Harriett's tomb was located. While living, Ralph tormented Harriett, and spewed his bitterness across the landscape of her life. Now dead and far removed from her, Ralph could torture her no more. If Hades was a place of pain and turmoil, Ruby Mae reasoned that Ralph should be right at home there.

As his only surviving heirs, Ruby Mae and her seven brothers inherited all of Ralph's remaining assets. The old farmhouse was in need of repair, and Ralph's tobacco fields had long since been abandoned by her brothers. The farmhouse was worth little, but the land on which it sat was valuable.

Trains were becoming the number one means of moving people and goods at the time, and railroads needed vast acres of land on which to lay tracks. Ralph Kelsey had one-hundred prime acres of land in his name when he died. Norfolk Southern Railroad was rapidly expanding its operations throughout the southeast. They proposed to the city of Durham to run a railroad line through the western part of Durham to provide a vital connection for transporting goods along the east coast. They would need a substantial parcel of land to accomplish their goal.

Ralph Kelsey's one-hundred acres happened to be located on the western end of the county line. Norfolk Southern Railroad extended an offer to the heirs of Ralph Kelsey. The brothers hired a lawyer to negotiate the price, and after many months of discussions, an offer to purchase the land was made, and accepted, on behalf of Ralph Kelsey's heirs.

Ruby Mae never knew the actual amount of money the railroad paid for the land, but it was substantial enough for her and her brothers, now ages 38 to 49, to afford better lives.

One by one, her brothers left the small, southern, tobacco town of Durham, North Carolina, in search of better opportunities for themselves and their families. Ruby Mae's brothers deeded a few acres of land to her prior to selling the remaining acreage to the railroad. For the first time in her life, twenty-six year old Ruby Mae faced living alone.

Her brothers put her portion of the proceeds from the land sale in a trust fund that would provide her with a monthly income for living expenses. Every month, Wilbur Eubanks, the head teller at Mechanics and Farmers Bank, wrote a check and deposited it into Ruby Mae's account.

Ralph Jr., Granny's oldest brother, prior to moving to Virginia to work with Norfolk Southern Railroad, warned Ruby Mae that her monthly stipends would not last forever, and that she should be frugal with her spending. Ruby Mae heeded Ralph Jr.'s warning and set aside a few dollars each month, for what she called her "rainy day" fund.

She attended the same church in which she had been reared every Sunday, and derived strength from Preacher Jackson's sermons. She found solace and friendship among the people in the church's congregation. When church services ended, she went faithfully to Harriett's gravesite where she removed stray weeds, smoothed the soil, and laid a handful of wildflowers she had gathered as she walked up the long, dusty, dirt road leading to the church. Not once did she visit Ralph's grave, or cast an eye in its direction.

Ruby Mae recalled her mother's dying words to her, "If you carry me in your heart, I will speak to you from there." Ruby Mae could not foresee the obstacles life would eventually put in her path, but like the mighty oak and the roots that anchor it, she would stand strong knowing that Harriett's silent spirit would guide and sustain her through whatever came her way.

THE GENESIS

The Good Book says that everything and everyone has a "beginning." This is mine.

My name is Mattie Rose Radley and I was born on September 18, 1952, in Durham, North Carolina, barely nine and a half months after my teenaged parents eloped and ran off to Ocean City, South Carolina. Whether conceived in love or conceived in lust, I did not come into this world alone. I had a companion, a womb-mate as it were, and her name was Annie Lizbeth, my fraternal twin sister.

My little corner of the world was located in Durham, North Carolina, a sleepy little southern town named after Dr. Bartlett Durham in 1853. The history books say that Dr. Bartlett Durham donated four acres of land to the North Carolina Railroad in 1853 to establish a new railroad station that would run east-west.

It was around this railroad station that the City of Durham sprang up, and many years later it was on this railroad that my maternal granddaddy was killed—a life-altering event for his kin that cast dark shadows on future generations of my family for many years to come.

Durham was a small, blue collar and agricultural community that was best known for producing tobacco. Sometimes simple acts can have a big impact. That was definitely the case with Dr. Bartlett's four acre land donation. Five years later those four little acres transformed Durham, North Carolina, into the leading tobacco stronghold in the South.

For as long as I can remember, most locals called Durham "The Bull City." At the time I did not understand the origin of the nickname, but I would soon become a scholar on the topic after writing and submitting a fictitious book report assigned to me on the subject during one of Miss Margaret McGee's fifth-grade civic lessons.

My life as a social butterfly was spent pollinating as many friendships as I could to add to my fertile, well-cultivated, garden of playmates. Mrs. McGee assigned a three-page book report, but due to the demands on my social life, I hastily wrote and submitted my own version of how I thought The Bull City got its name.

In my report I wrote that a special breed of bulls lived in Durham, North Carolina. The bulls were well known for spearing farmers in their behinds if they wore a red handkerchief in the pockets of their overalls, thus giving them the name, Bull Durham. I reported that the bulls were so famous the city was nicknamed after them.

After reading my report, Miss McGee hauled me to the front of the classroom and humiliated me by announcing that the only "bull" coming out of The Bull City was my book report. As punishment for making up the fictitious story, she assigned me extra homework: a five-page (vs. three-page) book report on the subject, as if that would correct whatever character flaw she saw in me, and my propensity for embellishing stories.

Funny, the things you can learn when you actually go to the library and look things up. In the end I submitted to Miss McGee the requisite five-page book report on the origins of The Bull City, and learned some interesting facts about the place I called home.

It was in 1858, when Robert Morris began manufacturing smoking tobacco, the spark was lit, igniting the city and fueling Durham's rapidly growing economic development. When Robert Morris sold his company to John R. Green in 1862, John Green began to manufacture "Bull Durham

Smoking Tobacco." John Green wanted to have a new label designed that would distinguish his cigarette packs from all others.

One day, while munching on a ham sandwich slathered with Coleman's mustard, John Green looked at its label and took an instant liking to the bull on the front of the jar. Mr. Green ordered the printer to put the same bull on his new cigarette label. Someone mistakenly told John Green that the mustard was produced in Durham, England, and he thought such serendipity would bring him luck in Durham, North Carolina.

Even though Mr. Green was mistaken about the origins of Coleman's mustard, Bull Durham was an instant success. By the time James B. Duke of American Tobacco Company purchased the Bull Durham Tobacco Company in 1898, Bull Durham was the most famous trademark in the world.

The Duke family became the wealthiest family in Durham, and American Tobacco Company became a source of steady jobs for local residents, including members of my own family.

Textiles and tobacco were the two major employers in Durham, North Carolina. My mama's side of the family worked in textiles at The Cotton Mill, and my daddy's, at American Tobacco Company.

My mama, Elizabeth Rose Childers, was the youngest daughter of Ruby Mae and Jackson "Jack" Childers. Ruby Mae married later than most women of her time, and her children came one right after the other. There was Jackson Jr., Sunny Rae, and Elizabeth Rose. Jackson, Jr., Sunny Rae, and Elizabeth Rose might have found themselves orphans had it not been for Ruby Mae's strong will and determination to keep her family together when she found herself a widow at thirty. Her husband, Jack, was killed in a tragic railroad accident when Jackson Jr. was four, Sunny Rae was three, and Elizabeth Rose was just two years of age.

We grew up hearing two different versions of our granddaddy's untimely demise. To this day, no one can verify the circumstances surrounding his death, except to say that in order to avoid buying a railroad ticket, he was jumping rail cars, a common practice during the Great Depression on his way back from a week's worth of work as a day laborer making furniture in High Point, North Carolina.

Times were hard, and money was even harder to come by, so Jack Childers went where the work was in order to feed and clothe his family. Some folks said Jack simply miscalculated his steps as he jumped from one railcar to the next, tripped, and fell under the train. Others said his love of moonshine was his ultimate sin, and drink cost him his life.

Whatever the reason for Jack's death, Ruby Mae was dealt a cruel twist of fate. Her family's destiny now lay in her hands alone. Though family and friends urged her to separate the children in order to lessen her own burden, Ruby Mae refused.

Her brother, John, and his wife, Laura, who were childless, offered to take Elizabeth Rose. Since she was the youngest, they reasoned, she would suffer few repercussions from being separated from her mother at such an early age. Ruby Mae lashed back at them: "How can you ask a mother to give up her children? I carried those babies inside me for nine months, I gave birth to those babies, and they are my living reminder of Jack. I know you mean well and all, but when my children look up to see someone standing over them, it's going to be their mama and not some stranger."

Ruby Mae had no idea of what the future would bring, but she knew she had three children to feed, house, and clothe, and in order to do that she had to find work. Ruby Mae had the will to keep her family together, but now, she had to find the way.

Her first order of business was to cash in the life insurance policy she and Jack had taken out when they first married. After Jack's death she received $950.00 from the policy.

Fearing negative publicity, the attorneys for the railroad offered Ruby Mae a one-time, cash settlement if she would not hold the railroad responsible for Jack Childers' death.

Ruby Mae did not have the financial resources to seek legal counsel, so at her family's urging she accepted the railroad's offer.

With the life insurance money and the railroad settlement check in hand,

Ruby Mae needed to put a roof over the heads of her children. She and Jack had been renting a small house near the cotton mills, but after his death, she decided that if she was going to pay rent, she might as well pay a mortgage towards a house she would eventually own and could pass down to her children.

Ruby Mae contacted her third cousin Jewel, who had married a ne'er-do-well construction worker by the name of Foy Whitters, about the prospects of building her a house. Foy Whitters was a disgusting figure of a man with a barrel chest, fat, overlapping belly, stubby beard, beady eyes and double chin. He was a man of low moral character with an insatiable appetite for easy money. Ruby Mae gave Foy $1,000 to build a home for her and her three children on the parcels of land her brothers' bequeathed to her.

The land was located on Peale Road one mile from the Bennett Place.

Ruby Mae originally hoped to sell off some of the acreage in order to build a nest egg for her family, but land buyers considered it farmland, and there was plenty of that in Durham already. Ruby Mae did not have the financial resources to build a farm, so she settled for a house instead.

When Foy Whitters finally completed the tiny, white, wooden framed house, it looked like a little doll house plopped down on acres and acres of land. It had four rooms; two bedrooms, a front parlor, and a kitchen. He told Ruby Mae that he had run out of money to install indoor plumbing, and built an outhouse instead.

Greedy Foy cut every corner he could in order to make money off of the recently widowed Ruby Mae Childers. He never hung one door inside the house which greatly limited the family's privacy. The house was supplied with well water, and its only source of heat was a woodstove in the kitchen for cooking, and a fireplace in the sitting room. That was home to my mama, and would eventually, as the years passed, become my home as well.

Ruby Mae then found a job sewing sheets at The Cotton Mill. She worked nights because she got paid twenty-five cents more per hour working the late shift, and she needed every spare penny she could make to keep her family afloat.

Moreover, Ruby Mae was a resourceful woman. As soon as the house was built and she had secured her job at the cotton mill, she promptly moved her spinster cousin, Fola Swilley, into the small, cramped, four-room house to watch over her children at night in exchange for room and board. Fola, grateful to be out of her parents' house, and away from their constant nagging about having to support an "old maid," shared one of the two bedrooms with Ruby Mae, while Jackson Jr., Sunny Rae, and Elizabeth Rose shared the other.

Fola worked as a waitress on the day shift at Wally's Diner, a rundown, hole-in-the-wall eatery on Ninth Street near the cotton mill where workers flocked in daily for Wally's economical blue plate specials.

Everyone in town knew of the Childers's family tragedy and the sacrifices Ruby Mae made in order to keep her family together. Wally had a big heart, and so, on those rare days when he was faced with leftovers at the end of working day, he would bag them up, and give them to Fola to take home to the Childers's family.

Fola was a meek and timid woman who knew full well that Ruby Mae was far too proud a person to accept charity in any form, and told Wally so. Wally told Fola to tell Ruby Mae that on the days she did not make her tip quota, they had an arrangement whereby she took home in leftovers that which she did not make in tips. Deep down Ruby Mae knew the truth, but was grateful for Wally's generosity. Every time her children sat down to one of Wally's "leftover" suppers, she knew she would be able to allocate some of her meager food dollars to other essential household needs.

The years passed, and though they lived a frugal existence, Ruby Mae remained true to her word and kept her family together. Fola eventually met a mild-mannered man who worked at the cotton mill, frequented Wally's Diner, and married him. However, the bond of friendship that had grown over the years between Ruby Mae and Fola would last a lifetime.

Jackson, Jr. was forced to step into the role as the only "man" in the family, and from the minute he could ride a bike, he had a paper route in the morning, and helped old man McDonald in his hardware store every afternoon after school.

At the end of every week, Jackson Jr. and Ruby Mae deposited their leftover pennies, nickels, dimes and quarters in a big glass pickle jar Ruby Mae kept on top of the chest of drawers in her bedroom. Ruby Mae told Jackson Jr., Sunny Rae and Elizabeth Rose in no uncertain terms that the jar held their "rainy day money," which would only be spent in emergency situations.

Unfortunately, much of the emergency fund went to pay for the doctors who treated Sunny Rae's asthma and other respiratory ailments. A deepening sibling rivalry was developing between Sunny Rae and Elizabeth Rose. Elizabeth Rose resented all the time her mother spent taking care of Sunny Rae, and acted out her resentment through rebellious behavior and temper tantrums.

Sometimes Ruby Mae felt a cold chill run up her spine when she looked at Elizabeth Rose. It seemed as if she was looking at the ghost of her father, Ralph. His spirit appeared to have been resurrected in Elizabeth Rose, particularly in her uncontrollable outbursts of anger and her bitter resentment of anyone that seemed to have more than she. As Elizabeth Rose grew older, she would badger her mother for money so that she could shop downtown and buy the latest fashion fad she saw in her stack of newspaper circulars. Ruby Mae felt guilty that she could not indulge Elizabeth Rose's fantasies of fancy dresses, patent leather shoes, and lacy undergarments, but she simply did not have the money for the uptown extras Elizabeth Rose craved.

One Friday evening after supper, sixteen-year-old Elizabeth Rose begged Ruby Mae to allow her to sleep over at her friend Frances Woodell's house, so they could catch the bus uptown on Saturday morning and spend the day together.

"Well, I don't mind if you stay over at Frances's house, and I can give you bus fare and lunch money, but I don't have any extra for shopping," Ruby Mae told Elizabeth Rose.

"Oh, that's okay," Elizabeth Rose replied nonchalantly. "I've been saving up my babysitting money for a month, so if I want something I can buy it myself." Elizabeth Rose packed up her things and took off to Frances's house for the sleepover.

Later that night when Ruby Mae was preparing for bed, she noticed that the glass pickle jar sitting atop her chest of drawers appeared lower than it had the day before. She pulled out the small notepad from her dresser drawer on which she kept a weekly total of the money they had saved. She went into the kitchen and poured the quart jar and its contents out on the kitchen table and started counting the money. When the last penny had been counted, the pickle jar was five dollars short.

Ruby Mae knew that Elizabeth Rose had stolen the money. This was not the first time money had been missing only to resurface in the form of nail polish, lipstick and cheap cologne that Ruby Mae found stashed under her daughter's mattress while changing bed linens.

When Elizabeth Rose finally sauntered in late Saturday afternoon with a couple of shopping bags in her hand, Ruby Mae confronted her about the missing five dollars.

"Oh Mama," Elizabeth Rose replied, "what's the big deal? That jar is always full of money, and since most of the money is spent on Sunny Rae and her respiratory ailments, why shouldn't I be entitled to spend some of it on my own ailments?"

"And what ailment might that be?" Ruby Mae demanded to know.

"Why, for my aching feet, Mama. I've needed a new pair of shoes for quite some time, and since I was short five dollars from my babysitting money, I figured you wouldn't mind if I borrowed it from the pickle jar. I'll pay back your precious five dollars if that's all you're worried about," she said sarcastically.

"Elizabeth Rose, it's not the paying back that's at issue here; it's the stealing. And you know good and well that I keep that money on hand to pay for emergencies."

"What you really mean is that the money is for Sunny Rae and her so-called respiratory ailments," Elizabeth Rose snapped back. "It seems to me the only time Sunny Rae has a respiratory ailment is when there's work to do!"

Elizabeth Rose was livid at being confronted by her mother; her cobalt blue eyes narrowed as she flashed sparks of rage at Ruby Mae. Her voice became a low-pitched growl. "I hate you, I hate you, and I hate the life I have to live because of you! Just you wait and see, Mama. The first chance I get I'm going to get out of this dump and find myself a house with doors, a real bathroom, and hot water for my bath, and then I won't be beholden to you or anyone else for a stinking five dollars!"

As much as Ruby Mae tried to console Elizabeth Rose and reassure her that she loved her with all her heart, Elizabeth Rose only measured Ruby Mae's love by the amount of attention she could take away from Sunny Rae, and the number of things she could convince Ruby Mae to buy for her. Elizabeth Rose had a hungry heart that, even when fed, wanted more.

I've heard it said that our daddy, James Matthew Radley, and our mama, Elizabeth Rose Childers, were introduced to one another by her sister Sunny Rae and Dewayne Bailey, a distant cousin of James who Sunny Rae was dating at the time. They met at a Sunday, supper-on-the-ground, church picnic in July 1951.

The story has it that Sunny Rae, Elizabeth Rose, and Dewayne had already spread out a blanket on the church grounds and were about to eat when Dewayne spotted James wandering around the church grounds, looking like a lost lamb, scanning the crowd for a familiar face with whom to share his meal. Dewayne, who had not seen James for a while, hollered his name out loud to get James' attention, and when he did, motioned for him to come over and share their blanket. James broke into an awkward grin, happy to see a familiar face, and walked to where the three were sitting and joined them.

After some initial small talk, Dewayne and Sunny Rae paired off on one corner of the blanket giggling and talking as they ate, leaving James and Elizabeth Rose to their own devices. They, too, made small talk, mostly initiated by James, but Elizabeth Rose liked the way he looked directly into her eyes when he spoke, as if no one else in the world existed. She liked his mild-mannered ways and soft-spoken voice. James made Elizabeth Rose feel special. Like a dry sponge dipped in water, she absorbed every drop of his undivided attention.

James Matthew Radley was a skinny, shy, awkward, eighteen-year-old, with the sharp, angular facial features of youth. His cheeks were flanked on each side by deeply-set dimples. His light blue eyes were small, but fringed in dark eyelashes and heavy eyebrows. He had the look of a serious young man. His lips were full and masked a slight overbite. His complexion had pink undertones that would flush with varying hues of red when he showed emotion of any kind. James was the next to the youngest of ten brothers and sisters, and grew up in a God-fearing home where Daddy worked, but Mama ruled the roost. He had an easygoing nature about him, and though shy and unsure of himself, was well-mannered and friendly to everyone he met.

Elizabeth Rose was, according to most folks, a Plain Jane. The only things that distinguished her tall and skinny frame as a girl were a few strategically placed bumps Mother Nature bestows upon the female gender. She had thick, curly, coppery red hair that framed her face in loopy ringlets that made her look even younger than she was. She had a smattering of freckles across her small, up-turned nose. She had inherited her mother's fair complexion, but also her grandfather's piercing cobalt-blue eyes.

As plain and unadorned as Elizabeth Rose was, her sister Sunny Rae was a budding beauty. Men seemed to liken her to a southern state, and much like geese in winter, flocked in the direction of her warmth. They said the local girls got their feathers ruffled the minute Sunny entered any room. She had a presence about her that filled any room she entered. At church socials or other public events, the girls hastened to attach themselves to their current beau as if making a public declaration of their personal property. Elizabeth Rose deeply resented Sunny Rae's physical beauty and personal charisma, and was bound and determined that, this time, Sunny Rae would not vie for James' attention.

After meeting James at the church picnic, Elizabeth Rose hounded Sunny Rae and Dewayne to include her and James on their dates. As charismatic as Sunny Rae was, Elizabeth Rose was conniving.

Within three months, Elizabeth Rose Childers and James Matthew

Radley were a steady item, and Elizabeth Rose intended to keep it that way. Little did James know that if he ever had any dreams about building a life of his own, they would soon vanish as Elizabeth Rose schemed and plotted her own dreams about a more permanent arrangement with James: that of man and wife. Marriage would be her ticket off of Peale Road and into the life of prosperity for which she longed. Longing is one thing, but attaining that for which you long is another story, as Elizabeth Rose would soon find out.

Like two mismatched puzzle pieces forced to fit into a bigger scheme, there were times when James struggled to retain his independence from the clingy Elizabeth Rose. However, his boyish innocence was no match for the Lolita-like charms of the seventeen-year-old woman-child.

When Jackson, Jr., Sunny Rae and Elizabeth Rose entered their teens, Ruby Mae switched from working nights to days. She left home every morning at exactly 6:30 to report for her shift at the cotton mill at 7:00.

On December 3, 1951, James Matthew Radley pulled into the driveway of Ruby Mae Childers at 6:45 AM, picked up Elizabeth Rose, and together they headed for Ocean City, South Carolina.

Elizabeth Rose penned a note to Ruby Mae that she had left the house early to meet some girls at school to work on a home economics project, and would be home later. Elizabeth Rose smiled smugly to herself as she wrote the note to her mother. After all, it wasn't really a lie. She was working on a home economics project...her own!

You had to be eighteen to marry in North Carolina, but sixteen was the magic age of consent in Ocean City, South Carolina. So, with a full tank of gas, a three-hour drive south, and five dollars for a marriage license, James Matthew Radley and Elizabeth Rose Childers said "I do" in front of the Clerk of Court in Ocean City, South Carolina, and headed back home to North Carolina as man and wife.

In a day's time—not counting the forty-five minutes they stopped for a greasy chili-cheese burger, fries, and a RC Cola at a truck stop right off the highway—they drove back across the North Carolina state line having made a decision that would forever alter the course of their lives. Their "honeymoon," and subsequent romantic interludes, were confined to the backseat of James' brother's car.

Knowing that Ruby Mae would have a fit if she found out that seventeen-year-old Elizabeth Rose had sneaked off and gotten married, she and James kept the marriage a secret. Each continued to live with their respective parents. But three months later, Elizabeth Rose was sprouting a new bump, and it was growing in size with each passing week. With nowhere to turn, they went to Ruby Mae, marriage license in hand, and told her what they had done.

At first, Ruby Mae sat quietly, contemplating the situation. But, ever pragmatic, she simply said, "Elizabeth Rose and James Matthew Radley, I do not think the two of you know what you've gotten yourselves into. You're still children yourself, and soon you will have a baby to care for. Have either of you given any thought as to how you are going to take care of it and support yourselves?"

James said nothing, but Elizabeth Rose retorted, "Oh, Mama, why are you always filled with doom and gloom! I've babysat Dorothy Alder's young'uns lots of times, and there ain't nothing to it. Besides, James and I are in love, and *love* will *always* find a way, won't it James?" By now, James had learned that, to get along with Elizabeth Rose, it was best to go along. James had adjusted his life to the ups and downs of Elizabeth Rose's wild mood swings. It just seemed easier that way.

"Mrs. Childers," James replied, his blue eyes cast downward, "maybe Elizabeth Rose and I allowed our feelings to run ahead of our thinking, but I do love her, and I will do the right thing as a father, I promise you. I've told my mama and daddy about the situation, and Mama says she will give Elizabeth and me the back room in their house to stay in since you don't have much space, if that's okay with you," he muttered quietly, his head lowered in shame.

And so, James and Elizabeth Rose moved into the back room of his parents' house, sharing one bathroom with the five remaining brothers and sisters still living at home.

Seventeen-year-old Elizabeth Rose suffered from unrelenting morning sickness. "If it's *morning* sickness, why does it last *all day*?" she would yell at James between bouts of nausea as he kept bowls of saltine crackers by the bed and near the sofa, while pouring glass after glass of icy-cold ginger ale in an effort to calm her stomach. If only he could find a magic potion to settle her nerves!

James had just finished high school the June before he had met Elizabeth Rose at the church picnic in July. After they eloped, Elizabeth Rose continued her senior year in high school, but by March, her morning sickness was so severe it forced her to withdraw from school.

With only his high school diploma, James had neither the trade skills that blue collar work required, nor the college degree needed to gain him entry into the white collar working world. He was stuck in the middle of America's great employment divide, and found himself packing cigarette crates by day, and pumping gas at his uncle's service station by night, all in an effort to save enough money so that he and Elizabeth Rose could move out of his parents' house into a place of their own.

Elizabeth Rose hated living at James' parents' home. It seemed as if his mother was running a boarding house; there was always something on the stove, and the smell of bacon grease and collards cooking only nauseated Elizabeth Rose more. His brothers and sisters had long grown tired of standing in line to use the one and only bathroom, because Elizabeth Rose had taken it over with her all-day morning sickness.

Elizabeth Rose felt isolated in the back room where she sequestered herself, and demanded that all her meals be brought to her there because she could not tolerate the smell of food that wafted throughout the house. She resented James for working day and night, which she never failed to remind him of in her nightly rants and raves the entire family could hear through the paper-thin walls that separated their rooms.

Tension in James' household was mounting. On Elizabeth Rose's eighteenth birthday in June, James' family, Ruby Mae, Jackson Jr. and Sunny

Rae all gathered together to celebrate her birthday. At first Elizabeth was full of joy, soaking up every bit of the attention that was solely focused on her. She opened all her gifts but one, telling everyone she was saving James' for last. When the time came to open James' gift, Elizabeth Rose carefully untied the pink ribbon that surrounded the rose-covered wrapping paper.

"Oh, I hope it's what I think it is," she exclaimed excitedly as she slowly lifted the top off of the small box.

"What's this?" she asked, glaring at James.

"Why it's a baby bootie to add to your charm bracelet. I thought you'd like it with the baby coming and all," James replied, feeling a groundswell of bitter disappointment starting to surround him.

"A baby bootie? Who wants a baby bootie on their birthday? People get those at a baby shower, not on their birthday," Elizabeth Rose retorted angrily.

"James Radley, you knew I wanted that bottle of perfume I showed you in the magazine, but instead you give me some cheap baby bootie for my charm bracelet! Some birthday this turned out to be!"

As if in slow motion, everyone sat in utter disbelief as Elizabeth Rose picked up the birthday cake that James' mother had painstakingly made for the event and threw it on the ground before running into the house, screaming horrible words at James as he ran helplessly after her.

The following Sunday, after lunch, James' father took him out on the front porch and told him that Elizabeth Rose was destroying the peace and harmony of the family, and he had no choice but to ask them to leave. Elizabeth was seven months pregnant.

He told James he had made arrangements with his brother Robert, James' uncle, who owned the service station where James worked at night, to use the garage apartment in back of the station. It had its own separate entrance from the garage itself, and consisted of one large open room that had a small utility kitchen at one end, and a small bathroom on the other. All they had to pay was gas and electric.

James thought that Elizabeth would be happy to have the privacy of her own place, but she flew into a rage over being asked to leave James' parents' home to live in one room above what she called, a filthy garage. Nevertheless, they moved, but Elizabeth spent her days treating herself to blue plate specials at Woolworth's Five and Dime lunch counter, and her afternoons in an air-conditioned movie theatre where she indulged her every craving for sweets at the concession stand, spending money on penny candy luxuries James could not afford.

Even working two jobs, James was having trouble making ends meet. Elizabeth Rose's due date was fast approaching and the doctor bills were mounting up. Her pregnancy had been difficult, and she never missed an opportunity to share her tale of woes with anyone willing to listen. The one thing that no one knew, including James and Elizabeth Rose, was that she was carrying not one baby, but two.

One month before she delivered, Elizabeth went into a rant that lasted for three days. She gave James an ultimatum; he either found them an apartment of their own, away from the smell of oil and gas, or she would leave, deny him all access to the baby, and move as far away as she could get. James, frantic with worry that Elizabeth Rose might actually take his baby from him, turned to Ruby Mae.

By now, Sunny Rae had graduated high school and was attending nursing school where she was living in student housing. Jackson Jr. had joined the Army and was living on a military base in Texas.

Ruby Mae had settled into a quiet, comfortable routine in the little four-room, white framed house on Peale Road. When James approached Ruby Mae about the possibility of he and Elizabeth moving in with her, he assured Ruby Mae they would only be there long enough for him to get on his feet financially. Little did James know that life on Peale Road would take on a more permanent arrangement as the months passed by.

On September 18, 1952, after a long and difficult labor, eighteen-year-old Elizabeth Rose Childers Radley gave birth. The waiting room was full of family; James, Ruby Mae, Sunny Rae, not to mention James' parents and his gaggle of brothers and sisters. Everyone was holding their breath in anticipation of whether the baby was a boy or a girl.

When Dr. Monroe came out of the delivery room to make the announcement, James could not take the suspense any longer and blurted out, "Okay, Doc, what is it?" Dr. Monroe looked at James, broke into a big grin and said, "James, you are not the father of one baby, but TWO! Elizabeth Rose just delivered twin girls, each one complete with ten fingers and toes! I thought Elizabeth Rose was a bit large during her last trimester, but I guess one of the girls was just curled under the other. Life is full of surprises, and I must say, this is one surprise I did not expect! The babies are small, but they are healthy, and we should all give thanks for that," Dr. Monroe said with a big smile etched across his face.

"Is Elizabeth all right?" James asked anxiously.

"James, Elizabeth Rose had a tough labor and delivery," replied Dr. Monroe, "but she'll be just fine. She just needs to rest now. Now, congratulations everyone, and might I suggest that you all go home, get some rest, and come back tomorrow to see the twins." The doc chuckled, shaking his head in amazement at what had just happened as he walked back towards the delivery room to check on Elizabeth Rose.

Everyone was more than a little surprised, though elated, that Elizabeth Rose had been carrying twins all along. James got more than his share of handshakes, slaps on the back, and congratulatory comments from all the family that had gathered at the hospital when Elizabeth Rose went into labor.

James was still in a state of shock as he and Ruby Mae drove back home that evening. There was a deafening silence between him and Ruby Mae, so much so that he suddenly heard his stomach rumbling and realized that he had not eaten all day. He knew nothing about birthing babies, but was convinced he felt every labor pain that Elizabeth Rose must have experienced as she labored to give birth to their daughters.

When they parked the car in the driveway and entered the house, Ruby Mae set about making a fresh pot of coffee, and pulled the last two pieces of sweet potato pie out of the refrigerator and set them on the kitchen counter. She fried James a couple of eggs, and re-warmed some biscuits she had made earlier in the day. James hungrily devoured the eggs and biscuits, knowing that Ruby Mae heard the rumblings of his stomach on the drive back home. Ruby Mae then set a slice of the sweet potato pie in front of each of them, and refilled their coffee cups with the dark, strong, aromatic brew.

As James ate his pie, he allowed its sweet and creamy texture to linger in his mouth. As he lifted his coffee cup, he inhaled the strong, rich, aroma of Ruby Mae's coffee. Ruby Mae broke the silence.

"James, I want you to know that I am tickled pink to be the grandmother of those baby girls, but young man, you now have quite a responsibility on your shoulders. Not only do you have to find a way to support you and Elizabeth Rose, you now have to find a way to support those two little babies who will depend on you for everything for many years to come. Having babies is one thing James; raising them is another." Ruby concluded.

"I know, Ruby Mae," James answered solemnly. "I know."

James' face suddenly looked weary and much older than his nineteen years. His mind was racing as he thought to himself. Yes, he and Elizabeth Rose had problems "adjusting" to married life, and the fact that she got pregnant so fast only complicated matters.

Elizabeth Rose was only eighteen years old, and James knew in his heart that she was not prepared to be a mother of one, much less two. Elizabeth Rose was self-centered and selfish, and he knew firsthand that her cold cobalt-blue eyes led to an even colder heart. All James could hope for was that motherhood would release Elizabeth Rose's maternal instincts and that, for once, she would be able to put someone else's needs before her own.

The next day, James got permission to take a long lunch hour from his job at the cigarette factory to visit his newborn twin girls. He arrived at the hospital right at noon and went straight to the nursery to see the miracles he and Elizabeth Rose had produced. The nurse saw him as he held up his visitor's sign that read, "Radley Girls," his hands shaking with nervous excitement. She then rolled the bassinets over to the viewing window for him to see us for the first time.

James was smitten at the first sight of his two little girls wrapped in pink blankets with scrunched-up little faces and tufts of soft brown hair sticking up on the top of their heads, both screaming at the top of their lungs. As the nurse held each of us up for him to see more closely, tears welled in his eyes as the joy of fatherhood engulfed him.

The nurse smiled reassuringly at James as she began to put us back into our bassinets, but not before James noticed that in the name slot of one bassinet was the name Radley, Mattie Rose, and in the other; Radley, Annie Lizbeth.

James' face was flushed with bright crimson red. He was furious. After all, he and Elizabeth Rose had agreed to name their child, depending on the sex, after one of their parents, as was tradition in the South. It took him only a couple of minutes to figure out what Elizabeth Rose had done. She had taken derivatives of her own name and used them to make ours. Elizabeth Rose Childers Radley was determined to leave her fingerprint some place in the world, and what better place than to name her twin daughters after herself.

When James confronted her about the names in her hospital room, she shrugged off his anger and said, "I don't know what your beef is about. I named Mattie after YOUR middle name Matthew, and besides, I'm their mother and I can name them what I please. And, let me give you something else to think about, James Radley. If you say another word on the subject, I'll change their last names from Radley to Childers and leave this stinking county so fast you won't be able to remember them in your dreams." And so, our names remained Mattie Rose and Annie Lizbeth Radley.

We were the first set of twins to be born on either side of the family, so we achieved a "down home" kind of celebrity status for which our young daddy and mama were ill prepared. Word had gotten out that a pair of twins had been born to a young, hometown couple, and so when we were released from the hospital, the local paper was there to snap pictures of the proud mother and father, each holding a baby girl in their arms. It seemed like everyone in the community wanted to see the Radley twins. Elizabeth Rose dragged us around like prize trophies and, like the sponge she was, soaked up every drop of attention she could get.

James was still working two jobs while we all lived with Ruby Mae in her little white framed, four-room house on Peale Road. But pretty soon, the excitement died down, and Elizabeth Rose was left with the day-to-day reality of caring for two infant babies. Elizabeth Rose rebounded quickly from our birth, but did not exactly take like a duck to water when it came to mothering. Eighteen-year-old Elizabeth Rose found herself housebound or, as she called it, "hog-tied" to two babies; something she deeply resented. Ruby Mae hired Oleta Massey to help Elizabeth Rose in the morning hours, knowing that she would be home by 3 PM from her job to pitch in when Oleta left.

By November, when we were two months old, the minute Ruby Mae walked in the door from work, Elizabeth Rose would practically throw us at her as she walked out the door, jumped in a car with anyone willing to give her a ride, only to return late that night.

If James would inquire as to where she'd been, she would shriek, "It's none of your business where I am! I'm stuck at home all day as it is, and I sure ain't going to be stuck here all night with the likes of you and those screaming babies."

Ruby Mae could see the marriage was deteriorating, but was helpless to change the course of events that would forever change our lives.

Elizabeth Rose grew more and more distant from James. She stayed out more and more, and it was rumored that she was hanging around the Blue Moon Drive-In, which was known for attracting shady characters. She started smoking, and James thought he could smell the faint aroma of beer on her breath when she came in late at night. If he dared ask her a question as to her whereabouts, a fight would break out and last until the wee hours of the morning. Elizabeth Rose was scratching and clawing at James to get out of the very cage she had constructed for herself.

Christmas and New Year's passed. James bought Elizabeth Rose a Whitman's Sampler for Valentine's Day, along with a card that he simply signed, "Love, James." The next day he found the card thrown in the trash can under the kitchen sink with the unopened box of chocolates.

James desperately wanted to hold the marriage together for the sake of his twin daughters, but Elizabeth Rose was growing more rebellious and irresponsible. She moved out of their bedroom and slept on the sofa in the front parlor.

By March, Elizabeth Rose Radley was leaving her five-month-old daughters with anyone and everyone who would keep them. She was gone more than she was home, and it was widely rumored that Elizabeth Rose had been seen with a character named Billy Bart Calhoun, a long distance truck driver, with tobacco-stained teeth and multiple tattoos up and down his arms. He had a reputation as a lady's man, and he was no stranger to trouble. James heard that Billy Bart was making frequent stops in Durham at the Blue Moon Drive-In to see some young woman with red, curly hair and fair skin.

In April, Elizabeth Rose did with Billy Bart Calhoun what she had done with James Matthew Radley. She left town bright and early one morning, but this time, she never came back. Billy Bart tattooed the word "Rose" above his heart and, apparently, that was all Elizabeth Rose needed for him to do to steal hers. They rode off down the highway together and, from that moment on, Annie Lizbeth and Mattie Rose Radley were motherless children.

The temporary living arrangement James had promised Ruby Mae now took on a more permanent tone. Ruby Mae left her job at the textile mill to take on the role of mothering two six-month-old twin girls. It was not a job she expected to assume at this stage in her life but, like James, she loved the girls and was determined that they would not suffer for the sins of their mother.

Eighteen months later, James Matthew Radley received a divorce decree from the State of Arkansas. It had been granted to Elizabeth Rose Childers Radley who had met state law requirements by living separate and apart from her legal husband in North Carolina for eighteen months. Elizabeth Rose signed away all parental rights to Mattie Rose and Annie Lizbeth Radley, giving James full and complete custody.

We were only two years old when our mother legally erased us from her life, but she had left us long before that. Elizabeth Rose Childers Radley did not have a maternal bone in her body, and we represented nothing more than an annoying reminder of a mistake she created with James Radley in the backseat of his brother's car. When I grew old enough to know about such things, I sometimes wondered if she made any more mistakes in the back of Billy Bart Calhoun's eighteen-wheeler.

We never heard or saw our birth mother again and, like an old valise put away and forgotten in the corner of a deep, dark attic, Annie Lizbeth and I relegated her to some deep, dark, corner of our minds as well.

The weight of the world was cast upon our daddy at an early age. It would have broken a lesser man.

But, from shattered beginnings come new starts, and to this day I hear Granny say:

"Houses are made of sticks and stones,
People are made of flesh and bone.
Don't take much to come together,
But when you're family, you're family forever."

SAME POD, DIFFERENT PEAS

Anyone who has ever ventured out of their safe little world will tell you they had doubts. But when it comes to making a major life change, not only is a certain amount of fear perfectly normal, it's actually helpful.

When you think about it, our healthy fears prevent us from jumping off of thirty-story buildings, or diving into deep water when you don't know how to swim. But the great thing about fear is that there are ways to get around it. You just have to be resourceful.

So, it was no coincidence when Mrs. Emily Johnson, the first female assistant principal ever hired at Carver Elementary, requested a year-end meeting with Daddy and Granny. Her goal? To convince Daddy and Granny that the time had come for Annie Lizbeth and me to be reassigned to different teachers for the upcoming fifth-grade school year.

Mrs. Darcy Earl, our fourth-grade teacher, brought the matter to Mrs. Johnson's attention during an end-of-year staff meeting when she was making recommendations regarding the promotion of various students in her fourth-grade class. Mrs. Earl was expecting her third child at any minute and, since she would not be returning to teach the following year, she felt the discussion with Mrs. Johnson was of an urgent nature. It was Mrs. Earl's opinion that, since we had been in the same classroom since first grade, and were approaching ten years of age, fifth grade might be an opportune time to separate us.

Mrs. Earl felt that if we were placed in separate classrooms, we would have the chance to explore our individuality, not only academically, but socially as well.

In our school records, Mrs. Earl wrote: "Annie Lizbeth and Mattie Rose Radley are 'fraternal twins' that have been dressed 'identically' since first grade. In this year's fourth-grade class, they have been the target of ridicule by other students."

She further noted, "I had a parent-teacher conference with Mr. Radley and Mrs. Childers earlier in the year, and briefly touched on the subject of separating the girls for the upcoming fifth-grade school year. Mrs. Childers was dead set against it, and Mr. Radley seemed to follow her lead. Please be aware that Mrs. Childers may be the roadblock around which you have to navigate."

Daddy's plant was on a production deadline, and he could not get off from work to attend the meeting. So, he called Mrs. Johnson and asked if Ruby Mae Childers, our granny, could attend the meeting on her own.

During their conversation, Daddy told Mrs. Johnson, "Ruby Mae is really the one who should be there, because she's the one who tends to the girls' needs. My job is to keep a roof over their heads and food on the table. Ruby has done a good job with the girls since their mama ran off, and I trust her, so it's best if you talk to her, and then she'll discuss your meeting with me."

"Ah... Mr. Radley," Mrs. Johnson hesitated. "I would like to tell you now the nature of the meeting, so you can let Mrs. Childers know what we'll be discussing."

"Sure," said Daddy. "What is it?"

"I really wish you could be here, Mr. Radley, because we want to discuss the possibility of placing Annie Lizbeth and Mattie Rose in separate classrooms this upcoming year," Mrs. Johnson concluded.

Daddy paused for a minute, knowing full well what Granny's thoughts were on the subject, but said, "I wish I could be there too, but I assure you, Ruby Mae is the one you need to talk to. She's funny about the girls, and she likes them to be together, but I will tell her what you've said, and let you two discuss the matter when you meet. I tend to go along with what Ruby Mae says when it comes to Annie Lizbeth and Mattie Rose. The woman may have gray hair, but where those girls are concerned, she has a heart of gold. We'll do the right thing by them, I can promise you that."

Mrs. Johnson asked Mr. Livingstone, the school principal, to join her at the meeting as a show of support for the recommendations she was going to make regarding Annie Lizbeth and me.

Emily Johnson had worked hard to climb up the ranks from teacher to Assistant Principal, a job she took seriously. She was an attractive woman in her early forties with dark brown hair. Although a few streaks of gray were beginning to show around her temples, she made no attempt to conceal them. She was of medium height, a little overweight, but she disguised it well by the conservative manner in which she dressed and carried herself. She was a stark contrast to the portly Mr. Livingstone, with his baggy eyes, prominent jowls, big pot belly, stubby legs, and food-stained ties.

It was a bold move on Mrs. Johnson's part to have a one-on-one meeting with Granny. At 5'11", 185 pounds, Ruby Mae Childers was a formidable woman. Her gray, cat-eyed eyeglass frames gave her gray-green eyes a stern appearance that belied the warm, fun-loving, optimistic person Annie Lizbeth and I knew and loved.

Every week, her salt-and-pepper tresses were washed, sculpted, lacquered, and forced into perfectly formed finger curls by Christine Brewer in the basement of her home beauty salon. To keep that fresh, "lacquered" look, Granny wore a nylon mesh hair net to bed every night to insure that her perfectly formed curls would stay that way.

Annie Lizbeth complained to me that she didn't know why Granny insisted on wearing that awful-looking hair net to bed. She said that, even without the net, Granny's hair could withstand gale-force winds. For once, Annie Lizbeth and I agreed on something.

Granny may have been "salt of the earth," but she was as meticulous in the way she dressed herself as she was in the way she dressed us. She wore the clean lines of crisply starched and ironed daytime cotton dresses, usually in small prints, and yet, she never appeared matronly. She preferred nylon stockings, with a reinforced heel and toe, tightly rolled in elastic garters above her knees because, as she explained to us, "they lasted longer."

At night, as Granny prepared for bed, we would watch her remove her stockings. Granny would put on a pair of five-and-dime white cotton gloves and gingerly roll her stockings down, to prevent nicking or snagging them. Wearing the same gloves, she carefully washed and rinsed each stocking by hand. Annie Lizbeth loved the glove part, but I liked seeing Granny lay the stockings out, full length, on a bath towel, which she folded and re-folded until it looked like a small package.

She would then walk all over the towel to remove the excess moisture from the stockings before hanging them to dry. If she caught Annie Lizbeth and me watching, she would do a little "Irish jig" on the towel and we would burst out laughing.

To this very day, as a grown woman with children of my own, whenever I wash out my stockings, I lay them out on a towel just as Granny did and, when I am sure no one is watching, I do a little "jig" on the towel, look towards heaven, and smile at Granny.

Granny's complexion retained the "essence" of the peaches and cream undertones of her youth; there was hardly a line on her face. A light dusting of facial powder and a swipe of her favorite coral-red lipstick to offset her perfectly straight, pearly-white teeth were the only makeup she wore.

She always pinched her cheeks to make them blush and if, by chance, we were around when she was applying her famous coral-red lipstick, Annie Lizbeth and I would line up right beside her, our chins tilted upwards and our lips pursed, waiting for her to stain our lips with a kiss. She would then tell us to "press, press, press" our lips together because Daddy would have a hissy fit if he thought we were wearing lipstick. I think the "press, press, press" part pretty much demolished whatever color she had planted there, but it was her way of making us feel grown up.

If I had to compare Granny to an animal, she would definitely qualify as a porcupine. Undisturbed, Granny was fine, but if you cornered her and poked at her soft spots, specifically where we were concerned, you might find your back side embedded with a shield of quills.

Mrs. Johnson heard through the teachers' grapevine that Granny could be prickly, so she set about the task of making her feel right at ease when the day of the meeting arrived. As Granny made her way up the schoolhouse steps and pulled opened the heavy, grey metal door leading into the entrance hall of the school, Mrs. Johnson was standing there waiting to greet her. Granny, wearing her Sunday best, looked like she just stepped out of a bandbox, neat, dapper and groomed to the nines.

Mrs. Johnson extended to Granny a welcoming hand, while Granny extended to her a bright smile and robust hello. Together, they engaged in small talk while walking down the seemingly endless corridor that led to the office where Mr. Livingstone had already gathered.

As Granny walked down the long hall, she could hear her voice echo against the barren schoolhouse walls typically filled with the artwork of Carver Elementary students. When she asked Mrs. Johnson about the missing artwork, Mrs. Johnson replied, "Well, it's summer vacation, and we always send the artwork home with the students for their parents to display and enjoy," giving Granny a grin and a wink as she emphasized the words "display and enjoy."

Granny smiled back, remembering that Annie Lizbeth and I had come home with a stack of artwork a mile high on our last day of school, and immediately converted the walls of our room into a mini art gallery.

After Granny and Mr. Livingstone exchanged basic pleasantries, Granny took a seat, her black leather pocketbook perched on her lap as she loosely clasped her hands around its single strap.

Mrs. Johnson began the meeting by saying, "As you know, Mrs. Childers, Annie Lizbeth and Mattie Rose are the only pair of 'twins' at Carver Elementary, and they are a wonderful addition to our student population."

"Thank you," Granny replied politely, delighted to hear the word "wonderful" used in Mrs. Johnson's description of us.

Mrs. Johnson continued. "At a recent staff meeting, Mrs. Earl, the girl's fourth-grade teacher, brought up the idea of assigning Annie Lizbeth and Mattie Rose to different teachers for the upcoming school year. When Mr. Radley called and said he could not attend this meeting, I mentioned the idea to him, but he said that you were the person with whom I needed to discuss the matter, so I am most interested in hearing your thoughts."

Granny looked over at Mr. Livingstone, as if she was waiting for him to confirm, or add something more, to what Mrs. Johnson had just said. Instead, he cleared his throat, shifted uneasily in his chair, and averted his eyes away from hers, fixing his gaze instead on the tomato stain his tie had acquired when he ate spaghetti for lunch in the school cafeteria that day. Mrs. Johnson's eyes begged Mr. Livingstone to step in and add support, but his preoccupation with his tomato-stained tie indicated that he was taking the coward's way out. Mrs. Johnson was on her own.

"Well," Granny began, "James did say you mentioned the idea of separating the girls this year and, I admit, I am none too fond of the idea. I don't know if you are aware of the girls' background, Mrs. Johnson, but their mama, my daughter, ran off and left those babies when they were only six months old.

Poor James, being so young and all, was devastated, but most of all, he was helpless to take care of two babies. So, when my daughter stepped out of the picture, I stepped in. James and I have done our best to create a sense of family for Annie Lizbeth and Mattie Rose and, to me, family means sticking together. I never wanted those girls to feel 'different' or 'not good enough' because of the poor choices their mama made, so James and I have purposely kept them together so they would always have one another on which to rely."

"Mrs. Childers, I certainly hear what you are saying about the girls, and I sense your concern for the overall well-being of both Annie Lizbeth and Mattie Rose," Mrs. Johnson replied empathetically.

"However," she continued, "being a twin is but one aspect of who Annie Lizbeth and Mattie Rose are, not the only. By always being together and dressing alike, the girls are looked at by their classmates as a 'matched set.'

"Annie Lizbeth and Mattie Rose are twins, and that bonds them in a special way, but they are individuals, nonetheless, and sooner or later they will have to learn to rely on themselves. I think we can start that process by placing them in separate classrooms next year." Mrs. Johnson, bringing her comments to a close, waited for Granny's response.

Granny knew she was being asked to step outside the safe world she had carefully constructed for us and reflect on what had been said in the meeting. She asked if she could excuse herself for just a minute or two to get a drink of water.

Mrs. Johnson replied, "Of course, take as long as you need. We'll be right here." Granny didn't need water; Granny needed time to think. As she walked down the long, wide, wooden corridor in search of a quiet place, she found an empty classroom and sat down at one of the desks that in a few weeks might very well belong to Annie Lizbeth or me.

She thought to herself that perhaps, even with the best of intentions, she had done Annie Lizbeth and me a disservice by presenting to the outside world an appearance of "sameness." She had spent the last ten years of her life believing that if she kept us together, even to the point of dressing us as mirror images of one another, that no matter where we looked, we would always see the other's reflection standing nearby as a safe harbor in times of need.

We had now reached our fork in the road. And even though no one could predict which one of us would take the road less traveled, it was time for the journey to begin.

Granny walked back down the hall and re-entered Mr. Livingstone's office. A feeling of calm replaced her earlier apprehension. Sensing that all was well between the ladies, Mr. Livingstone suddenly came to life as he shifted his attention from his tomato-stained tie to the meeting that was now winding down.

"Mrs. Childers," he eagerly chimed in for the first time, "I cannot tell you how delighted I am that we were able to have this meeting today and talk about the future of Annie Beth...uh, excuse me, I mean, Annie

Lizbeth and Mattie Rose. Mrs. Johnson and I want nothing but the best for our students here at Carver Elementary, and you have our commitment that your girls will receive nothing less!"

Granny thanked Mrs. Johnson for her time, shook her hand, and assured her she would discuss the matter with Daddy and get back in touch with her quickly regarding his decision about separate classrooms for Annie Lizbeth and me.

Before she exited the door, Granny looked over at Mr. Livingstone and said, "Tell your wife to put some cornstarch on that tomato stain and let it sit awhile before she brushes it out. It works every time." And with that, Granny turned on her heels, left the building, and headed for home.

Later that evening, as we sat down to a supper of cold sliced ham, potato salad, fried green tomatoes, and biscuits, Annie Lizbeth and I sensed something was "up." First, after Daddy said evening grace for the food we were about to receive, the table was quieter than usual. Our supper table was always filled with lively conversation. No sooner did Annie Lizbeth stop talking than I would pick up where she left off. Granny was always fussing about us interrupting one another, or talking with our mouths full, but tonight, our transgressions seemed to go unnoticed.

Second, I noted that Daddy and Granny occasionally exchanged knowing looks with one another, but quickly shifted their eyes to their supper plates the minute I caught them in the act of their visual conspiracy.

Third, and most telling, was that Daddy and Granny had barely touched any of the food on the plates set before them. This was highly unusual because Daddy was like a hungry grizzly bear when he got home from work, and he always looked forward to one of Granny's home-cooked meals.

Like a pressure cooker on the verge of exploding, Granny blurted out, "Annie Lizbeth and Mattie Rose, your Daddy has something he wants to tell you."

And out it came, simple as could be. "Mattie Rose and Annie Lizbeth," he said, "the school is recommending that you girls be assigned to different teachers this upcoming year, and Granny and I think it's a good idea. The school thinks different classrooms and different teachers will present you with chances to learn new things on your own."

And, just like that, our world changed. The Radley twins were about to undergo the physical and academic separation for which we silently longed.

It took a wise and compassionate educator named Mrs. Emily Johnson to translate that longing into meaning for Granny. Moreover, it took wisdom and understanding for Granny to recognize that the time had come to let go of the old, so that Annie Lizbeth and I could embrace the new.

Annie Lizbeth gave me a quizzical look and shrugged her shoulders as if saying, "Can you believe this?" as she sprinkled extra salt on her fried green tomatoes. Daddy asked Granny for another piece of ham, and Granny suddenly regained her appetite as she helped herself to a big scoop of potato salad.

Suddenly, our kitchen table was alive again with conversation, laughter, and the tingling sensation that things were about to change for Annie Lizbeth and me.

There would be plenty of time to think about the changes that lay ahead, but for tonight, in this moment, surrounded by Annie Lizbeth, Granny and Daddy, I happily surrendered to the sweet familiarity of sameness.

THE LETTER

Shortly after Granny and Daddy's surprise suppertime announcement to us, Granny contacted Mrs. Johnson to tell her that she and Daddy agreed that Annie Lizbeth and I should be assigned to different teachers for the upcoming school year. Within a week of Granny's call, an official Carver Elementary School envelope arrived in Friday's mail addressed to Mr. James Radley. Granny knew it was the all important letter that held the news of our teacher reassignments. "Darn," Granny thought as she put the day's mail on the kitchen table. "Why couldn't they have put my name on the envelope as well? Then at least I would have a reason to open and read it!"

For a fleeting moment, she considered putting the tea kettle on to boil so she could steam open the envelope, read its contents, and then reseal it without Daddy being the wiser. Instead, she resisted the devil's temptation and put the envelope on top of the other mail that had arrived that day, making sure that Daddy would see it first thing when he arrived home from work.

When we were about a year old, Daddy's brother, Frank, helped him land a full-time job at American Tobacco, a local cigarette manufacturing company. Frank worked in sales and was well-connected inside the company. Frank used those connections to get Daddy an interview where he was subsequently hired to work in the shipping and receiving department. It was a physically taxing job, but at the age of twenty, Daddy was young enough to handle the constant lifting and unloading of boxes into eighteen-wheeler trucks that, when filled, would drive off and deliver cartons of cigarettes to retail customers all across the country.

Daddy was a quiet man who never missed a day of work and did whatever was asked of him without complaint. Daddy's work ethic did not go unnoticed by his supervisors, and so, at the ripe old age of twenty-five, he was promoted to a "desk job" within the company, where he now sat, instead of stood, for eight hours a day. The heaviest thing Daddy now lifted was a bill of lading or packing slip for the dock loaders to put into the crates they were preparing for shipment.

Daddy was so dependable you could set your watch by him. He left for work every morning at seven, and returned every evening at five. You didn't even have to look at the clock to know that five o'clock had arrived because you could hear the mufflers on Daddy's 1957, black Ford Fairlane banging and popping the minute he cleared the overpass and headed up Peale Road towards home.

If we happened to be in the yard, Annie Lizbeth and I typically ran over to greet Daddy, as the car swayed back and forth as he tried to avoid the numerous pot holes left by summer rainstorms in our red clay driveway before pulling up alongside the house to park his car for the night. When Daddy exited the car, he would begin to loosen the tie that held his Adam's apple hostage throughout the day. This particular evening, as he walked from the car towards the house, he saw Granny perched on the steps outside the screen door waving some white envelope in his direction like a flag at a Fourth of July parade. It was obvious she was excited about something.

The letter had been staring at Granny all day, quietly beckoning her to cross over to the dark side and read it first, but she had resisted the urge. But now that James was home, the seemingly endless wait was finally over. Scurrying over to him, waving the envelope wildly about her head, Daddy wondered what the commotion was all about.

"Look James, look! Look at what I've got!" Granny said excitedly as she handed him the envelope.

Daddy took the envelope from her hand, studied it briefly before eyeing the return address of Carver Elementary School in the upper right hand corner.

"Look at what, Ruby Mae?" he replied quite calmly, knowing perfectly well what was inside the letter and that the suspense was killing her.

"Well, for heaven's sake, James Matthew Radley, aren't you going to open it?" Granny asked impatiently.

"Well, if you'll give me a minute Ruby Mae, I will. But can we at least go in the house and open it, or are you going to have a hissy fit out here in the yard if I don't?" he replied, doing his best to keep from bursting out laughing at her obvious exasperation with him.

With that, Granny lifted her chin, turned on her heels, huffing and mumbling under her breath as she headed back towards the house, slamming the screen door behind her as she entered the house. Daddy knew he had tested the limits of Ruby Mae's patience and sheepishly followed her into the kitchen He quietly sat down at the kitchen table, pulled out his pocket knife and slashed open the top of the crisp, white envelope. When he removed the letter and unfolded it, he handed it to Granny and said, "Here, you read it, Ruby Mae."

"James," she said, as she caught her breath. "Listen to this," as she began to read the letter."

June 12, 1961

Mr. James Radley
4001 Peale Road
Durham, North Carolina

Dear Mr. Radley,
    The following fifth-grade classroom assignments have been made:
Annie Lizbeth Radley: Assigned to Mrs. Alice Cozell
Mattie Rose Radley: Assigned to Miss Margaret McGee

The new school year begins on September 4, 1961. Classes start at 8:10 AM. We look forward to seeing the girls in the fall.

Sincerely,
Mrs. Emily Johnson, Assistant Principal
Carver Elementary School

Granny clasped her hand over her mouth in disbelief. It was now official. Annie Lizbeth and I had been assigned to different teachers for fifth grade. "Oh my goodness, James, wait until Annie Lizbeth and Mattie Rose hear the news! James, can I tell them, *please*? Would you mind?" she asked anxiously in anticipation of sharing the news with us.

"Of course you can tell them, Ruby Mae. After all, you're the reason the change was made in the first place," Daddy said, as he picked up the next piece of mail to open, a smile slowly creeping across his face.

Granny, holding the letter in her hand, exited the kitchen in a flash as she headed for the screen door and down the steps into the backyard where she had seen us playing right before Daddy came home. She found us out on the old black tire swing Daddy had suspended with a rope from an oak tree in the back yard. We had been taking turns to see who could push who the highest. Annie Lizbeth was in the tire swing and I was pushing her as hard as I could, as she yelled, "Higher, Mattie Rose, higher!"

Annie Lizbeth was suspended in mid-air when Granny came running towards us, waving the letter above her head and yelling, "Annie Lizbeth, Mattie Rose... quick, quick, get off that swing right now and come over here. We got your teacher assignments today, and I bet you can't wait to hear in whose classroom you're going to be!"

Annie Lizbeth bailed from the swing like a tree squirrel and went flying over to meet Granny at the picnic table that Daddy built years ago for our occasional barbeques and messy arts and crafts projects.

When Annie Lizbeth jumped off the swing, it swung back with enough force to knock me to the ground. At first I was a bit stunned, but when I realized what Annie Lizbeth had done, I was furious. How dare she jump out of a moving swing like that, leaving me to absorb its full impact? As I got up off the ground and dusted myself off, I could have cared less about my teacher assignment, because I was going to get even with Annie Lizbeth and knock her to the ground so she could get a taste of her own medicine. I didn't care if Granny sent me to my room for the rest of my life. Annie Lizbeth was going to pay for what she did to me!

"Mattie Rose, don't make me call you again," Granny said. "You come over here right now. I have important news to tell you."

I sullenly walked over to the picnic table, my eyes shooting darts in Annie Lizbeth's direction. Annie Lizbeth acted oblivious to my rage, so I looked at Granny and said, "Annie Lizbeth let that tire swing come back on me and it knocked me to the ground. I'm going to push her to the ground so she knows how it feels," I declared, defiantly.

"You are not pushing anyone to the ground, much less your sister, now come on over here and sit next to me. And since you two cannot get along for a minute, Annie Lizbeth, I want you on the other side of the table. Why you girls are always fighting is beyond me," Granny said, annoyed that we were ruining her news.

"Okay, now where was I?" Granny said, flustered by the fact that I had interrupted her train of thought with threats of physical violence against Annie Lizbeth. "Oh yes, I was about to tell you your teacher assignments for next year." Granny took a deep breath, gave us one of her wide, bright smiles, and announced, "Mrs. Johnson has decided that Annie Lizbeth will be in Mrs. Cozell's class, and Mattie Rose will be in Miss McGee's. Now isn't that something about which we should all be excited?"

Annie Lizbeth leapt up from her seat across from me at the picnic table and started jumping up and down. "Oh boy, oh boy, oh boy, I got Mrs. Cozell! She's the BEST fifth-grade teacher at Carver! Wait until Daddy hears this!" she joyfully exclaimed, as she took off running towards the house to find him, unaware that he already knew who was going to be in whose classroom that fall.

I felt like I had been hit by the tire swing again, but this time, right smack dab in my face. Oh my goodness, what had I done to deserve a year of solitary confinement in Miss Margaret McGee's dark den of learning? She had the reputation as the meanest fifth-grade teacher at Carver, and I was the unlucky stiff who drew the losing fifth-grade lottery ticket. I was still sitting beside Granny when she looked at me and said, "Mattie Rose, what's wrong with you? Are you still pouting about the tire swing? Why aren't you all excited like Annie Lizbeth?"

"Because Granny," I said, tears welling in my eyes, "Miss McGee is the meanest teacher at Carver, and Annie Lizbeth is the meanest sister in the world, and while I know I can be mean too, I'm not mean enough to deserve all this." I started to sob, my pent-up emotions released at last as I buried my head on the big fluffy pillow of Granny's bosom. I pressed my head against her chest for quite some time, finding comfort there as she held me close and stroked my hair.

"Now, now, Mattie Rose," Granny said soothingly, as she lifted my chin, looked me in the eye and spoke. "If any kid is smart enough to find a way to get along with Miss McGee, it will be you. You may not always agree with what she says, but you must always be respectful, because she is your teacher. In life, Mattie Rose, you have to learn to get along with all sorts of people, and this may be one of those times. I guarantee if you do what is expected, and mind your manners, you and Miss McGee will get along just fine. Just you wait and see."

I took some solace in Granny's words, but I still had a sickening feeling in my stomach that September 4, 1961, was going to be my own personal D-Day.

Suddenly, Daddy and Annie Lizbeth came outside, while Granny gave me a quick kiss on the head, and told me to wipe my eyes, as she got up from the picnic table and turned to go inside to get supper on the table.

"James?" she hollered back to him over her shoulder as she entered the house.

"Yeah, Ruby," he answered.

"I have a bunch of fresh strawberries I picked this morning, and if I don't use them up they'll go bad. Maybe we could pull out the ice cream maker and hand crank us some strawberry ice cream for dessert later. I'm sure Annie Lizbeth and Mattie Rose wouldn't mind a bowl or two, do you think?"

Daddy could see my eyes were red and swollen from crying. He looked lovingly at me and winked. "No, Ruby Mae, I reckon they wouldn't."

They say that in life you have to learn to take the bitter with the sweet. The news of my assignment to Miss McGee's fifth-grade class had been a bitter pill for me to swallow that day. But Granny, in her infinite wisdom, knew that a bowl of her homemade strawberry ice cream would sweeten my day and that, in time, I would learn that life is rarely all bitter or sweet, but a combination of the two. The trick is learning how to swallow both with grace.

DON'T MESS WITH GRANNY

It didn't take long for Annie Lizbeth and me to find out who had been assigned to whom for the upcoming fifth-grade year. Our community was small, and the kids attending Carver Elementary were the same kids you saw at the public swimming pool, in Vacation Bible School, at church, or, as playmates in the neighborhood.

Miranda Stone had also been assigned to Miss McGee's class. Miranda Stone was the only daughter of Herbert and Evelyn Stone. They were grooming her to be the next Princess Grace of Monaco, and she took to the role like a duck to water. Annie Lizbeth and I could not stand Miranda because she was spoiled, snooty and, worst of all, a tattletale.

Her Mother, Evelyn, took great pride in telling all her lady friends that Miranda only wore the finest; Peaches and Cream dresses and Life Stride shoes.

Annie Lizbeth and I wore designer dresses too; homemade dresses designed by Granny and shoes by Buster Brown. If we did get a store-bought dress, it was usually off the discount rack at Sear's Department Store in downtown Durham.

One Sunday morning in early July, while in Bible study class, Evelyn Stone heard Granny mention to one of the church ladies that Annie Lizbeth and I would be in different classrooms for the first time. Evelyn's ears perked up when she heard that Annie Lizbeth was going to be in

Mrs. Cozell's class and that I was going to be in Miss McGee's. The minute Evelyn received her letter that Miranda had been assigned to Miss McGee, she had done her best to have her reassigned to Mrs. Cozell.

Evelyn tried to plead her case to Mrs. Johnson by stating that Miss McGee had a reputation as a tyrant teacher, and that Miranda was far too sensitive a child to be placed in that type of classroom environment. Mrs. Johnson refused the request by stating that Miss McGee was held in high regard at Carver Elementary, and that all classroom assignments were final. Evelyn had played her final hand with Mrs. Johnson and had come up short. So, it did not take Evelyn long to make a bee-line for Granny after church services.

"Oh, Ruby Mae, do you have just a little minute to spare? I'd like to speak with you about something regarding the girls," she said, sugar oozing out of her mouth.

"Well, of course, Evelyn," Granny replied. "What can I do for you?"

"Ruby Mae, they've made a terrible mistake over at Carver Elementary," Evelyn stated dramatically.

"What kind of mistake?" Granny asked.

Evelyn continued. "Ruby Mae, they put my Miranda in Miss McGee's fifth-grade class, when I specifically requested that she be put in Mrs. Cozell's. Miranda is such a special child. I don't know how well she will cope in Miss McGee's highly structured classroom."

Evelyn barely came up for air before continuing in the same syrupy, sweet voice Granny despised. "I think I overheard you say in Bible study class that your Annie Lizbeth has been placed in Mrs. Cozell's classroom and that Mattie Rose is going to be in Miss McGee's. Is that correct or am I mistaken?"

"That's right, Evelyn," Granny replied, her spine stiffening. "James and I decided the girls should be in separate classrooms next year."

Granny was a formidable woman and not a person you wanted to mess with, but Evelyn was oblivious to anything but her own self-interests.

"Well, Ruby Mae, don't you think that might be a mistake considering that the girls are twins and have never been separated before? I mean, it could be very traumatic for them, considering their 'past' and all," Evelyn said, as she whispered the word "past." "I just want you and James to know that should you reconsider separating those precious girls, Miranda will be happy to exchange teachers with Annie Lizbeth," she concluded, as she cleared her throat uneasily. Seeing Granny's icy stare, Evelyn's radio dial suddenly tuned into Granny's station, and she had a foreboding sense that her favorite record was not the next one in the queue.

"Well, my oh my," Evelyn said looking nervously at her watch. "I've taken up too much of your time, and Herbert will kill me if I don't go and say my goodbyes to Pastor Lewis so we can go home and have Sunday lunch. Ruby Mae, please give my regards to James and the girls," Evelyn mumbled as she shuffled over to thank Pastor Lewis for his inspirational sermon.

Granny always said you can't hold a child responsible for the actions of their parents, but that Sunday Evelyn Stone stepped into her "quill zone." Daddy had already left the church and taken us to the car, where we all sat, windows rolled down, sweating, fanning ourselves with cardboard church fans with stick handles furnished by Parson's Piece Goods Store, whose motto for the week was… "Blessed are the seamstresses for they keep us in stitches."

Granny walked over to the front of the vestibule where Evelyn was saying her goodbyes to Pastor Lewis and tapped her on the shoulder. When Evelyn looked back and saw Granny standing there, she did her best to make a quick exit. But it was too late.

"Ah, excuse me, Evelyn, but I have given our conversation as much thought as I'm going to give it. The Pastor can correct me if I am wrong, but it is my understanding that the good book teaches that everyone has their cross to bear in life and, if Mattie Rose can bear a year with Miss McGee, so can Miranda. I've also heard it said that busy souls have no time to be busybodies, and since I know you are a woman of substantial faith, surely you have more important things to ponder than the girls' classroom assignments."

Granny then turned her attention to Pastor Lewis. "Good day, Pastor," she said as she exited the church vestibule.

"Good day, Ruby Mae," replied Pastor Lewis.

Granny, never being one to let a sleeping dog lie, turned around one more time to address Pastor Lewis in front of a stunned Evelyn Stone.

"Pastor Lewis, James, the girls, and I look forward to hearing another one of your fine sermons next Sunday, and hope to have you and Mrs. Lewis join us for Sunday lunch real soon."

"Well, I never!" huffed Evelyn Stone, trying to mask the embarrassing encounter she had just had with Granny in front of Pastor Lewis.

"Well now you have," Pastor Lewis replied as he secretly asked the Lord to forgive him for the delight he took in Granny's "designer" put down of Evelyn Stone.

COPPER PENNIES

The only things we had in common that first day of school were white cotton bobby socks and brown penny loafers. That was the one thing on which Granny refused to compromise. She said we could select our own clothes, style our own hair, but as long as she could buy socks in six packs from the "employee outlet store" at The Cotton Mill, where, as a retired employee she received a discount on all "outlet" products, we would wear white cotton socks.

As for the penny loafers…they were all the rage at school, and Annie Lizbeth and I desperately wanted a pair. Granny argued that our black leather Mary Janes still had plenty of wear in them, but Daddy sensed our desire to "fit in," and not "stand out" among the other kids at school. So he worked the day shift every Saturday during the horrifically hot month of July, loading and unloading finished goods into eighteen-wheeler transport trucks on the docks of American Tobacco in order for us to have them. When Daddy would drag his tired, sweaty body through the door late Saturday afternoon, Granny never failed to give the two of us one of her "I-hope-you're-proud-of- yourselves" looks, and then say aloud so Daddy could hear, "I hope you girls realize how lucky you are to have a daddy like yours!"

We would always respond the same… "We know, Granny, we know," though we had no clue as to the multitude of sacrifices Daddy made to provide not only the basic necessities of life, but a few of the extras as well.

The afternoon before the first day of school, Annie Lizbeth was running around like a gerbil in a cage, going through her closet inventory to decide which dress she was going to wear, while my stomach burned in anticipation of the next day's events. Daddy had put two, brand new, shiny, copper pennies in the slots of our loafers to give us good luck. I knew I would need more than new pennies to bring me "luck" in Miss McGee's class.

I had been pouting all afternoon, knowing that my destiny in Miss McGee's classroom was only a day away. Later that evening at the supper table, I burst into tears when Granny scolded me for pouting. "Mattie Rose," she said, "I've had enough of your doom and gloom. You've had your feathers ruffled ever since you learned about Miss McGee. Now, I've 'bout had enough of it, so if you cannot be pleasant at the supper table, then you can excuse yourself and have your supper later."

Annie Lizbeth locked eyes with mine, somewhat empathetically, but not empathetic enough to dampen her appetite as she chomped down on one of the cucumbers Granny had fried in bacon drippings to go alongside the golden-brown salmon patties that Daddy liked so much.

I jumped up from the table, sobbing, and ran into my room where I threw myself on my bed and buried my face in my pillow. It wasn't long before I felt the presence of someone in the room, someone who sat down beside me on my bed and began patting my back.

"There, there, Mattie Rose," came a soothing voice. "Everything's going to be all right. Granny didn't mean to hurt your feelings." It was Daddy.

As I sat up and looked at him, big tears flowed down my face. Trying to talk, I stammered, "I - I - I - I –" but couldn't get the words out as I tried to tell Daddy that I didn't think I could bear Miss Margaret McGee's class for an entire year. "It's not fair, it's not fair," I sobbed, tears still streaming down my face. "Why couldn't they put Annie Lizbeth in her room instead of me?"

Daddy pulled his clean, white, freshly-pressed handkerchief from his pocket and gently dabbed the tears from my eyes. "Mattie Rose," he began, "I told you when I received the teacher reassignment letter that the school uses an alphabetical system for student placement, and since Mrs. Johnson could not go by your last names, she used your first," he sighed, having explained this to me at least once a week since the letter arrived. "Your first name begins with an "M," which is closest to McGee. Annie Lizbeth starts with an "A," which is closest to Cozell, and that's why you are in Miss McGee's room and Annie Lizbeth is in Mrs. Cozell's."

"It's still not fair," I lamented.

"Mattie Rose," he said, "life is not fair, but you are going to have to accept what is and try to make the most of it. Every accomplishment starts with the decision to try. I have all the faith in the world that if you try your best in Miss McGee's classroom, at the end of the school year you will reap the rewards of your efforts."

Exhausted from crying, but surrendering to the sweet release of weeks of pent-up emotions, I closed my eyes and rested my head on Daddy's shoulder for a moment.

"Mattie Rose," he whispered softly as he stroked my hair. "Will you promise me you will try with Miss McGee?"

Knowing I was facing the inevitable, I lifted my head from his shoulders, eyes swollen and red from tears, looked him in the eye, and answered, "Yes, Daddy, I'll try."

"And don't forget, Mattie Rose," he said, smiling broadly.
"Remember:

Find a penny
Pick it up
All day long
You'll have good luck."

OH, HOW THEY HATE TO GET UP IN THE MORNING!

"BURR-ring, BURR-ring" rang the big, brass alarm clock that sat on the nightstand between our twin beds at exactly 5:25 AM, as it did every school day morning. The monstrous little hammer positioned between the two bells sitting atop the clock struck them both with infuriating speed, creating a metallic jarring sound that rattled our teeth and startled us into early morning wakefulness.

It was September 4, 1961, and the much-dreaded first day of school had finally arrived.

Still groggy from sleep, it took me a moment to register my surroundings before I reached out my hand to push down the alarm clock's hammer. However, Annie Lizbeth, queen of sibling rivalry, had already beaten me to it as she reached over and smashed the hammer down with her fist to stop the loud and obnoxious noise. Next, moaning unintelligible words, she flipped on her stomach and covered her head with her pillow to protect her ears from "round two" of our morning revelry.

The alarm clock was our first "wake up" call of the day, but the second, and most dreaded, was Daddy's unsolicited, endless caterwauling of Irving Berlin's World War I song, *"Oh, How I Hate To Get Up in the Morning."*

Daddy's singing was so bad that I once considered sticking a Q-tip through my eardrum just to deafen the sound, but Annie Lizbeth convinced me not to do it. She said we were losing enough brain cells just listening to him without inflicting further damage on ourselves. We could never decide which was worse, the metallic jarring sound of that hideous clock, or Daddy's torturous vocal rendition of *"Oh, How I Hate To Get Up in the Morning."* Both were an assault to the senses and provided ample motivation for us to pry our skinny little bodies out of the cozy confines of our beds and head in any direction furthest from all the noise which, for us, meant the bathroom located at the back of the house.

My eyes were still puffy from sleep as I shuffled through the kitchen on my way to the bathroom to prepare for school. As I glanced outside the kitchen window, I could see the sun was waking up too, and wondered if that dreadful alarm clock, combined with Daddy's singing, had the same effect on it that it had on us. How could anything or anyone ever stay asleep when those two forces were in concert with one another?

The coolness of the hardwood floors felt good against my bare feet. I paused for a moment as I caught a glimpse of the old "outhouse," now sitting all alone and forsaken behind the makeshift shed where Daddy kept his tools and yard stuff. Its only companion that morning was the kaleidoscope of red and orange hues as the sun rose in the southern sky that overlooked our little corner of the world.

Our family had abandoned the "outhouse" four years ago when Granny and Daddy decided to convert a small utility closet located right off the kitchen into a teeny-tiny bathroom the summer before Annie Lizbeth and I entered first grade. Granny feared that the kids at school would make fun of us, and call us names if word got out that our "indoor" facilities were actually located "outdoors."

The bathroom was literally the size of a closet, so economy of space was the number one consideration when it was constructed. Our next-door neighbors were Carl and Millie Forbush. They were a childless couple, who, in many ways, looked upon us as their own. Carl was a plumber, so when the time came to add on the bathroom, he volunteered to help, knowing that he could purchase the supplies second-hand, provide the labor for free, thus saving Daddy some much-needed pennies.

When Carl completed the bathroom, it had all the key necessities: a small white ceramic sink attached to the wall with a mirrored medicine cabinet suspended above it, a toilet, and a dinky corner shower stall made of galvanized steel we nicknamed the "bullet" because of its spherical shape and shiny exterior. To enter or exit the tiny bathroom, you did so via a pocket door that you pulled out or pushed into the wall. A single light bulb, activated by a pull chain, was the only light source for the room.

Our little bathroom was not up to the standard of the Vanderbilt or Duke family but, to Granny especially, it represented that we had raised our standard of living and, by doing so, achieved another small piece of the American Dream.

After Daddy's solo performance, it was no wonder that Annie Lizbeth was the original "Miss Crank" in the morning. She refused to speak to anyone and walked around like a zombie out of a B-list horror movie. One side of her hair lay flat against her head where she had pressed it against her pillow all night, while the other side stuck out in all directions like a zillion little brown pine needles.

Annie Lizbeth had a thing about bathroom and food cooties. She did not want anyone touching her things. Every morning, as we prepared for school, a fight would break out between us over who touched the bar of soap first, who screwed off the cap of toothpaste first and, heaven forbid, who moved or touched her hairbrush first! "Granny," Annie Lizbeth would yell at the top of her lungs, "Mattie Rose is touching my stuff again! Make her stop! Granny...."

Granny and Daddy were getting tired of hearing us fight every morning. In an effort to reduce Annie Lizbeth's morning cootie tantrums, Granny took her to Woolworth's Five and Dime store on Main Street and let her select her own powder-pink plastic soap container, and a matching powder-pink plastic toothbrush tube for her toothbrush. And, though our family used Palmolive bath soap and Pepsodent toothpaste, she bought Annie Lizbeth a four-pack of Ivory soap and a tube of Ipana toothpaste. Granny never bought for one without buying for the other, so I, too, got my own plastic soap/toothbrush containers. Granny chose my favorite color, "baby blue," so that there could be no confusion as to who's was whose in the mad rush to get ready for school each morning.

Annie Lizbeth seemed reassured knowing that she could now wash-up to her heart's content using the "soap that floats," and could "brusha, brusha, brusha" without fear that her personal hygiene products, now protected in plastic containers, were being contaminated by other people's cooties.

Still, in spite of Granny's efforts to bring peace to our morning routine, Annie Lizbeth always found a way to exercise one-upmanship on me. She found one of Daddy's old shoeboxes in the back of his closet, and, using a black magic marker wrote on the top in big, bold, letters... "Annie Lizbeth's Personal Hygiene Box... KEEP OUT OR ELSE!"

She lined her "personal hygiene box" with wax paper, which she faithfully changed every Saturday night while she soaked her hairbrush and comb in ivory soap and water. She would then rearrange her "personal hygiene products" in her box, and place it on a freshly-folded towel before stashing it underneath her bed for safekeeping.

One of Annie Lizbeth's most valued treasures in her personal hygiene box was a tiny bottle of Evening in Paris *eau de cologne*. While Granny argued that soap was the "perfume of kids," every now and then, at church or some other special occasion, I could smell the faint aroma of Evening in Paris on Annie Lizbeth. In an effort to make it last as long as she could, she would add little drops of water to it when its fragrant oils were running low.

At the age of ten, I don't think Annie Lizbeth figured out that oil and water do not mix, but she had figured out something more important: that, like the life that lay ahead of her, better it be half-full than half-empty.

After we washed up and dressed for school, we choked down pasty, sticky bowls of Granny's oatmeal, as she carefully watched the clock on the wall. "Hurry up or you are going to miss the bus," she said in an exasperated tone. "And, wouldn't that be a fine how-do-you-do, missing the bus on the first day of school!" With that, she burst out laughing, tickled pink that she had made a rhyme.

I thought Granny was a hoot, so I burst out laughing too, the oatmeal in my mouth spewing forth everywhere. "Ewwwwwwwh," Annie Lizbeth screeched as she jumped up and shoved her chair as far back from the table as she could, almost falling over it, fearful that a single, cootie-laden rolled oat might find its way in her direction. She quickly grabbed her school bag, gave me the evil eye, huffed a big sigh of righteous indignation, turned on her heels, and made a quick exit out the kitchen door heading towards the bus stop.

As I headed out the door right behind Annie Lizbeth, I took a final look at the calendar, my stomach tightening a bit in anticipation of what the day would bring.

A simple twist of alphabetical fate had landed me, and not Annie Lizbeth, in Miss McGee's fifth-grade classroom.

It would turn out to be a year I would never forget.

ME AND MISS MCGEE

It was the first day of school. Annie Lizbeth and I could see Bus #419 making its way around the curve heading towards our bus stop. You could hear the brakes come to a grinding stop before Mrs. Olive placed her hand on the manual release that opened the two-part, split-type door that allowed us to board.

Annie Lizbeth and I must have made school bus history that day. For one brief moment, when we stepped inside to make our way to the first available seat, the bus went silent. Our fellow riders were wide-eyed and speechless, their mouths hanging open in disbelief as they witnessed, for the first time, our dramatic transformation. It was a transformation that began after Granny's meeting with Mrs. Johnson, and continued throughout summer vacation after the decision was made to separate us for fifth grade.

Even Mrs. Olive asked, half joking, "Annie Lizbeth, Mattie Rose, is that you?"

"Of course it's us," I replied, a slight tone of indignation in my voice. "Who else would it be?" However, deep down inside, I was delighted that the change in us was striking enough that even Mrs. Olive, who looked at the same busload of faces year after year, had taken notice.

Annie Lizbeth had no interest whatsoever in current hairstyles, so she continued to wear hers in a bob cut with fringe bangs. I, on the other hand, had allowed mine to grow out to where it now reached slightly below my chin and naturally curled under.

For the first time in four years, the kids on the bus were not "seeing double." We were wearing outfits *we* had chosen, and *not* matching outfits chosen *for us*.

Patti Summerhill, my best friend since third grade, had saved Annie Lizbeth and me a seat on the crowded bus, which we eagerly accepted. Patti was short for Patricia. She and her family had relocated to North Carolina from California after her father was transferred by IBM. Patti was a ten-year-old, plucky tomboy with sun-bleached blond hair, round, expressive, bright-blue eyes, and skin the color of honey.

Our skin was so pale the kids called us "lilies." Annie Lizbeth said that Patti had been permanently "stained" by the sun because that's what happens to people who live in California and play on the beach all day. I don't know if Patti was "stained" or not, but she was a striking young girl whose potential as a natural beauty nature would later reveal.

When Bus #419 picked up its last student that morning, it lumbered down the long, bumpy, back roads of our bus route until it finally arrived at Carver Elementary School. Mrs. Olive pulled the bright-yellow bus into the circle entrance of Carver Elementary, where we found ourselves behind a line of other bright-yellow buses that had arrived before ours.

Most of the kids were antsy, excited to find their new classrooms and meet their new classmates and teachers for the new school year. Patti and I knew where we were headed, and there was certainly no excitement to be found in that.

One by one, as the school buses emptied out their cargo of students, the next school bus inched forward until, at last, it was Bus #419's turn to unload. Before Mrs. Olive opened the door, she turned around in her seat and yelled at the top of her voice that everyone better exit the bus in a single file, and that no pushing or shoving would be tolerated. "Just because this is the first day of school doesn't mean I won't write a bus misconduct report for anyone breaking the rules!" she threatened, as if her verbal warning was going to act as a deterrent to a bunch of elementary school juveniles.

I liked Mrs. Olive, I really did, but her warnings and veiled threats fell on deaf ears. With the exception of a few of us, most of the kids on our school bus route would probably, one day, have their yearbook pictures posted in the "Most Wanted" section of post offices all across America.

In my opinion, Melvin Sparks and Sammy Hicks should save everyone the trouble, and turn themselves in now. They were criminals-in-waiting, cunning and sharp, looking for loopholes in the system, which they usually found.

No sooner had she issued her verbal warning and opened the school bus door than a mass exodus of kids, with Melvin Sparks and Sammy Hicks leading the pack, charged out of the Bus #419. They were pushing and shoving any and everybody out the door as fast as they could, creating a massive pile-up of students.

The lucky ones landed on their feet outside the open school bus door. However, some unfortunate few, including Miranda Stone, got knocked to the ground, their arms, legs, and brand-new book bags flying in every direction.

Miranda Stone was shoved off the bus by Sammy Hicks who plowed into her, hurling her off the bus and onto the ground. At first stunned, she started to whimper. Patti and I watched as she picked herself up, her elbows and knees scraped, frantically dusting off the dirt that soiled her brand-new, pretty, pink dress, and scurrying around to pick up the pens and pencils that had fallen out of her brand-new pink book bag and scattered in all directions.

Annie Lizbeth was also one of the enthusiasts making her way to the front of the bus. She climbed over poor Cookie Ketchum's back to make her great escape. I yelled at Annie Lizbeth to wait for me, but she yelled back that she wasn't going to wait on my "snail's tail" and be late for class.

Sometimes Annie Lizbeth could really burn me up. I immediately thought of a word that rhymed with "class," and was a synonym for "tail," but knew if I called her by that name, she would tell Granny, and that would mean my mouth would be washed out with soap, so I thought better of the idea.

I was fuming. Just because we were in separate classrooms did not mean Annie Lizbeth had to run off like that. But, like a puff of smoke, she did, and for the next nine months, most of what I remember seeing was the back of her head as she darted from the bus to run up three flights of stairs to Mrs. Cozell's classroom, eagerly anticipating each new day of learning.

Patti and I sat in amazement at what had just transpired on Bus #419. Mrs. Olive was frantically writing out pink bus misconduct reports that she would be passing out to Melvin Sparks and Sammy Hicks, along with any other bus violator she could identify. Annie Lizbeth and her partners in crime received "warnings."

The last two people off Bus #419 that first day of school were Patti and me. Mrs. Olive did not have to worry about writing a bus misconduct report for the two of us, that is, unless you got one for refusing to leave the bus.

Carver Elementary School was a three-story, square, red brick building, with evenly cut windows across each of the four classrooms located on each floor. To the left of the main building was a bell tower with a huge bell that Mr. Livingstone rang at 8:05 every morning, alerting students that they had five minutes to find their way to class. He also rang the bell at the beginning and end of recess and lunch, and, most important to me and the other hostages in Mrs. McGee's class, at 3:10 PM to signal the end of the school day!

Class started at 8:10 every morning. A stately flag pole stood in front of the school house, and only members of the all-male Carver Elementary Safety Patrol, led by Mr. Ed Birmingham, Eagle Scout and boy's physical education teacher, were allowed to raise and lower the American flag. Whoever had the special honor bestowed upon him for the week had to be at school at 8:00 AM to raise the flag, and then lower it in synch as Mr. Livingstone rang the final school bell at 3:10 PM, all under the watchful eye of Mr. Birmingham.

The first floor of the building contained the first- and second-grade classrooms, along with a large auditorium plopped right in the middle of the large square that was designated for PTA meetings, school plays, and other large group activities. Behind the auditorium was the school administrative area where Mr. Livingstone, Mrs. Johnson, the school secretary and school nurse were located.

The second floor was home to the third- and fourth-grade students. As if climbing the chain of command, the third floor was reserved for the fifth- and sixth-grade classrooms. Melvin Sparks told Sammy Hicks, who told Tommy Jones, who told Patti Summerhill, who told me, that the reason we were on the third floor of the building was so Mr. Livingstone and Mrs. Johnson could not hear all the screams coming from Miss McGee's classroom!

With the exception of the first floor that had the big auditorium plopped right in the middle of it, each of the four, rectangular, cinderblock classrooms sat opposite from one another with a long, wide, wood plank hallway running down the middle of them. At one end of the lengthy hall was a girls' restroom, and on the opposite end was the boys'. Mounted on the wall outside of each restroom were two water fountains designed to accommodate thirsty students throughout the day. Those water fountains would ultimately lead me to my own personal "Waterloo."

To the right of the main building was a flat-roofed, one-level school cafeteria. The original cafeteria had been located in the school's basement, but when we entered third grade, they added the new space to accommodate more kids. The cafeteria seemed more like an afterthought than anything else, but then, so did the food it served.

Why anyone would pay to stand in an endless line of hungry, irritable kids, only to end up with some grisly, cheap meat baked into submission and hidden in some kind of hideous gravy on a metal tray was a mystery to me. Granny's brown bag lunches may not have won awards for creativity, but at least when I removed the wax paper from my sandwich, I knew what I was eating.

Miss Margaret McGee must have laid the first brick at Carver Elementary, and her reputation as a tyrannical taskmaster was legendary. She had been teaching fifth grade at Carver for forty-three years, and she was the oldest teacher at the school. Either she had taught everyone in town, or everyone knew some poor soul that survived the ordeal of having been taught by her.

Miss McGee had a reputation as a strict, nit-picky, crabby, old-maid school teacher who, with the exception of a broomstick, pointy black hat, and green complexion, bore a striking resemblance to Margaret Hamilton, who played the wicked witch in the movie *The Wizard of Oz*.

Melvin Sparks, whom Patti Summerhill and I voted "Future Snake Oil Salesman of America," had convinced many of the younger kids at Carver Elementary School that Margaret Hamilton could not find work after the movie. He was most persuasive as he argued, "Who would want to hire her after she stole Dorothy's dog Toto, set the scarecrow on fire, made the tin man cry and rust, and frightened the cowardly lion out of his wits?" He was convinced she changed her name from Margaret Hamilton to Margaret McGee and left Hollywood to work undercover as a teacher at our school.

Every kid at Carver Elementary froze in their tracks when they heard the "click, click, click" of Miss McGee's black leather, Enna Jetticks's shoes, with their two-inch square heels, coming down the hall. She was a tough old biddy who, upon spotting you in the hall at any time other than designated breaks, would grab you by the arm and demand to see your teacher's pass. If, by chance, you did not have one, off to Mr. Livingstone's office you went, where you received a demerit. Three demerits landed you in Miss McGee's after-school detention program for rule violators.

Neither Annie Lizbeth nor I had ever received a demerit, so all we knew of Miss McGee's after-school detention program was hearsay, but those that went once were rarely repeat offenders. The rumor was if you were sent to Miss McGee's after-school detention program, into the coat closet you went. The only light source in the coat closet was a single overhead bulb whose on/off function was controlled by Miss McGee. If Miss McGee banished you to the coat closet, you stood in the dark. Because many of my fifth-grade classmates were afraid of the dark, going to the coat closet was the worst possible punishment they could imagine. You could see chins quiver and eyes swell with tears once the decree was handed down by Miss McGee that the offending party was going into the coat closet. You could hear the sobs of repentant boys and girls begging for one last pardon, which Miss McGee never granted.

Once time had been served, the prisoner of the coat closet would come out blinking and shading their eyes from the onslaught of light that flooded the bare windows of the classroom. They would quietly take their seat and fade into silent oblivion for the rest of their time in her after-school detention program.

As Annie Lizbeth and her new classmates ran through the open double doors of Mrs. Cozell's classroom that were covered in bright-yellow construction paper with big orange letters that spelled "Welcome Back Students" that first day of school, Patti and I, along with eighteen fellow inmates, were lined up like members of a chain gang along the outside cinderblock wall of Miss McGee's class.

The doors to her classroom were closed. There was no bright-yellow construction paper, or bright orange letters spelling out "Welcome Back Students" covering her doors. Instead, the steel-gray doors looked more like the entrance to a prison cell where we would be detained for the next nine months.

As she checked off our names in alphabetical order, her beady eyes looked over the half-frame glasses she balanced on the bridge of her bumpy, pointed nose at each of us, up and down, as if we had some communicable disease.

"Hicks, Samuel?"

"Here," he replied, giving his best James Dean, Rebel WITH a Cause, imitation.

"Jones, Thomas?" "Here," he mumbled nervously as he looked at the floor and his scuffed-up shoes.

"Radley, Mattie Rose?"

"Here," I replied, thinking of Daddy's words, "Promise me you'll try."

"Sparks, Melvin?"

"Here," he replied, jerking his overactive body side to side, like one of the tough guys representing the Lollypop Guild from *The Wizard of Oz*, trying to see if she recognized his character imitation from the movie, so he could blow her cover.

"Stone, Miranda?"

"Here," Miranda said, sugar dripping from her mouth, just like her mother. "And may I say what a pleasure it is to meet you Miss McGee."

"Summerhill, Patricia?"

"Present, but my *friends* call me Patti," she replied gaily.

"Well, P-A-T-R-I-C-I-A, let's get this straight from Day One. You are not my friend. You are a student. You will be addressed as 'Patricia,' and only 'Patricia,' when in my presence. Do you understand?"

"Yes, I understand: *you are not my friend*," Patti replied, her blue eyes glaring directly into Miss McGee's beady brown eyes.

I could feel the cinderblock starting to crumble when Miss McGee looked at Patti and said, "Young lady, I have a feeling you and I are going to see a lot of each other in my after-school detention program." Plucky Patti said not a word, choosing instead to shrug her shoulders as she continued her stare-down with Miss McGee.

When Miss McGee completed checking off the twenty names that comprised our classroom on the metal clipboard she held close to her bony chest, I wondered if she was guarding some top school security secrets that she had gathered surreptitiously in the dead of night, to use against each of us for an extended "sentence" in her class at some later date.

When she was satisfied that roll call was completed, she opened only one door to her classroom, instructing us to enter, single file, and locate our desks, which we would find marked with name cards.

Funny how Miss McGee's request was taken much more seriously than the one that came from Mrs. Olive, less than fifteen minutes earlier. There was no shoving, no pushing, and no massive clumps of kids trying to get ahead of one another. Instead, we marched in silent unison and entered Miss McGee's stark and barren prison cell of a classroom.

There on our wooden flip-top desks were name cards that simply read: Mr. Samuel Hicks, Mr. Thomas Jones, Miss Mattie Rose Radley, Mr. Melvin Sparks, Miss Miranda Stone, and Miss Patricia Summerhill, along with fourteen other Misters and Misses, identified by their "proper names" only.

Walking back and forth across the front of the room, Miss McGee picked up her wooden yardstick and loudly tapped the blackboard three times. "Class," she said, "whenever you hear me tap this blackboard three times, that means your full attention is to be on me. Does everyone understand?"

There was silence in the classroom.

"I'm sorry, I didn't hear you!" she replied condescendingly, her voice growing louder. "Does everyone understand that when I tap this blackboard three times, your attention is to be on me?" she snarled.

"Yes, Ma'am, we understand," we replied in harmony. The "Yes, Ma'am, we understand" regurgitation would become our class mantra for the next nine months.

"Very well," Miss McGee continued, tap, tap, tapping against the blackboard with the soon-to-be-hated ruler. "Let's begin our first day together going over classroom rules and regulations."

"She means prison rules," Patti whispered to Melvin Sparks and me, as we stifled a laugh, fearful of drawing Miss McGee's attention to ourselves.

"And, in case anyone has doubts," Miss McGee continued, "please be aware if you do not follow MY rules, there will be consequences," she added, her toxic tone communicating two parts threat combined with three parts power.

Tap, tap, tap went her yardstick on the blackboard, and we instinctively knew Miss McGee could and would use it to inflict pain or humiliation. The stinging blow of a swinging yardstick can work like an electric shock treatment for those students that fail to respond to other methods of classroom discipline. Miss McGee did not have the reputation of sparing the yardstick for her rule violators.

To begin, she stated, attendance roll call would be our first order of business every morning and, unless we had a bus or principal's pass, we were to be standing in the hall outside her door for roll call at 8:05 AM. As she continued walking up and down the front of the room, her black leather, Enna Jetticks's shoes, click, click, clicking across the wooden plank floor, she reminded me of a prison warden giving new inmates their official first-day orientation before they were sent off to their cells.

Miss McGee laid out the rest of her rules and regulations for the new school year:
- There would be no dilly-dallying in her classroom. Any dilly-dallying would result in a demerit.
- If we were not in our seats at exactly 8:10 AM, when Mr. Livingstone rang the bell, we would receive a demerit.
- We were to be in our seats, shoulders squared, facing forward, notebooks opened, pencils poised, brains alert and ready to give full attention to her daily lesson plans. If she noted any infractions, we would receive a demerit.

In other words, anyone caught moving, breathing, or acting the least bit human would receive a demerit.

If any student accumulated three or more demerits, they would automatically be assigned to her after-school detention program. Miss McGee made it quite clear that, since she had no pressing domestic responsibilities, she could spend as much time after school as needed for rule violators, focusing her gaze on Patti.

Outside of a thirty-minute, mid-morning playground/bathroom recess, a thirty-minute lunch break, and a ten-minute afternoon bathroom/water break, we spent the remaining six hours of each day in Miss Margaret McGee's version of "lock down."

Confined to our desks, our brains went through Miss McGee's daily drills that she executed with military precision. Whether as individuals or groups, our class dropped and gave that woman twenty every single day for nine long, miserable months. Patti and I kept both kept pocket calendars in our book bags, marking off every single day spent in Miss McGee's prison with a big red "X!"

Never a day passed that Miss McGee did not torture us with her endless "tap, tap, tapping" of the much-hated yardstick against the blackboard as she leapt from subject to subject, forcing our minds to do mental back flips, reminding us daily that "the brain has muscles for thinking as the legs have for walking."

I told Patti at recess one day that, if I could take my leg muscles and put them in my brain, I'd be walking out of Miss McGee's classroom as fast as I could. Patti responded, "You can walk all you want; I'm running!"

And while Annie Lizbeth spent her nine months cutting out paper jack o' lanterns for Halloween in Mrs. Cozell's class, we were forced to listen to Vincent Price's recording of Edgar Allen Poe's "The Raven." As we listened to the scratched and muddy sound of the old 78 record on Miss McGee's Vitrola phonograph, with all its pops, ticks and rumbles, Patti looked at me with a poker face, her big blue eyes full of mischief, and passed me a note.

It read:

> Once upon a midnight dreary,
> while I pondered weak and weary,
> Will this record ever end?
> Before Halloween passes,
> And Christmas begins?
> *Patti*

I did my best to stifle a giggle, but Patti's note struck a funny bone in me, and so I quickly scribbled back a note to her that read:

> My head is hurting,
> And my back is sore,
> Let's hope after hearing this,
> The Raven quoth NEVERMORE!
> *Mattie Rose*

Miss McGee seemed lost in the recording of her yesteryears, so I passed the note to Melvin and pointed for him to give it to Patti. Stupid Melvin opened the note and read what we had written, snickered, and passed it to Sammy Hicks. But, before it found a safe haven in Sammy's hand, Miss McGee, whose ears I was convinced were active receiver antenna, picked up Melvin's snort, saw the note being passed, and snatched it out of Sammy's hand. As she inspected the torn piece of lined paper on which Patti had scrawled out the note, my heart stopped beating and my face was flushed with color. Annie Lizbeth would be happy to know that the "honey" color of Patti's skin could now be classified as "Lily-white."

"Well, well," Miss McGee began, "what have we here?" she asked out loud as she held our note in her hand. She took great pains in unfolding the note as slowly as she could, her beady eyes peering down at every word over the half-framed glasses perched over her own raven's beak, before saying, "Class, it looks like we have two poets among us. I was unaware that such talent existed here at Carver, and, right here in our own classroom nonetheless! Let's stop our recording so that I can introduce you to these two resident poets and their work. Surely Edgar Allen Poe is no match for the eloquent prose of these two young ladies."

"Patricia Summerhill and Mattie Rose Radley, will you two budding rhymesters please come to the front of the room, so that you can share with the entire class your rendition of Edgar Allen Poe's 'The Raven'?"

Melvin Sparks put his head in his hands, shaking it back and forth, knowing that Patti and I were about to undergo public humiliation of the worst kind. For the first time since school began, Sammy Hicks sat silent, looking guilty that it was from his hand our note had been plucked.

I looked at Patti and she looked at me as we slowly rose from our seats and walked the gangplank to the front of the room where Miss McGee stood holding our note. "Class," she said, "this poem is in two parts. The first part will be read by its author, Miss Patricia Summerhill, and the second part will be read by its author, Miss Mattie Rose Radley. Both verses are compelling examples of the unique insight these two young ladies have into Mr. Poe's work."

Patti and I read our "prose" in front of the entire class, who burst out in loud fits of laughter, bent over double, enjoying the humiliation we were enduring under the gloating eyes of Miss McGee. She made us read our "prose" to Mr. Livingstone, who said that we would each receive three demerits, which automatically put us in Miss McGee's after-school detention program.

Granny and Daddy passed the note off as mere "child's foolishness," but made me do my time in Miss McGee's after-school detention program, explaining that she was the teacher and I was playing around when I should have been learning.

Patti and I spent our time in Miss McGee's detention coat closet practicing our Jack LaLanne figure-enhancing exercises in the dark, and playing our favorite clapping game, "I am a Pretty Little Dutch Girl," barely touching one another's hands for fear of making noise. The time went quickly, and we were happy to have been banished to the closet instead of having to do some extra homework assignment from Miss McGee.

Annie Lizbeth never missed an opportunity to look at Patti and me as we lined up for roll call each morning, taunting us in her deepest voice: "Quoth the Raven, Nevermore," as she went running and laughing into Mrs. Cozell's class.

And while Annie Lizbeth and her class did a re-enactment of the first Thanksgiving feast in the school cafeteria, we had to write an essay on the Voyage of the Mayflower.

And while Annie Lizbeth enjoyed a Christmas party hosted by the parents, including Granny, who made sugar cookies sprinkled with red and green sugar, our class project was Deck the Halls with Science.

And while Annie Lizbeth was dyeing and decorating Easter eggs for their class Easter egg hunt, we had to write a three-page, single-lined notebook paper essay on the religious differences between Easter and Passover.

And so it went for nine long, miserable months, locked up in Miss McGee's penitentiary. Patti, Tommy, Melvin, and Sammy accumulated the most demerits that year, and spent endless afternoons in Miss McGee's after-school detention program.

LAST DAY OF SCHOOL: 8:05 AM

After line-up and head count, we entered Miss McGee's classroom for the final day of school. While I looked out of the window with envy as Annie Lizbeth and her classmates were outside on a nature hunt, Miss McGee was about to engage us in one final lesson. The topic: Her recommended summer reading list.

"Now class, just because this is the last day of school does not mean we are going to abandon our regular classroom schedule. I want you to think of this day just like any other regular school day, so we will continue with our customary lesson plan right up until the 3:10 bell rings. As usual, I expect your full attention. Do I have everyone's full attention?" she queried, her beady brown eyes peering over those half-framed glasses as she scanned the room for potential rule violators.

"Yes, Miss McGee, you have our attention," we all repeated in unison, like the mindless robots we had become.

"Very well then class, we shall continue," she said briskly, as we heard the all too familiar "tap, tap, tap" of her wooden yardstick against the blackboard.

As she picked up a piece of chalk to write, our backs stiffened in anticipation of the screeching sound the chalk made as it came into contact with the blackboard and reverberated down the base of our spines.

While Miss McGee was in search of rule violators, all I could see was a bunch of wilted kids, sweating and squirming in their seats, straining their overheated bodies to catch a brief and passing breeze from the one oscillating floor fan that stood at the front of the classroom, conveniently located right beside Miss McGee's desk. I and nineteen of my fellow student inmates anxiously awaited their final release from Miss Margaret McGee's rigid, harsh, demanding, and highly-disciplined fifth-grade classroom.

She turned our attention to the recommended summer reading list she had typed and reproduced on the duplicating machine located in Mr. Livingstone's office. "Now class," she continued, "I want you to pass this list around the room and place it in the front of your notebook for quick reference when visiting the library or bookmobile this summer."

"Does everyone have a copy?" she asked, lilting her voice in her all too condescending fashion. As the list was passed from student to student, I watched Sammy Hicks's eyes glaze over as he inhaled the aroma of the still slightly damp ink of each newly-copied paper as he passed them to those around him.

Though I partially tuned her out, I kept one ear open as Miss McGee's tinny voice continued to recite from her never-ending list of recommended books for summer reading.

Most of my attention stayed squarely focused on the big, round, black IBM clock mounted on the wall above the coat closet as I began my countdown to freedom. My heart skipped a beat each time the minute hand jumped from one minute-marker to another with an accompanying audible clunk.

2:30 PM (40 MINUTES TO FINAL FREEDOM)

Rule Violator #1: Tommy Jones

Sleeping in Class

Whether overcome by the stifling heat that filled the room that last day of school, or just too full from the monstrous lunch he had just consumed, Tommy Jones was Rule Violator #1 as he drifted off into a world of his own. Tommy Jones was the only child of an extremely over-protective mother. He was not allowed to ride the school bus because his mother feared it was contaminated with germs from the people that rode it, so she faithfully and dutifully transported him to and from school daily.

Tommy was overweight, and nicknamed "doughboy" by all the kids at school. Because of his weight, he was sluggish, and because of his mother, he was spoiled. However, Tommy's worst offense was that of class whiner. In Tommy's world, nothing was "fair," everyone was "picking on him," and the "dog ate his homework" several times a week. Miss McGee could not stand Tommy's constant whining, and he spent a great deal of time either in the hall, or in Miss McGee's after-school detention program.

That afternoon, Tommy's arms and elbows rested atop Miss McGee's freshly-duplicated, highly-prized, recommended summer reading list, his shirtsleeves smearing all the ink and titles Miss McGee had so meticulously typed and copied while bunching up the paper on which they were printed.

Tommy may have been in Miss McGee's fifth-grade class, but he had entered the fifth dimension of sleep, a world in which he doused Miss Margaret McGee with a bucket of water as he watched with delight as she melted before his very eyes.

Trying to camouflage the fact that he was sleeping, Tommy had buried his head in the cradle of his elbow and clasped his hands in front of his face as he positioned himself behind Kenny Kilpatrick in an effort to hide from Miss McGee's prying eyes. Little did Tommy know that a twister named Miss McGee was about to come his way and, like Dorothy, he would never make it to Auntie Em's storm cellar for safety.

Tommy had just gotten to the best part of his dream, where everyone was singing "Ding dong, the witch is dead, which old witch, the wicked witch," before he was awakened by three incredibly loud whacks across the top of his desk. Miss McGee hit his desk with such force that her ruler broke in half, sending the splintered end flying halfway across the room. Tommy's legs were already spread eagle in front of him, and his bottom was barely making contact with the edge of his seat, when his body and mind were suddenly awakened to the "WHACK, WHACK, WHACK" of Miss McGee's ruler.

Poor Tommy was so startled that his body jerked back, his bottom losing what little contact it had with his seat, and he fell, KER-PLOP, on the floor.

Melvin Sparks and Sammy Hicks snickered, but their smiles quickly disappeared when Miss McGee cast them an evil glance. The rest of us sat in total silence as we stared at a dazed and bewildered Tommy Jones. Sitting on the floor, he had not quite grasped what had happened to him.

In an instant, Miss McGee grasped Tommy by the scruff of his shirt collar and yanked him up from the floor before leading him out the door to put him on public display in the hall. Inside the classroom, we heard Tommy whimpering, "It's not fair."

Rule Violator #2: Melvin Sparks
Throwing Objects with Intent to Cause Harm

Melvin Sparks—originator of the Margaret Hamilton conspiracy theory, instigator of trouble, and paper plane wizard of the entire fifth-grade class—was Rule Violator #2.

He occupied his last forty minutes of classroom confinement by aiming paper airplanes at the back of Miranda Stone's head, the most hated girl in our fifth-grade class. Miranda had spent the entire school year vying for teacher's pet. What Miranda never figured out was there were no teacher's pets in Miss McGee's class, only potential rule violators who needed to be identified and publicly humiliated at all costs.

Melvin launched a stealth attack of paper airplanes at the back of Miranda's head whenever he thought Miss McGee wasn't looking. Miranda, though obviously annoyed, successfully warded off his mission by swatting them away with the back of her hand, turning in her seat, and firing off dirty looks to Melvin. At the exact moment when Miranda finally had enough and raised her hand to report Melvin to Miss McGee, he successfully landed the sharpest point of his paper plane marvel in the back of her neck. Miranda let out a yelp so loud the entire classroom held its breath, fearful for Melvin's life.

After Miss McGee tore his paper plane into a zillion pieces and threw it in the trash for all to witness, Melvin Sparks was sent out of the room to stand against the wall with the sobbing Tommy Jones as Miss McGee's Hall of Shame for Rule Violators continued to grow.

Rule Violator #3: Patti Summerhill
Improper Doodling

That afternoon, Patti did not even pretend to listen to Miss McGee's recitations. She had pretty much checked out of Miss McGee's class the minute she was checked in during roll call. Instead, she spent her last forty minutes doing what she loved best, sketching horses, dogs, and cats on the front and back of Miss McGee's typed and mimeographed summer reading list. She had moistened her finger with her tongue, and was smearing away as many book titles as she could to make more room for her animal doodles.

"And might I also suggest Jane Austen, Charles Dickens, Anne Frank, and Agatha Christie for those of you interested in classic literature," Miss McGee droned on. As soon as she completed her sentence, I could hear Patti mumbling under her breath. She was writing something on one of the few remaining unfilled spaces on Miss McGee's summer reading list. Patti, like Tommy, had drifted off into her own world, and I could tell she was having more fun in hers than I was sitting here in mine.

"Classic literature? With this group of morons? Who is she kidding?"

Patti whispered to me. "The only summer reading this class is going to do is pull out the comic section of the Sunday paper," she continued, obviously agitated by Miss McGee's pompous suggestions.

Oh my goodness, I thought to myself. Had Patti been overcome by the heat in the room and suffered a heat stroke? I heard that heat strokes could make you delirious and say strange things that you would later regret.

"Miss Summerhill, would you like to repeat what you just said so that the entire class can hear you?" a smug Miss McGee asked.

"No, I would not," replied a defiant Patti.

Miss McGee walked over to Patti's desk and saw her neatly typed and mimeographed list of recommended summer reading smeared and completely covered in animal sketches. Miss McGee was doing a slow burn. "Well, Miss Summerhill, since you obviously have no interest in improving yourself this summer, you can join your fellow underachievers, Mr. Jones and Mr. Sparks, in the hall."

Patti rose from her seat, but before she left the room she looked straight at Miss McGee and shouted defiantly, "I just want you to know I made a summer reading list of my own, and it begins with *The Wizard of Oz*, featuring you as the Wicked Witch of the West!" She paused for a minute before shouting even louder, "Oh excuse me...I should have used your proper name, MISS Wicked Witch of the West!"

And with that, Patti marched out of the room and joined Tommy Jones and Melvin Sparks in the hall.

Rule Violator #4: Sammy Hicks
Disruptive Behavior in the Classroom
Possession of a Nuisance Item
Physical assault of a fellow student
Inhaling noxious fumes

Sammy Hicks was the "bad boy" of our fifth-grade class. In fact, Sammy was the "bad boy" of the entire school. He wasn't mean, as in evil, he was just an independent kind of guy who had a special talent for getting into trouble. He and Miss McGee were like oil and water. She was determined he was going to abide by her rules, and he was determined to break them every chance he got.

We had a classroom of twenty students, and Miss McGee had the room arranged so that there were four rows of five students each. When school started, Sammy sat in the last seat of Row #2, directly out of Miss McGee's line of sight.

However, by week three, it had become abundantly clear that Sammy would require a lot more supervision when Miss McGee discovered he had snuck a comic book into class and placed it in the middle of Charles Dickens' *Great Expectations*, choosing to read it instead of our assigned chapter that day.

Sammy's antics did not stop at comic books. He chewed gum in class and, when caught by Miss McGee, would automatically swallow it and feign innocence.

He would wad up pieces of notebook paper, put them in his mouth, drench them in spit and then throw them at the backs of the heads of other students when Miss Margaret McGee was not looking.

He once stole a pack of matches out of his dad's shirt pocket and lit the end of a #2 pencil, which he pretended to smoke during recess. Miranda Stone, tattletale of all tattletales, was the first to report this outrageous violation to Miss McGee, who kept Sammy in her after-school detention program for a week.

By the end of the first nine-week grading period, Miss McGee, fed up with Sammy's theatrics, placed his desk right beside hers in the front of the entire classroom. She figured that if she isolated Sammy and kept him right by her side, his classroom antics would stop disrupting the class. Boy was she wrong, because Sammy's antics would extend well beyond the classroom walls.

Three weeks before the end of school, Sammy became the proud owner of a brand new Duncan yo-yo. If a boy owned a Duncan yo-yo, he became an instant celebrity among the other boys at school, attention that Sammy enjoyed. Instead of spending hours doing the homework assignments Miss

McGee handed out at the end of every day, Sammy had spent his time perfecting his yo-yo tricks.

On that last day of school, during morning recess, Sammy wowed a bunch of us with what he had learned. We watched with open mouths as Sammy showed us how to Walk the Dog and Rock the Baby with his yo-yo. He said he knew how to do Around the World, but just as he was warming up, the bell rang signaling the end of recess. Sammy, undeterred by a bell of any sort, started to whirl his yo-yo around and around over his head, with as much speed as he could muster. I later learned the secret to Around the World is to make sure there is no slack in the string. Slack in the string can make the yo-yo pop back before you anticipate it. Unbeknownst to Sammy, he had too much slack in his string, so as he whirled it as hard as he could around his head, the yo-yo spun out of control and hit Miranda Stone squarely on her forehead.

Miranda still resented Sammy for taking her seat in the early weeks of school, removing her from the spotlight of Miss McGee's beady eyes. Yes, she was bopped on the head, but Miss Drama Queen fell to the ground, holding her head in her hands and screaming at the top of her lungs as if she had been assassinated.

All the kids scattered when they saw Miss McGee running to see what in the world had happened to Miranda. Sammy ran too, but, out of fear of being caught, tossed his yo-yo onto the ground and under the crawl space of the white wooden gymnasium. I knew if Miss McGee found the yo-yo, she would destroy it. Even if it was the last day of school, Sammy had finally excelled at something, and I was not going to let Miss McGee rob him of his moment of glory, even if Miranda Stone's forehead had been sacrificed in the process.

"Sammy hit me, Sammy hit me," moaned Miranda as Miss McGee helped her to her feet.

"Hit you with what?" a flustered Miss Margaret McGee demanded.

"He," she sobbed, "he," she gasped for breath, "he hit me with his yo-yo."

"What yo-yo?" Miss McGee's high-pitched voice queried.

"The yo-yo he brought to school to show off to the kids," Miranda pressed on, rubbing the red spot on her forehead.

"Well, young lady, we'll see about this after you see the school nurse!" Yep, Miss McGee was on the case. She and Miranda had already tried and convicted poor Sammy, and I dreaded the thought of what his final sentence would be.

When the drama finally ended, and Miranda returned to class holding a cold compress against her head, Sammy had already taken his place in the Hall of Shame for Rule Violators.

Miss McGee sent him to Mr. Livingstone for a pat down in search of the missing yo-yo. He even had Sammy empty his pockets, but, outside of a couple of pennies covered in lint, the yo-yo was never discovered. Instead, it remained safely hidden in my skirt pocket. In the crazed bedlam of Miranda's accident, I ran over to the gymnasium's crawl space and saved not only Sammy's prized possession, but his dignity as well.

Rule Violator #5: Mattie Rose Radley
Improper Behavior Unbecoming to a Young Lady

June's early summer heat was unrelenting as the sun's rays poured through our open and unadorned classroom windows. As the day passed, the temperature of the room continued to inch upward while the perspiration dripping from my head and neck spiraled downward, creating huge wet circles under my arms and soaking through the back of my favorite robin's egg blue cotton shirt.

The sweat from the back of my bare thighs had formed a tight seal to the bottom of my seat. I tried to loosen them, but they were stuck like two helpless flies that had made a horrible error in judgment by mistaking flypaper for something more welcoming. The heat was taking its toll on everyone, especially me. I was more concerned about releasing the vise-like grip that was holding me to my seat than listening to Miss McGee's final words about how to turn your summer into a learning adventure.

What if the 3:10 PM bell rang and I could not get out of the seat that had held me captive for nine months? Could there be a fate worse than that? My mind went through a quick checklist and, no, I could not think of a fate worse than being stuck, literally, in Miss McGee's classroom for another minute.

Every day before morning recess, Miss McGee turned out the lights, turned on the projector, and made us watch one of her "mental hygiene films." They were designed to reinforce manners and moral behavior. These ten-minute, black and white films had titles such as, *Develop Your Character, Social Courtesy, Mind Your Manners, Appreciating Our Parents,* and my favorite, *Friendship Begins at Home,* a film I thought should be on Annie Lizbeth's "must see" list.

I must have missed the film that dealt with girls exposing the ruffled ends of their white cotton petticoats to boys, because I became the final rule violator in Miss McGee's Hall of Shame that very afternoon.

At 2:50 PM, Miss McGee excused the class for five minutes to get a drink of water from the water fountain at the end of the hall. As we filed past Tommy, Melvin, Patricia, and Sammy, who had to remain standing upright against the wall outside our classroom, Snot-Nosed Billy Brown dared me for the umpteenth time to do the twist, the latest dance craze, right there in line as we waited our turn at the water fountain. We all knew that dancing, running, jumping, skipping, or hopping in the hall was strictly prohibited by Miss McGee.

I was dared a lot, probably because I usually took them on. The way I saw it, if I "did the twist," then Snot-Nosed Billy Brown who had dared me in the first place would have to shut up, and I wouldn't have to hear him telling everyone in the class that I was a "chicken."

So I accepted his dare and began twisting my waist from one side to the other, all the while revealing the edges of my white ruffled petticoat. Before I could twist another rotation, Miss McGee grabbed my wrist and walked me briskly back to the classroom where I received a stern lecture on moral character and behavior unbefitting a young lady. As my fellow classmates and Snot-Nosed Billy Brown filed back in from their water break, snickering all the way, I filed out of Miss McGee's class and took my place among the rest of the inmates standing in the hall.

Standing in the hallway alone, we were forgotten like unwanted toys or broken objects left to perish under the layers of educational dust. We were excluded from the last day's classroom activities. We were not normal or acceptable. We were not good student material.

When the 3:10 bell rang, we were still standing in the hall, our backs as straight as Miss McGee's yardstick, pressed up against the cinderblock wall. As the kids fled out of Miss McGee's classroom that last day, they looked like prisoners who had been deprived of water and sunlight for nine months, scattering everywhere, anywhere, to be free of the wicked witch's grasp.

Miss McGee's Rule Violators stayed in the hall until 3:30 PM when she finally exited the classroom and commanded us to come back inside.

She told us she had contacted everyone's parents, and that we would remain in her custody until 4:45 PM that afternoon. The rule violators would dust all the erasers, sweep the classroom floor, wash the hated blackboard and all desktops, making sure to remove wads of gum and other foreign objects stuck under them, re-arrange all the reading books in alphabetical order, and tidy up the coat closet.

At exactly 4:45 PM, Patti, Melvin, Sammy, Tommy and I stood, lined up outside on the sweltering sidewalk of Carver Elementary with Miss McGee by our side.

Miss McGee made a point of telling each parent the infraction their child had committed that last day of school, further driving home the point that, in all her years of teaching, she had never experienced such disrespectful, unruly children. Before Sammy got into his mother's station wagon, I walked over to him and handed him his yo-yo. "Thanks, Mattie Rose," he said with gratitude in his voice. "For a girl, you're not so bad after all."

When Granny arrived to pick me up, she listened patiently as Miss McGee expressed her outrage over my behavior unbefitting a young lady. I could see that whatever punishment I had received from Miss McGee would pale in comparison to what I would get from Granny. Annie Lizbeth was sitting in the backseat of the car, snickering and waving her finger back and forth at me through the window, mouthing na, na, na, na, na!

Before we got home that afternoon, Granny made it a point to stop at the public library where she checked out Munro Leaf's *How to Behave and Why*.

While Annie Lizbeth was outside playing with Cookie Ketchum, celebrating the last day of school and the beginning of summer vacation, I sat at the kitchen table reading the chapter "You Have To Be Wise" out loud to Granny. At the end of the chapter, Granny asked me what on earth could make me want to show my underwear to Billy Brown, or anyone else for that matter. She said that, while she was no fan of Miss McGee, her point about my behavior being unbecoming to a young lady was correct.

"Do you see me showing my underwear to strangers," she asked.

"No," I replied.

"And do you know why?" she asked, looking at me point blank.

"Because you're a lady???" I responded uncertainly, trying to figure out the right answer so I could get this lecture over with.

"That's right. I'm a lady, and I expect no less from you or Annie Lizbeth. It matters not if you are ten or twenty years old, if you want people to think of you as a lady, you have to act like one! So, I better not hear of you showing your underwear again, or you are going to regret it, do you understand me, Mattie Rose Radley?"

"Yes, Ma'am," I answered sheepishly.

I asked Granny if she was going to tell Daddy, and she said, "No, this will be a girl's secret." I asked if Annie Lizbeth was going to open her big trap and tell him, and Granny said again, "No," that Annie Lizbeth knows this is a girl's secret, and if she wants to keep her bottle of Evening in Paris, she'll keep it to herself. Knowing that Granny's ace card was Annie Lizbeth's most prized possession, her bottle of Evening in Paris, I felt pretty sure Daddy would never know about the underwear incident.

As I sat reading aloud yet another chapter of *How to Behave and Why*, Granny was putting the finishing touches on supper. I looked up for a minute to see her looking towards heaven, shaking her head back and forth and saying, "Lord, give me strength."

When we came back to school the following year and entered sixth grade, I learned that Miss McGee had resigned her position from Carver Elementary right after we left for summer vacation. They said she told Mr. Livingstone she needed a rest and was going to live with her sister in Kansas.

I was secretly delighted that Miss McGee's reign of terror was over, but I have to admit I learned a lot that year in her class. Though she ruled with an iron hand, she was, unknowingly to us, molding our character and bringing out the talents that would prepare us for the time when we would take our rightful place in the world.

Years later, I became a teacher and had my own classrooms filled with the personalities of a Tommy Jones, Melvin Sparks, Sammy Hall, Miranda Stone, Patti Summerhill, and yes, even a Mattie Rose Radley.

I learned there was a fine line between controlling a classroom and it controlling you. And though Miss McGee's teaching style was far different from mine, you could find the following inscription written across the top of my blackboard at the beginning of each new school year: "The brain has muscles for thinking, as the legs have for walking."

Thank you, Miss McGee.

BUSTED ON THE BUS

"Only one more week of school to go," I lamented to Annie Lizbeth that Friday morning as we waited to be picked up by Bus #419 at our usual stop.

"Oh, hush your mush, Mattie Rose. I'm so sick and tired of hearing you moan and groan every day about Miss McGee. It can't be that bad," Annie Lizbeth shot back, which annoyed me to no end.

"That's easy for you to say since you've spent your entire year on field trips, reading aloud in circle groups, and learning math by flip cards," I replied sarcastically.

Before we had the opportunity to bicker more, Bus #419 approached. As Mrs. Olive brought the bus to a halt and swung open its double doors, I shoved Annie Lizbeth as hard as I could up the first step, causing her to miss the handrail, stumble, and bump her shin against the hard edge of the second step.

At first startled, she turned around in a flash, daggers shooting from her eyes, before hissing the words, "I'll get you for this, Mattie Rose."

Lucky for me, Mrs. Olive missed the incident and said, "Okay girls, let's get going, I have more students to pick up, and for once, I would like Mr. Livingstone to see this bus arrive at school on time!"

Annie Lizbeth wasn't going to do anything to me. Our school had a three-strikes-and-you're-off-the-bus policy. Annie Lizbeth already had two, so she had to be particularly mindful of her P's and Q's.

She received strike one the very first day of school when she, along with the likes of Melvin Sparks and Sammy Hicks, trampled over poor Cookie Ketchum, Miranda Stone, and others, knocking them to the ground, their brand new book bags and lunch boxes scattered in every direction, in their uncontrollable desire to be the first ones off the bus.

Her second offense came later that year when she laid herself out flat like a corpse on her seat, refusing to allow Purvis Brickle to sit beside her, fearing "cootie contamination."

Granny had signed both of the bus misconduct reports, but told Annie Lizbeth if she got another one, she'd bring Daddy into the matter, so I felt pretty secure that the little bump on her shin would remain just that...a little bump on her shin, its origin unknown, should Granny ask.

Mrs. Hilda Olive, our school bus driver, was a pudgy, middle-aged homemaker who parted her salt and pepper hair right down the middle of her head, tightly braiding each side before securing the braids to the top of her head with a couple of bobby pins. A few of the wispy ends of each braid managed to escape the grasp of the bobby pins and stuck straight up, like a small patch of unruly weeds in an otherwise manicured lawn which, according to Patti Summerhill, could be easily managed if Mrs. Olive would apply some hair pomade to the offending strands.

Why anyone would want to drive Bus #419 was a mystery to me, but Mrs. Olive seemed to have made it her life's profession since we entered first grade.

Every morning when we boarded the bus, there sat Mrs. Olive, a reliable and comforting sight, her eyes still puffy from sleep, her ample bosom squeezed into a too tight, short-sleeved, white cotton blouse whose front pocket bore the Carver Elementary School insignia. Her arms reminded me of sausages in casings, pinched off by the bands of white fabric that cuffed the sleeves of her blouse. Her bosom rested atop a mountainous belly that cascaded down her navy blue skirt onto her heavily dimpled knees. Her thick, stubby calves were covered in opaque, flesh-toned support stockings. Her feet looked like two of Granny's oversized biscuits shoved in black oxford lace-ups with crepe soles.

Mrs. Olive's substantial rear end could not be contained in the compact driver's seat, and so its fleshy excesses spilled over and wobbled like Jell-O whenever her feet hit the floor pedals to shift the school bus's gears. Annie Lizbeth, Patti Summerhill, and I would watch and snicker as Mrs. Olive's rear end wiggled and jiggled as we made our way to and from Carver Elementary.

To serve as a constant reminder to anyone contemplating bus misconduct of any kind, Mrs. Olive kept a fresh, thick, pink pad of bus misconduct reports attached to a ballpoint pen sticking out of her front pocket. Typically, after a single day of picking up and dropping off the kids on Bus #419, her thick pink pad had thinned down considerably.

Our route generated more bus misconduct reports than any other school bus at Carver Elementary School. More likely than not, by year's end, Bus #419 was half-empty, and there was a reason for it. Mrs. Olive had the worst bus route of any of the other drivers. Why? Because her route had to stop and pick up the kids from "The Park."

"The Park" was located about a half-mile behind our house. Its only access was right off Peale Road. Barely suitable for cars, the drive down to the Park was a foreboding one; the steep and winding road was nothing more than red clay and gravel that eventually came to a dead end.

Granny called it the "Road to Nowhere," and said the people living down there were living on the Road to Nowhere, and that if we wanted to stay on the Road to Somewhere, we were to stay away from the road and the people from nowhere.

Since the kids from "The Park" attended Carver Elementary, Annie Lizbeth and I had, on a couple of occasions, gotten off Bus #419 at their bus stop and walked back there, more out of curiosity than anything else. Granny was right. It was the road to nowhere.

The dense growth of trees, plants, and underbrush over the years gave the area an eerie darkness, and your breath quickened by the stillness of the forest that surrounded and yet, in some sense, protected it from outsiders who might venture down there as unwelcome visitors.

There were eight ramshackle shanties located down there that had originally been bathhouses back in the 1930s. Granny said that, in its heyday, it was one of Durham's most prestigious public parks, complete with three swimming pools, walking trails, a natural spring, and a moving carousel with horses for children to ride. She said by the end of the Great Depression, "The Park" had fallen into disrepair and was eventually closed. The pools were drained, dense forest was allowed to grow, and it became a deserted island unto itself.

A local real estate developer named Clyde Sumter bought the abandoned property at a city auction in the early 1940s. He put in the one-way road full of ruts and mud holes, and had the shacks supplied with electricity for lighting. With electricity to light the "shacks," they were suddenly transformed into "rental houses," from which Clyde profited.

The people that rented the shanties became known as "Park People." They were a transient group of folks who could be here today and gone tomorrow.

These three-room shanties used woodstoves for heating and cooking, and had no indoor plumbing. If you needed to do your "business," you did so in an old wooden "outhouse" located at the top of the hill in back of the house.

Their main source for water was a natural spring which still flowed abundantly at the end of a well-worn path, and from which the women and children filled buckets for their daily needs.

Annie Lizbeth and I visited the natural spring and marveled at its never ending source of clear, cool, flowing water. We took great care to stash our shoes and socks at the top of the path leading down to the spring so that Granny would see no telltale traces of wet socks or muddy shoes as we sat on the rocks and allowed the cold, refreshing water to run over our feet and tickle our toes on a hot summer's day.

Most yards were adorned with two or more rusted-out, broken-down trucks hiked up on cement blocks, giving the impression that someday, if the mood struck, someone might get around to working on them and maybe even putting on some tires.

Hubcaps were used as yard art, or for feeding the four or five junkyard dogs that were considered members of the family. It was not unusual to see chickens walking around the yard, having escaped their poorly-constructed prison coops.

No front porch was complete without an abandoned wringer washing machine alongside an old, worn-out sofa where the menfolk, with tobacco-stained teeth, passed out drunk on Saturday night from drinking too much hard liquor.

The Park People had a communal structure all their own. The men and women of the Park were no more bound to marriage than they were to a steady job. There was no such thing as "family planning." Children just got born, and like untended ivy, they seemed content to coexist with other family foliage.

None of the men worked day jobs like our daddy. Granny said they made most of their living selling moonshine, and that only the Park People could make sitting on the porch seem like a noble profession.

You could always find clothes, mostly denim overalls, faded flannel shirts, and long john underwear, hanging out on some homemade clothesline strung between two trees.

The smell of pork drippings used to season a pot of beans or greens that simmered all day on the back of the woodstove wafted through the air in the Park. Beans, greens, and cornbread. That was the *menu du jour* for the Park People. And if there was meat on the side, it came from something they hunted, and not something Granny brought home from the store wrapped in butcher paper.

The most notorious of the Park kids were the Brickle Brothers: Billy Ray, Purvis, and Earl. And much like the untamed forest in which they lived, they were loud, unruly and, most of the time, uncontrollable. We never arrived at school on time because Mrs. Olive would inevitably have to stop the bus at least one or two times, and break up a fight initiated by the Brickle Brothers. Then she had to apply first aid to some unfortunate soul that failed to duck when the Brickle Brothers threw some flying object through the air.

Granny told us to steer clear of those boys because they were mean and always up to no good. But no one could steer clear of the Brickle Brothers if they set their eye on you as their next victim. No one, as they were soon to discover, except the Radley sisters and their best gal pal Patti Summerhill.

The 3:10 PM final school bell rang, and I was out of Miss McGee's classroom in a flash, looking for Annie Lizbeth. We always met in the middle of the hall between our two classrooms, and raced to the bus to secure one of the prized front seats, but today, Annie Lizbeth was late. Unbeknownst to me, she had been named "Student of the Week" by Mrs. Cozell, and her reward was the last baby turtle from a family of turtles the class had been raising as part of a nature study project.

It had taken her several extra minutes to put the baby turtle in its special shoe box with holes cut into the sides so that it could travel safely from school to home. I was pacing up and down the hall, wondering where she was, but more worried that Miss McGee might spot me, demand to see my after-school teacher's pass, which I did not have, and give me a demerit.

All of a sudden Annie Lizbeth came running down the hall, her book bag under one arm, a shoe box under the other. "I won! I won!" she yelled at the top of her lungs, barely able to contain her excitement.

"Won what?" I replied, trying to figure out what all the commotion was about, and growing increasingly anxious about the passing minutes and the possibility of missing the bus.

"I won 'Student of the Week,' Mattie Rose," Annie Lizbeth replied. "I won, and guess what my prize was?"

"What?" I answered impatiently.

"I won a baby turtle that I am going to name Myrtle. Look at her, Mattie Rose, isn't she the sweetest thing you ever saw?" Annie Lizbeth cooed as she carefully opened the top of the shoe box for me to see the little turtle inside.

"Why are you calling it Myrtle? How do you know she's not a he?" I asked.

"Be-cause," Annie Lizbeth replied indignantly, rolling her eyes at me in utter disbelief at my inability to recognize the gender of turtles.

"Because what?" I asked, my agitation with Annie Lizbeth growing.

"Because we learned in class that girl turtles have flatter shells on their bellies and shorter tails, and double because since Mrs. Cozell said so!" she replied adamantly.

Annie Lizbeth, being Annie Lizbeth, then began giving me a list of to-do's for the care and feeding of a baby turtle. "We have to feed her lettuce and carrots and earthworms, and we have to keep her safe. I'm going to ask Granny if she can sleep with me! Do you think she'll let me sleep with Myrtle, Mattie Rose, do you?" she implored, as if I had a crystal ball into Granny's thoughts.

"I don't know, Annie Lizbeth. You know Granny's funny about that kind of thing, but if you hurry up, we can ask her when we get home," I replied, trying to get Annie Lizbeth out of fantasy land and onto the bus.

Bus #419 always departed the school around 3:20 PM, and I could see that Annie Lizbeth was more concerned about sleeping with the turtle than getting to the bus, so I grabbed her book bag, and pleaded, "Come on, Annie Lizbeth, come on. You know Daddy has the car today, and if we miss the bus, how are we going to get home…walk? You know it's hotter than Hades outside!"

As a further incentive to get her moving, I said in my most serious tone, "Annie Lizbeth, if we have to walk home your turtle is going to get hot and run a temperature, so for the sake of Myrtle's health we better get to the bus!"

That proved to be just the motivation Annie Lizbeth needed, so she picked up her pace, and we made our way down the steps to the main floor, and out the heavy, gray, metal door of the schoolhouse to the circle drive where Bus #419 and Patti Summerhill were waiting. Patti was obviously irritated that we were late because the line to get on Bus #419 was already growing long and she was standing near the end of it waiting for us.

"I hope you're happy, Annie Lizbeth," I snapped. "Because of you and that turtle we'll be standing out in this line forever, and if we have to stand up because we can't get a seat, it will serve you right! And don't ask me to hold your books so you can hold that turtle because I ain't."

Pushing and shoving at the back of the line were the infamous Brickle Brothers: Billy Ray, Purvis, and Earl. Billy Ray, as a gesture of pure meanness, shoved Purvis as hard as he could and, like a domino effect, Purvis fell into

Earl, who fell into Patti Summerhill, who fell into me, as I fell into Annie Lizbeth who was holding Myrtle the Turtle's box.

"Hey, cut it out!" Annie Lizbeth yelled at the top of her lungs, as she held the box tightly to her chest, lifting the lid to make sure her prized possession, Myrtle, had not been injured in the scuffle.

Billy Ray was eleven, and in Mrs. Watson's sixth grade class. Purvis was ten, and in Annie Lizbeth's class. She could not stand him or any of his brothers, and avoided them like the plague, saying they had Park cooties. Earl, the oldest, was twelve, but had been retained in sixth grade for another year by the school's truant officer because he skipped more days than he attended the year before.

"Okay, kids, listen up!" Mrs. Olive bellowed. The heat and humidity had taken their toll on the braided ends of her hair, and the few unruly strands that Patti said could be controlled with just a dab of hair pomade would now take an entire jar to conquer the mass eruption taking place on top of her head.

"I have an announcement to make," she continued. "We're taking extra passengers on our bus because Bus #410 has a flat tire, so it's going to be a tight squeeze. It's three to a seat, and if you're real skinny, there may be four. I better not see any less than three in each seat, and if I see anyone hogging up space or misbehaving you're going to get a bus misconduct report. Let… me…repeat…myself…again," she said slowly and deliberately, "if I see any misbehaving, you'll be getting a pink slip. Does everyone understand?"

None of us spoke, choosing instead to shake our heads up and down in agreement.

"All right then, saddle up cowboys and cowgirls," she hollered as she boarded the bus, plopping her generous, wiggling, jiggling behind in the driver's seat before giving the long line preceding us the go ahead to begin boarding the bus.

Because Annie Lizbeth had dawdled with Myrtle the Turtle, we found ourselves taking our seat in the next to the last row at the back of the bus. Cookie Ketchum was already seated by the window when we scooted in to sit beside her. Patti Summerhill ended up taking the aisle seat directly across from us sitting with Kathy Dinette and Sweet Pea Warson. Following behind us, were the Brickle Brothers, pushing and shoving one another as they fought for seat positions in the last row at the back of the bus.

Cookie Ketchum, who was one of Annie Lizbeth's "fallen" victims the first day of school, wasted no time in moving to the middle of the seat when Annie Lizbeth insisted that she needed to sit by the window so that Myrtle the Turtle could stay cool on the ride home. With Annie Lizbeth sitting by the window, Cookie Ketchum sitting in the middle, I happily took the aisle seat so I could talk with Patti on the ride home.

It was the first week of June. Anyone who has ever spent a day in North Carolina during the summer months knows the days are sweltering and sticky hot, enough so to make even the calmest of temperaments run short.

None of the school buses were air-conditioned, so Mrs. Olive had opened all the windows to allow for as much breeze as possible as we began our ride home. On that particular Friday afternoon, all the collective breezes in North Carolina would not have been enough to "cool down" what was about to brew in the back of Bus #419.

We were pretty much minding our own business, bumping along down the road, Patti and I talking about our upcoming summer vacation plans, when Billy Ray Brickle, with his nasty, matted, blond hair and dirty fingernails stuck his head between Annie Lizbeth, Cookie Ketchum, and me and said, "Hey, Annie Lizbeth, what you got in that there box?" Purvis and Earl stuck their heads between us as well, trying to see what Billy Ray was so curious about.

"It's a baby turtle," Annie Lizbeth replied smugly, "and I won her for being 'Student of the Week,' something you'll never be, Billy Ray Brickle. Now, get your nasty, cootie-ridden self away from me and my turtle."

Patti Summerhill heard Billy Ray nagging Annie Lizbeth and turned around in her seat, her sparkling blue eyes taking on an icy-blue stare as she looked at Billy Ray and warned, "You better leave Annie Lizbeth and her turtle alone, or I'm telling Mrs. Olive, and you'll get thrown off the bus. How'd you like to walk halfway home in this heat, cootie head?"

Billy Ray, Purvis, and Earl sat back in their seats for a couple of minutes contemplating Patti's warning, but wasted no time as they began taking turns tapping Annie Lizbeth's shoulder in order to distract her attention away from the turtle.

Now I was starting to get mad. I turned around and told Billy Ray, Purvis, and Earl that they better leave Annie Lizbeth and her turtle alone or they were going to be sorry.

"Sorry for what, you stupid, wimpy girl?" Billy Ray taunted in my direction.

Mrs. Olive was making stop after stop to accommodate the extra passengers she was carrying, oblivious to what was going on in the back of the bus. We were hot and sweaty, and the Brickle Brothers were becoming increasingly irritating. Billy Ray wadded up a piece of paper and proceeded to make a spit ball, which he aimed for the center of Patti's head. "*Eeewhhhhh*," she squealed, as the spit ball hit her squarely in the back of her head.

Patti turned around in her seat, knowing full well that Billy Ray Brickle had thrown the spit ball at her, and told Cookie Ketchum, who was sitting between Annie Lizbeth and me, to get up and change seats with her. Cookie knew trouble was brewing, so she willingly exchanged seats with Patti. Kathy Dinette and Sweet Pea Warson seemed to be contemplating the pros and cons of jumping out the window of a moving school bus in order to avoid what was about to happen.

Now, it was Annie Lizbeth by the window, feisty Patti Summerhill in the middle, and me sitting by the aisle in the next to the last row of the Bus #419, the Brickle Brothers behind us.

"Hey, Annie Lizbeth," Billy Ray taunted, "I'll give you a penny for that turtle. My Daddy likes turtle soup, and that would be one less he'd have to catch," he said as he threw his head back laughing, Purvis and Earl joining in unison.

"Oh yeah," I hollered back. "Well, my Daddy likes chicken, and I know where he can find three!"

All of a sudden, I felt my head jerked back, my hair pulled so tightly in Billy Ray Brickle's dirty hand I could feel the roots straining to stay attached to my scalp.

"We ain't no chickens, Mattie Rose Radley, so take back what you said, and take it back now," demanded Billy Ray.

"I w-o-n-'t," I groaned as I gritted my teeth and reached over my shoulder to dig my fingernails as hard as I could into his hand to release his grip. Billy Ray screamed in pain and immediately released my hair, but that was just the beginning of it.

By now, Purvis had a throat hold on Patti, pushing her head back and forth as she screeched for help in between gulps of air. After digging my nails into Billy Ray's hand in order to stop him from pulling my hair, I now, as Granny would say, "in a manner most unbecoming a young lady," climbed over the back of the seat and lunged at Purvis, grabbing a chunk of his hair, trying my best to tear it out of his scalp.

As he begged for me to let go of his hair, I was yelling, "Now who's a chicken, who's a chicken, Purvis Brickle? I'll tell you who's a chicken...you're the chicken, and if you don't let go of Patti's throat I'm going to pluck you bald!"

Earl Brickle grabbed the hand Annie Lizbeth was using to clutch Myrtle the Turtle's box to her chest and started bending her fingers back so she would release her grip on the box. "Ouch," she cried, "you're breaking my fingers!"

That was it. By now, I had scratched and clawed Purvis enough so that he released Patti. Patti and I were consumed with revenge, so the next thing I knew Pattie had bawled up her fist, reached across the back of the seat, and punched Earl in the eye. Annie Lizbeth quickly passed Myrtle the Turtle to Cookie Ketchum for safekeeping and threw herself into the pile of flailing arms and legs, getting in her fair share of licks while taking a few of her own.

Tommy Jones saw what was happening, and pushed his way to the front of the crowded bus to alert Mrs. Olive of the fight going on in the back of the bus. "Mrs. Olive, Mrs. Olive," he panted, gasping for breath. "They're going to mur...mur...mur..DUR one another back there! Come quick, come quick!"

All the kids on the school bus had their eyes transfixed on the ruckus at the back of the bus. "Fight, fight, fight!" they all chanted in unison.

Mrs. Olive slammed on brakes and stopped the school bus on the side of the road before making her way to the back of the bus to see what all the commotion was about. From a distance, I could hear the squishy sound of her crepe soles as she made her way back to where we were, but I didn't care. No one was going to break my sister's fingers, steal her turtle, or choke my best friend and get away with it. Especially the Brickle Brothers.

"What on earth is going on back here?" Mrs. Olive yelled, shocked by the display of flailing arms and legs in mortal combat. When Mrs. Olive finally pulled us off of one another, I had, in my hand, a wad of Purvis Brickle's nasty, matted, cootie-ridden hair.

"Yuck," I said in disgust, throwing it to the floor and wiping my hand repeatedly on my skirt.

Patti had handprints around her neck where Purvis tried to choke her, but he was beginning to sport a black eye from where she punched him. Billy Ray had practically ripped my peter pan collar from my blouse; however, he had several red lines of fingernail scratches up and down his right hand and arm to serve as a reminder of what would happen to him if he ever pulled my hair again.

Annie Lizbeth had pushed Earl on the floor and begun stomping his fingers, as she later said, to show him how it felt. Earl was clutching his hand to his chest, pleading his case to Mrs. Olive that Annie Lizbeth had broken his fingers.

"Move your fingers up and down," Mrs. Olive commanded, her patience with the boys worn to a frazzle. Earl slowly moved his fingers up and down, pretending to be in great pain. "Well, if you can move them they ain't broke, so sit down, or I'm throwing you off the bus and you can walk the rest of the way home!" Mrs. Olive threatened.

Before Mrs. Olive hauled Annie Lizbeth, Patti, and me to the front of the bus, Annie Lizbeth retrieved Myrtle the Turtle from Cookie Ketchum, turned around, and stuck her tongue out at the Brickle Brothers as her farewell parting shot.

When Mrs. Olive dropped the Brickle Brothers off at their stop, she wrote each of them a pink bus misconduct report. As the bus pulled away,

Billy Ray, Purvis, and Earl, with the "broken fingers," picked up rocks and started throwing them at the back of the bus, along with the wadded up pink bus misconduct reports.

As she dropped us off at our stop, she handed us a bus misconduct report as well. "Annie Lizbeth, this is your third strike, so you are off the bus for the rest of the year," Mrs. Olive declared.

"Wait until your daddy and Mrs. Childers hear about this. I know they didn't raise you girls to fight like a bunch of banshees, especially with those Brickle Brothers," she said disgustedly as she closed the school bus door in our face and pulled away.

Patti Summerhill hung her head out of the window and yelled at us as the bus started off down the road, "Annie Lizbeth, Mattie Rose, I'll call you later. I'll tell your daddy and Granny you didn't start it, I promise!"

The peter pan collar of my pink pinstriped blouse was ripped off on one side after my encounter with Billy Ray, and my hair was wadded up and sticking straight out from the back of my head where he had pulled it. Both Annie Lizbeth and I had scraped elbows and knees. It was obvious we had been in some kind of altercation.

As we walked in the back door, Granny took one look at us and said, "Great day in the morning, what happened to the two of you?"

With great drama we retold Granny detail after detail of our encounter at the back of the bus with the Brickle Brothers, and watched as the color of crimson spread up her neck and across her cheeks. "Well!" she said indignantly. "We'll just see about this when your daddy gets home."

"Now, you girls go clean up and change your clothes. Annie Lizbeth, bring me some mercurochrome from the medicine cabinet so I can paint both your elbows and knees. And Mattie Rose, I want that blouse so I can show the collar to your daddy, and don't you dare touch your hair. I want your daddy to see it just like it is!"

And with that, Granny went about the task of assembling supper which, every Friday night, consisted of all the leftovers we had not eaten during the week. As Granny pulled out Wednesday's meatloaf and Thursday's mashed potatoes, Annie Lizbeth asked her if she thought Myrtle the Turtle would like mashed potatoes.

Granny, still exasperated by what had transpired, looked at Annie Lizbeth and replied, "Annie Lizbeth, do you eat earthworms?"

"No," replied a solemn Annie Lizbeth.

"Well then, what makes you think that turtle wants potatoes? If I find out you are feeding 'people food' to that turtle, you are going to be in big trouble, do you understand me, young lady?"

"Yes, Granny," Annie Lizbeth pouted. Later, with paper cup in hand, she went outside to look for earthworms to feed Myrtle the Turtle.

Later that evening when Daddy got home, Granny was like a chicken with ruffled feathers. She was furious that Mrs. Olive had issued Annie Lizbeth and me bus misconduct reports, when the fight had been started by the Brickle Brothers. As further evidence that we were the "victims" and not the "instigators," she showed Daddy my reddened scalp and the bunched up hair where Billy Ray had pulled it, along with our mercurochrome-painted, scraped elbows and knees, and the torn collar of my blouse.

She looked at Daddy, and with a stern voice said, "Now James, I know we've told Annie Lizbeth and Mattie Rose that we don't want them fighting, but this time they were defending themselves. Those Brickle Brothers are always up to no good and something needs to be done about it!"

"Don't worry, Ruby. I'll take care of it after supper," was all Daddy said before we sat down at the table to eat. Daddy's jaw was set, and we knew when his jaw was set, he meant business. Supper that night was not filled with lively conversation of the day's events. Everyone already knew the "lively events of the day," so we all sat quietly, and ate Granny's Friday night leftovers while Annie Lizbeth stashed a little piece of meatloaf and a fingernail sized serving of mashed potatoes in her paper napkin to give to Myrtle the Turtle later that night when no one was looking.

After supper, Granny "volunteered" to do the dishes while Daddy told us to go outside and get in the car. Annie Lizbeth and I held tightly to one another's hand and said not a word as Daddy, his jaw clenched, backed out of the driveway and pointed the car in the direction of the Park.

He slowed down as we approached the line of beat-up mailboxes indicating the last names and house numbers of the people living down there. The Brickles' was the last mailbox in the row, with the number #08 hand painted on the side.

Now, our Daddy was a pretty even-tempered kind of guy, but he did not take too kindly to boys beating up his girls. As we turned onto the one-way, steep and winding, red clay and gravel dirt driveway, my stomach felt tied in knots. I was growing increasingly nervous, my mind racing with thoughts of doom and gloom.

What if the Brickle Brothers' daddy had a gun and shot our daddy? What if he shot us? How long would it take Granny to notice we were gone too long, and would she remember to feed Myrtle the Turtle? What if she found the meatloaf and mashed potatoes in the paper napkin Annie Lizbeth had hidden under her pillow?

It was twilight as Daddy maneuvered his car down the Road to Nowhere, trying to avoid as many potholes as he could. There were lights on in most of the shanties, lending credence that life did exist down there. A trail of smoke escaped from a fuel drum sawed in half and fashioned into a pig cooker at shanty #07, filling the air with the smell of roasting meat and burning wood. There, at the end of the Road to Nowhere, was Park house #08, home of the Brickle Brothers.

Though Annie Lizbeth and I had walked through the Park on a couple of occasions, we had never been in one of the shanties. Daddy took our hands when we got out of the car and told us to be careful as we walked through the yard, littered with cast-off car parts, hubcaps, pieces of rusted bikes, and flat tires stacked on top of one another. The dogs were barking, but they had long chains attached to their collars around some trees to keep them from running away at night, or from attacking strangers like us who were invading their territory.

As we started to climb the few steps leading to the front porch, every step we took was met with a creak, squeak, or sagging floorboard announcing our arrival. Before Daddy could even knock on the door, a torn screen door was opened, and we were facing a tall thin man in blue denim overalls and a dingy, ribbed T-shirt peppered with small holes. There were yellow stains from perspiration under each arm. He had the deeply-lined face of a man twice his age. His was not the face of a man weary from a day's work. His was the face of a man weary from life itself.

"What can I do for you folks, this time of evening?" he asked in a slow, southern drawl. I thought I could smell the faint aroma of alcohol on his breath as he spoke. Annie Lizbeth and I exchanged a quick glance and held tighter to Daddy's hands.

"Are you Mr. Brickle?" Daddy inquired.

"Yes sir, I am. Now what can I do for you and your little missies here?" he asked, slowing taking in the strangers standing on his front porch.

Daddy paused for a moment, but pressed on. "Well, Mr. Brickle, if you don't mind, I would like to speak with you about an incident involving your boys and my girls on the school bus today."

Without saying a word, Mr. Brickle opened the door and motioned for us to come inside the house. Annie Lizbeth's eyes grew big as saucers, as did mine, at what we saw. Inside the shanty was one main room that was divided by a woodstove. The front part was some version of a living room, and the back part must have been the kitchen with a door leading outside to the johnny house.

It was hot inside the house, and there was a rotating fan in front of an open window, humming away. Only when its spinning blades moved in our direction did we feel any movement of air. The knot in my stomach had crept upwards and now formed a lump in my throat. I tried to swallow, but my mouth was dry.

There were two faded, mismatched couches: one without legs, just sitting on the floor in the front parlor, and the other so threadbare you could see its inner springs. There were a couple of distressed wicker chairs whose seats were in need of repair positioned around the woodstove. In back of the big room was a long wooden table with benches on each side for seating. In the middle of the table lay an open loaf of white bread, a jar of mayonnaise, two half-eaten cans of something labeled "potted meat" alongside some empty bottles of RC Cola, and a mason jar half-filled with some clear liquid.

"You'll have to excuse the mess," Mr. Brickle said. "The Missus ain't here right now. She took the little ones over to help out her sister in Alamance County. Her husband run over her foot the other night with his truck and broke it. It was an unfortunate accident is all it was. His tail lights were burnt out and she was trying to direct him out to the road, but I reckon he cut it too close and run over her foot. No bad feelings, though. The Missus said she'd be back in a few days, and since the little ones ain't in school, it don't make no nevermind. I told her I'd be here to keep an eye on the boys."

Mr. Brickle offered us a seat, but Daddy told him we wouldn't be staying for long, so we just stood in the middle of the room, holding tight to Daddy's hands as he began telling Mr. Brickle about the school bus incident. Mr. Brickle just stood there, no expression on his face, his eyes glassed over, as if he was hearing a re-run of a story he had heard time and time again.

Daddy finished his peace by saying, "Now Mr. Brickle, I want you to know I have already given my girls a good talking to about fighting. They know their granny and I do not approve of such unladylike behavior, and they will be punished for their actions. However, I don't think your boys acted like gentlemen by deliberately provoking a fight with my girls over a turtle that did not belong to them."

The next thing we knew Mr. Brickle was hollering at the top of his lungs, "Billy Ray, Purvis, and Earl, you get out here right now!" From behind a door located not far from where the long wooden table sat emerged the Brickle Brothers. You could see the dread in their faces and eyes as they timidly entered the front part of the room, their heads down, shoulders slumped forward, to face their father.

"Well, now," replied Mr. Brickle, surveying the three boys with a look of disgust on his face. "Seems like you boys have been in trouble again, and this time you picked on a bunch of girls. What's the matter with you? Have you boys turned into such sissies that you now have to fight with girls to show how tough you are?" The Brickle Brothers kept their heads down and uttered not a word. I could see Billy Ray's hands trembling ever so slightly.

"And what's this I hear about you trying to steal this little girl's turtle? We got enough animals around this place, and I sure don't need nothing else to feed, so you better come up with some good reason about doing what you did, before I whup yew good," Mr. Brickle said as he narrowed his eyes and looked over at a wide leather strap hanging off a rusted hook on the wall.

Annie Lizbeth and I could see the Brickle Brothers were frozen in fear, and we knew by looking at them that they were quite familiar with the wide leather strap hanging on that rusty hook. Funny, they didn't look so tough now. We looked up at Daddy, our eyes pleading with him to do something, anything, to keep the brothers from being whupped with that leather strap.

Daddy looked over at the leather strap, and then at Mr. Brickle, and began speaking in a quiet tone. "Mr. Brickle, I did not come down here to get your boys a whupping. I came down here to show my girls that people can talk out their differences without resorting to hitting. As a father, I know you work hard to set a good example for your boys, as I do for my girls. The turtle is fine, no damage done there, so why don't we just have the kids apologize to one another, so that there's no hard feelings on the bus next week. As a matter of fact, I will be happy to stop by Mrs. Olive's house on the way home and settle the matter with her. What do you say?"

"Well," slurred Mr. Brickle. "I reckon if you say no harm was done, I can let the matter pass this once, but you boys be warned, if I hear of such a thang happening again, you won't get off this easy! Do you hear me?" he said with a menacing tone, his glassy eyes squinting as he looked each of the boys up and down.

"Yes sir, we understand," the brothers replied in military precision.

Daddy pushed Annie Lizbeth and me forward to offer our apologies to Billy Ray, Purvis, and Earl for our part in the fight. The boys, sensing that the leather strap would stay on the wall that night, were breathing big sighs of relief and told us they were sorry too.

Daddy shook hands with Mr. Brickle, and then walked over and shook each of the boy's hands, a gesture with which they were unfamiliar and awkward. He then took us by our hands, said good evening, led us off the porch, through the yard with the barking dogs, and back to the car.

Annie Lizbeth and I sat in total silence in the backseat of the car during the short ride home. Daddy stopped by Mrs. Olive's house, and we watched as he stood under her front porch light, saying words we could not hear, but watching until we saw Mrs. Olive nod her head up and down before Daddy shook her hand goodbye and said goodnight.

When Daddy got back in the car, he turned around, looked at us, and said quite matter of fact, "You girls are to be at the bus stop Monday morning at your regular time. Mrs. Olive is going to seat you right behind her all next week so she can keep her eye on you. You can tell Patti she'll be sitting with you as well."

Annie Lizbeth and I remained silent until Daddy pulled the car, bumping and grinding its way up our red clay driveway, into the yard and parked it. Granny had left the back porch light on for us, but as we exited the car and made our way towards the house, Daddy stopped us, the back porch light glaring into our eyes causing us to squint as we waited to hear what he had to say.

"Girls, I want to make sure we understand one another," he said. "There is to be no more fighting on the bus. Two wrongs don't make a right, Annie Lizbeth and Mattie Rose. You had a choice to make and you made the wrong one. You should have gotten up and told Mrs. Olive what was going on so that she could have moved you to a different seat, but instead, you chose to let your anger get the better of you, and where did that get you?" he concluded, awaiting our response.

"Thrown off the bus," we replied, our chins quivering as we held back tears. I think we would have preferred the sting of Mr. Brickle's leather strap to the stinging words of our daddy expressing his disappointment in us.

"Annie Lizbeth and Mattie Rose," Daddy said in his most serious "Daddy" voice, "I expect you to do unto others as you would have them do unto you, and I also want you to remember as you think about those boys living down there in the Park, through no choice of their own I might add, that there but by the grace of God go you and I."

Annie Lizbeth was starting to sniffle and tears were beginning to roll down my face.

"Okay, I've said my piece," Daddy concluded. "It's late and we could all use a good night's sleep. I'll tell Granny that the matter with the Brickle Brothers has been settled and there will be no more trouble on the bus."

Annie Lizbeth and I just stood there, our chins still quivering, an errant tear occasionally escaping down our guilt-ridden faces when all of a sudden Daddy's voice quickened. "Know what girls? I was thinking about going fishing in the morning. Wonder if anyone will want to go with me to help catch tomorrow night's supper?" Annie Lizbeth and I burst out giggling as Daddy pulled us close and kissed the tops of our heads, letting us know that all was forgiven.

As I snuggled between the clean, cool, cotton sheets of my bed that night, I thought about Billy Ray, Purvis, and Earl and wondered what kind of beds they were sleeping in? Were their sheets as cool and clean as mine?

I thought about the potted meat sandwiches, and how the only things potted in our house were plants. I could never remember a day when Granny didn't put a real supper with real food on our table, even on leftover night, and I thought about how hard Daddy worked to make that supper possible.

I thought about Mr. Brickle, and how he used the fear of the leather strap to keep Billy Ray, Purvis, and Earl in line. I had no reason to fear my daddy, and every reason to respect him.

Before I drifted off to sleep, I glanced over at Myrtle the Turtle, happily grazing on a piece of lettuce in an old fish bowl we had long ago abandoned, sitting on the beside table between Annie Lizbeth and me. Granny found the napkin in which Annie Lizbeth had stashed the meatloaf and mashed potatoes under her pillow when she turned down her bed for the night, and replaced the "people" food with some lettuce in a clean napkin for Myrtle's "late night snack." Annie pleaded with Granny to allow Myrtle the Turtle to sleep with her, but Granny persuaded her that Myrtle would be much more comfortable in her own "bed."

There's an old saying that one man's ceiling is another man's floor. There could have been no clearer example of that than the night we visited the Brickle Brothers.

All I knew, as my lids grew heavy and I entered into the safe sanctuary of sleep, was that I grateful to have both.

PICK A PECK OF PICKLED PEPPERS

We looked forward to the end of every school year. It was a time when summer turned baking hot and the sunlight cast long shadows across rural yards, tempting us to linger in its golden pathways for as long as we could.

The syrupy sweet smell of wild honeysuckle, nature's candy, growing alongside the road never failed to captivate us as we inhaled deeply its fragrant aroma the minute we exited the insufferably hot school bus.

As we walked home, Annie Lizbeth and I would stop and help ourselves to a handful of the bell-shaped yellow flowers, pinching off the little green ends of the blossoms in order to extract the stamen, which we removed ever so gently in order not to disturb the luring, single, clear drop of sweet nectar that never failed to delight the tips of our tongues.

We lived at the top of a small plateau on Peale Road. The white frame, shotgun-style house was situated under a thick cluster of ancient oak trees. This canopied, leafy forest was bordered on one side by a thick, dense, area of woods. There was a vine of some kind that wrapped around several of the trees. It was a substantial, fibrous strand, certainly strong enough to support the weight of me and my inseparable sidekick twin sister, Annie Lizbeth. We called it the "Monkey Tree Vine," and we spent many happy hours swinging on it—Tarzan-style.

In the sweltering heat of a North Carolina summer day, the grove of trees provided us with our own little oasis. Cool and private. The growth was so thick that it provided the perfect hiding place from the prying eyes of adults that might want to come searching for us—to intrude upon our play long before we were ready for it to end.

Our yard was, likewise, heavily shaded; a combination of red clay lay beneath the sandy loam. The soil was so heavily shaded and sandy that for years it would not support the growth of grass. Our yard grew dusty when the area was bereft of rain, and when the rain finally arrived, it washed away the sandy loam, leaving nothing but the thick, sticky, red clay beneath it—red clay that betrayed our every step by leaving a trail of footprints that Granny used to track our whereabouts.

Behind our house and down the hill was where the Park People lived. The Park was a dark and mysterious place to us, probably because we were forbidden to go there under one of Granny's thinly-veiled threats of, "If I ever catch you down there, young ladies, you'll be sorry for the rest of your life!" It is said that curiosity killed the cat, and for two inquisitive girls like Annie Lizbeth and me, the word "forbidden" was nothing more than an open invitation to "explore."

When, at long last, the final schoolhouse bell rang that first week in June, we knew that summer had arrived and we ran to embrace it! Mind you, we had been cooped up for nine months in dusky old classrooms that seemed, at times, more like chalk-encrusted prison cells than hallowed halls of learning.

Off went our toe-strangling shoes and socks, our bare feet longing to feel the cool, green grass between our toes. Like snakes, we shed the outer layers of the prison uniforms we had worn throughout the year: freshly-washed, starched, and ironed dresses, along with all the girl stuff Granny made us wear underneath them. On went cotton shorts and sleeveless shirts and, if we had to wear any shoes at all, we reached for our flip flops.

School ended on Friday, so Granny arranged for us to have our summer haircuts at Aunt Maggie's beauty salon bright and early the following Saturday morning. Granny liked our hair to be short in the summer since we spent so much time outside. Every evening when she called us in for supper, she would line us up and do a "tick inspection" of our scalp, ears, and neck to make sure we had not picked one up somewhere in the woods from our day of swinging from tree to tree on the Monkey Vine.

Aunt Maggie was Daddy's oldest brother's wife. She was one of the few women in town who actually owned her own business. Aunt Maggie was a kind and gentle woman, and we liked her a lot. Since she gave us a "family discount," we had to be worked in between her regular paying customers, which meant sitting, for what seemed to us like hours, as she moved around the salon like a tall, graceful gazelle from customer to customer, applying hair color to one, curling solution to the perm of another, cutting and styling still another of her regular Saturday customers, all wanting to look their best at Sunday church services.

When Aunt Maggie finally got around to us, she had to stack old Hollywood magazines in her salon chair because we were too short, and she was too tall to cut our hair, even with the chair pumped up as far as it would go. There we sat, covered in black nylon capes that draped to the bottom of the chair and covered our toes as Aunt Maggie snipped, snipped, snipped away at our freshly-washed hair. We watched as locks of hair cascaded down the capes forming little piles of curls on the floor.

"If you cut a little more off the sides, and shorten those bangs a bit, I think we'll be in business," Granny would say to Aunt Maggie as she supervised our haircuts. "These haircuts need to last through the summer!"

When Granny was satisfied that our haircuts fit the category of "wash and go," she thanked and paid Aunt Maggie, and down we came out of the salon chair, off the pile of stacked up Hollywood magazines, and out of the beauty salon with Granny, little pieces of freshly-clipped hair still stuck to our faces.

To prepare us for church the following Sunday morning, Granny ceremoniously washed our freshly-cut bobs on Saturday night after supper. Annie Lizbeth and I took turns lying on the ironing board so Granny wouldn't have to strain her back as she scrubbed our heads with dishwashing detergent in the kitchen sink, towel-dried it, and sent us off to bed.

In church the next morning, Annie Lizbeth and I got into a singing contest as the church congregation was led in song by the choir director, Mrs. Lucille Harper, to the hymn *I'll Fly Away*. There's a line in the hymn that goes "When I die, Hallelujah, bye and bye, I'll fly away." When the time came to sing the word "Hallelujah," Annie Lizbeth and I yelled it out at the top of our lungs. There was a brief silence as everyone in church turned their attention to us with a look of shock on their faces before continuing with the hymn!

Even Daddy, who was sitting on the last row of the choir behind the pulpit where Pastor Lewis preached, heard us as he focused his attention on the hymn book in front of him, his neon and cranberry red face telling us all we needed to know.

At the beginning of church services that morning, Granny was sitting in her regular seat at the end of the pew while Annie Lizbeth and I sat next to one another. However, by the time the last refrain of the hymn was sung, Granny had repositioned herself squarely between the two of us.

Annie Lizbeth and I first looked at one another and slowly tilted our heads upward to get a read on Granny's facial expression. An imposing woman, she wasn't smiling, and we knew we wouldn't be either when we got home.

Once the congregation was seated, Pastor Lewis walked up to the lectern and, in an effort to be break the tension in the room caused by Annie Lizbeth's and my outburst, said, "Yes, my brethren, through music our love for God is both nurtured and expressed. So the ancient psalmist says, 'Make a joyful noise to the Lord,' and if Annie Lizbeth and Mattie Rose Radley did not do just that today, I don't know who did!"

Pastor Lewis then winked at us and the entire congregation laughed—everyone, that is, except Granny, who remained stone-faced.

As we made our exit from the church that morning after services, Pastor Lewis looked at us, then at Granny and Daddy and said, "Ruby Mae and James, those girls were making a joyful noise unto the Lord, and it is in that spirit you should celebrate their youthful exuberance. Please do not punish them for that which the good Lord bestows upon young people…unbridled enthusiasm. Heaven knows, we need all of it we can get!"

Annie Lizbeth and I exchanged a quick look and a sign of relief. "Whew," I thought to myself. If Pastor Lewis was willing to give us a reprieve, surely Granny and Daddy would as well.

We left the church and walked down the gravel parking lot where the car was parked. Daddy and Granny always sat in the front seat while Annie Lizbeth and I sat in the back. Granny was the last one to close her door, but this time, she closed it a little harder than usual. The only sound you heard was the squishing of the fake leather car seats as we nervously shifted our weight from one leg to the other. I looked over at Annie Lizbeth who looked at me. We both knew something was coming.

Granny turned around in her seat, looked at us and said, "Pastor Lewis thought you two made a joyful noise today in church. I just thought you made a lot of noise! You not only embarrassed your daddy and me, you embarrassed yourselves by acting so disrespectful in the Lord's house. I'm going to let you off with a warning, and chalk this up to what Pastor Lewis called your 'youthful exuberance,' but if it happens again, there will be consequences. Do you understand me?" she concluded with a level of sternness in her voice that meant business.

"Yes Ma'am," we replied in unison, looking directly into Granny's gray-green eyes. "We understand."

Then Daddy turned around in his seat and said, "What in the world would possess you two to do such a thing in church?"

"I don't know, Daddy," I replied, trying to sound as remorseful as I could. "I guess we were just playing around and didn't think."

"Well, remember this. You play outside. You do not play inside the church. Do we understand one another?"

Once again, in unison, we replied, "Yes, Daddy, we understand."

Daddy put the keys in the ignition of our black Ford Fairlane and turned it on. As we backed out of the church parking lot and proceeded for home, the tension in the car was palpable. No further words were spoken on the subject, but Annie Lizbeth and I got Daddy and Granny's message loud and clear.

From that day forward, whenever we entered the church we could hear Daddy's words echo in our heads: "You play outside, you do not play inside the church." It served as a constant reminder that we were to remember where we were at all times and act accordingly.

When we got home, we changed into our play clothes and proceeded to help Granny prepare Sunday lunch. Her mood had lightened considerably, which, in turn, lightened ours. Sunday lunch in our house consisted of certain staples: fried chicken, mashed potatoes with gravy, seasonal vegetables, biscuits, sweet iced tea, and, in summer, freshly-picked, sweet and juicy strawberries from Granny's garden, piled on top of vanilla shortcake and topped with a generous dollop of hand-whipped, sweetened cream.

Granny did not allow us to fry chicken, fearing we might get popped by hot grease, but Annie Lizbeth and I took turns each week as to who would mash the potatoes and who would whip the cream for the strawberry shortcake. No matter what job you were assigned, after completing the task, Granny gave you what she called a "cook's treat." If you mashed the potatoes, you got to lick the potato masher, and if you whipped the cream, you got to lick the beater. Annie Lizbeth and I often took turns sharing our "cook's treats," because that way you got two instead of one!

As we prepared lunch, Daddy changed out of his Sunday best, sat in his favorite chair, and read the paper. There was a comforting rhythm to our daily lives, but it was about to be altered, at least temporarily.

As we were finishing up our lunch, Daddy pushed himself away from the table and said, "Ruby Mae, no one makes fried chicken like you! Tender on the inside and crunchy on the outside. And whoever mashed those potatoes did themselves proud. There was not a lump in them!"

I was about to take credit for the mashed potatoes when suddenly the phone rang.

"I'll get it, Ruby Mae," he said. "You and the girls take your time finishing up."

Daddy picked up the phone and said, "Hello. Why yes, Ruby Mae Childers lives here. You'd like to speak with her? Well, can I tell her who's calling?"

All of a sudden Daddy's face grew solemn and his voice got quiet.

"Just a minute, please. I'll get Ruby Mae to the phone."

We were all looking at Daddy rather quizzical, including Granny, but he simply held the phone out and said, "Ruby Mae, it's Donnie, Ralph Jr.'s boy from Virginia, and he'd like to speak with you."

Granny took the phone and said a lot of "uh-huhs" and "okays." When she hung up, she sat down at the table and said, "Ralph Jr. has passed away. That was Donnie who called to let me know and said that most of the family would be attending his funeral, and they would like me there as well."

Ralph Jr. was Granny's oldest brother. He and his family lived in Short Pump, Virginia. Since he was twenty-two years older than Granny, they were more like familiar strangers than brother and sister.

Annie Lizbeth and I had never met him, because the only contact he and Granny had was limited to a yearly Christmas card and the occasional postcard with a few scribbled lines noting some milestone event in the family's life. Nonetheless, Granny wanted to attend his funeral and pay her final respects, not only to her brother, but to his family as well.

Granny later returned her nephew Donnie's phone call and informed him that she would be traveling to Virginia to attend the funeral of her brother. Donnie suggested, that since the family rarely got together in one place, he wanted her to stay for a while so she could see and visit with her remaining brothers, reacquaint herself with their families, and meet a new generation of great nieces and nephews. He extended an invitation for Granny to stay with him and his family during her stay in Virginia, which Granny graciously accepted.

Daddy made all the necessary arrangements for her train trip to and from Virginia, and though Granny was torn about leaving us for a month, Daddy encouraged her to go by saying, "Ruby Mae, this may be one of the last times you get to see your entire family together, so you should go. Don't worry about us, we'll be fine."

And so, the following Wednesday at 6:00 AM, Daddy, Annie Lizbeth, and I waved goodbye to Granny as her train departed the railway station in Durham bound for Richmond, Virginia. Donnie would pick her up and drive her to Short Pump, where he and his family lived, and where Ralph Jr., would be laid to rest.

Before Granny left, she made arrangements with Margaret Holladay, a local woman who worked as a day housekeeper, to tend to Annie Lizbeth and me while Daddy worked. Margaret was to cook, do laundry, and other light housekeeping duties during Granny's absence.

Margaret Holladay was a frumpy, middle-aged woman married to an alcoholic named Ray, whose nickname was "Pickle," because he was always brined in something! She also had a thirty-two-year-old son, Bobby, still living at home.

Though no one ever talked about it, everyone knew Bobby was different. We once heard Granny tell Daddy that Bobby was "slow" and his capabilities were that of a twelve-year-old boy. With "Pickle" for a husband, and a son who required a lot of care, Margaret was the only breadwinner for the Holladay family.

At Christmas time, people in the community would always take boxes of food and other basic supplies over to their house, and quietly leave them on the front porch, knowing that Margaret was a prideful woman who would not accept charity of any kind.

Margaret was neat in appearance, but wore her gray, mousy hair in some sort of misguided pageboy, not at all flattering for someone with a square face and even squarer figure. She wore eyeglasses whose thick lenses were scratched from years of wear and tear. Improperly fitted, if fitted at all, they constantly slid down her stubby nose, causing an almost knee-jerk reaction as she pushed them back up on the bridge of her nose time and time again.

Margaret had a mousy personality to go with her mousy, gray hair, which made her perfect fodder for the antics of two highly-spirited, ten-year-old girls named Annie Lizbeth and Mattie Rose Radley.

During Granny's absence, Margaret worked Monday through Friday, tending house, cooking, doing laundry, and searching our heads for ticks at the end of the day from the "to-do" list Granny left on the kitchen table before she left for Virginia.

Late one morning, bored, with nothing better to do, Annie Lizbeth and I snuck off and went down to the Park, the mysterious and forbidden place Granny and Daddy forbade us to visit.

We ran into Tommy House, a retired car mechanic, working in his vegetable garden. The only way we knew Tommy was, on occasion, he would wander up to Peale Road looking to fix someone's car in order to make a few dollars. Granny and Daddy warned us to stay away from him, as he was a person of "shady" character.

His most outstanding feature was his nose. Annie Lizbeth once commented that Tommy House's nose was bigger than George Washington's entire face on Mount Rushmore, and that she didn't think a bigger nose existed on the planet Earth.

Daddy once let Tommy do some work on his beloved Ford Fairlane, and while he was working on the car, I asked Granny why Tommy's face was so red, why his nose was soooo big, and why it looked like a road map was sketched across it?

"Well," Granny replied, "that's what happens to people who drink moonshine and don't go to church." At ten years of age, Annie Lizbeth and I didn't even know what moonshine *was*, but we knew we were going to stay away from it to keep our noses from looking like Tommy's!

Well, Tommy must have been drinking moonshine that day because he was in an awful good mood when we happened upon him, his cheeks a bright rosy-red. He hollered out to us to come over so he could show us his garden.

The garden was impressive, with rows of corn, collards, cabbage, potatoes, tomatoes, squash, cucumbers, okra and green peppers. But Tommy's green peppers were not like any we had ever seen. The only green peppers Annie Lizbeth and I had ever seen were the *bell peppers* Granny grew in her modest patch of garden on the side of our wood-clad house. Tommy's green peppers were not bell-shaped. They were smaller, greener, and more elongated than Granny's.

I'd never seen a green pepper like it before, so I asked Tommy what it was. He told me it was a real special green pepper and asked me if I wanted to taste it. As a devoted member of the Weekly Reader's Food Explorer Club, I thought I could write an article on my new food adventure when I returned to school in the fall, so I enthusiastically replied, "Yes, I'd like to taste it," as Tommy pulled it from the warm summer soil.

Tommy dunked the green pepper in a bucket of water to rinse it off and handed it to me.

"Just bite into, little lady," Tommy cajoled. "It may be a little 'louder' than what you're used to, but that's the reason I grow them. I like things loud!"

Annie Lizbeth was looking suspiciously at the pepper and at Tommy, but before she could warn me, Miss Devoted-Member-of-the-Weekly-Reader's-Food-Explorer's-Club chomped down on that innocent looking little green pepper and began chewing it.

To this day I can still remember the slow, searing burn that started in my mouth and traveled to my stomach as I bit into and swallowed Tommy House's green pepper. It was hot, so hot I could feel it blistering my insides. I broke out in a heavy sweat as I spit. I spat trying to get rid of the awful fire inside my mouth, but Tommy House was bent over double laughing. He laughed so hard he couldn't catch his breath. I was crying so hard I couldn't catch mine.

"What's the matter, little girl? Never had a jalapeño pepper before?" the wretched Tommy House said, his laughter as loud as the pepper he had just given me.

Annie Lizbeth's eyes were as big as quarters as she stared at me in horror, watching as I grabbed my throat gasping for air, tears filling my eyes and spilling down my face. I still had half the uneaten hal-luh-PAIN-yo pepper in my hand, and without realizing it, stuffed it in the pocket of my shorts before Annie Lizbeth grabbed my hand and yelled, "Run, Mattie Rose, run!"

In the background I could hear Tommy House wheezing and coughing from laughing so hard. "Y'all come back now, you hear? I have other garden delights you can try!" he hollered as Annie Lizbeth and I ran for what seemed like miles, toward home.

We ran past Margaret hanging clothes on the line, up the back steps of the house and into the kitchen. My mouth, throat, and chest were in a state of fiery agony. I was out of breath from running, sweat was pouring off of me, and I felt sick and dizzy.

I feared the pepper had traveled to my brain as part of my punishment for visiting the land of the forbidden Park and it would now look like an over-roasted marshmallow. I had one thought and one thought only…water! Though I didn't know what moonshine was or how it tasted, I would have risked my nose and drunk a bucket full had Tommy House offered anything to cool down the smoldering remnants of what used to be my tongue.

Annie Lizbeth poured me glass after glass of water, her face as white as the sheets Margaret Holladay was hanging on the line as I gulped them down, one right after another.

"Gargle, Mattie Rose, gargle," Annie Lizbeth implored. "Maybe that will help cool down your throat, and besides, you don't want Margaret coming in here asking what's wrong, do you? If she finds out we've been in the Park and tells Daddy, your mouth won't be the only thing burning!"

Annie Lizbeth was right. I didn't want Margaret to know what happened, so I just kept on gargling, most of the water missing my mouth and spilling down my chin onto my green gingham sleeveless shirt and bright yellow shorts.

Annie Lizbeth kept asking, "Is it better now, do you need more water… here, eat a piece of bread." Slowly, the heat subsided, but the stinging humiliation of Tommy House and his pepper ruse remained.

My shirt and shorts were drenched in water, and I knew I had to change them fast before Margaret came back in from hanging clothes on the line. As I removed my shorts, I discovered the uneaten half of Tommy House's pepper I had shoved in my short's pocket. I pulled it out and examined it closely. It was filled with little white seeds that clung to its insides for dear life. I wondered if some of those little white seeds were clinging to my insides, ready to erupt like molten lava from the volcanoes our teachers had told us about in geography.

It was at that moment, a poor, unsuspecting Margaret Holladay came in from hanging clothes. Sweat was pouring off her from the summer heat, her glasses were barely hanging on the tip of her nose, and it was in that moment, my over-roasted-marshmallow brain decided to see if the other half of the uneaten pepper would have the same effect on someone else that it had on me. That person would be Margaret Holladay.

Margaret was not a bad person, in fact, quite the contrary. She arrived on time for work, did all the chores Granny left written on the kitchen table, let us drink Kool-Aid instead of milk with lunch, and generally ignored our daily antics. I thought Margaret might enjoy a little practical joke, and that we would all get a big laugh out of it at the end of the day.

So, it was a hot, tired, and grateful Margaret Holladay that accepted my invitation to make her a cool cucumber sandwich for lunch that summer's day. Only this cucumber sandwich would be different from any cucumber sandwich she'd ever eaten. This cucumber sandwich would give refuge to Tommy House's half-eaten, hotter than hot, green jalapeño pepper.

I said not a word about it to Annie Lizbeth, figuring she might protest my little joke or, worse yet, snitch to Margaret. To distract her, I gave her my latest copy of *Highlights Magazine* to read. She especially enjoyed reading Goofus and Gallant, the boys who approached right and wrong in different ways. Content, Annie Lizbeth went into the living room, sat in Daddy's chair, happily absorbed in the magazine, and not in anything I was doing.

As I began constructing Margaret's sandwich, I started with the usual two slices of Merita white bread. I slathered both sides in a thick coating of Duke's mayonnaise, knowing I would need a thick base in which to bury the remaining half of Tommy House's now thinly sliced hal-luh-PAIN-yo green pepper.

I meticulously layered the cucumber slices on top of the pepper pieces, doing my best to conceal them as I pressed them deep in the bed of mayonnaise. I knew better than to slice the sandwich in half, because Margaret might, just might, notice the different shades of green and look closer. I put the entire sandwich on a plate and on the kitchen table as I sweetly called out to Margaret… "Your lunch is ready!"

Margaret came into the kitchen and sat down at the table. She seemed relieved to be off her feet for a while.

"My, my, isn't this a treat?" she said. "It's not every day when someone makes me a sandwich!"

My heart pounded with anticipation as I watched. In what seemed like slow motion, Margaret lifted the sandwich to take the first bite. As she began to chew, all seemed fine. She even smiled at me. But after she swallowed, things began to change.

I couldn't tell if what I heard was the sound of cucumbers crunching against her dentures, or if it was the sound of her upper dentures grinding on her lower ones as Tommy House's jalapeño pepper melted the adhesive holding them to the roof of her mouth.

What I saw was a very startled Margaret Holladay, trying to figure out what was happening in her mouth once she realized something very hot had attacked her taste buds! Margaret threw the sandwich down and jumped up from the table in a panic, her hand over her mouth.

She ran over to the kitchen sink, her hands shaking as she struggled to turn on the water spigot. Margaret took an emergency detour from the conventional etiquette of drinking from a glass, and stuck her mouth directly under the faucet, and held it there spewing and spitting copious amounts of water until the fire subsided in her mouth.

Annie Lizbeth dropped the *Highlights Magazine* and came running into the kitchen to see what all the commotion was about.

"What's the matter, what's the matter with Margaret, Mattie Rose? Is she having some kind of seizure or something?" she asked anxiously. "Do we need to call Daddy?"

I had never seen Margaret Holladay so angry, but I guess the fiery peppers that were setting off Fourth of July fireworks in her mouth lit the end of her fuse. She walked over to the table and began peeling the sandwich apart, the thick layer of Duke's mayonnaise refusing to release its grip on the Merita white bread that held it together.

Like a forensic detective she slowly dissected the inner contents of my sandwich *du jour*, picking off the first layer of thinly sliced cucumbers before she discovered, tucked beneath them, the enemy…the jalapeño pepper, ribs, seeds, and all!

The peppers had brought tears to her eyes, and when she turned to glare at me, they were red-rimmed and watery. The area around her mouth was reddened, and her lips were slightly swollen.

"Mattie Rose Radley, I don't know what would possess you to do such a mean thing to a person, but you better believe I'm telling your daddy the minute he gets home, do you hear me young lady?"

"Yes, Ma'am," I replied, my face bright red, no longer from the heat of Tommy House's jalapeño pepper, but from shame.

"Now you go to your room and stay there before I do something that I might regret," she said, the anger still present in her voice.

Next, she turned to Annie Lizbeth and asked, "Did you know anything about this?"

"No Ma'am," Annie Lizbeth replied. "I knew about the pepper, but I did not know about the sandwich. I'm innocent."

I flashed Annie Lizbeth a hateful look as I exited the kitchen for my room, where I stayed for the remainder of the afternoon. I thought about what I had done, and realized that I was no different than Tommy House. He played a mean trick on me, which I, in turn, played on Margaret. No doubt, Daddy was not going to be happy when he heard about this.

Later that day when Daddy came home from work, he found Margaret, eyes still red from crying, her cheeks flushed, sipping a glass of water at the kitchen table. She told him about the sandwich and had wrapped its remains in wax paper as evidence. She also told him I was the one who did it, and that she was shocked that a child as innocent looking as I, could have such a devious mind.

"Mr. Radley, I did exactly as Mrs. Childers instructed during the entire time I have been here. I have tended the girls, taken care of the house, cooked supper every night, and this is the thanks I get!" she said, her eyes welling up again with tears.

"Mattie Rose Radley, I want to see you right now," Daddy commanded.

It was the moment I had been dreading all afternoon—facing Daddy. By the tone of his voice, you'd have thought he'd eaten one of Tommy House's peppers as well.

"Yes, Daddy," I said, as I timidly walked out of my room and into the kitchen.

"First, I want to know how you came in possession of a jalapeño pepper since Granny doesn't grow them in her garden. Then, I want to know why they were put in Margaret's sandwich?"

"Well," I hemmed and hawed.

"WELL, what?" Daddy said impatiently.

"Well, Annie Lizbeth and I snuck off to the Park earlier today and ran into Tommy House. He told us to come over and look at his garden, which we did. I saw some funny-looking green peppers growing. I asked him about them because I thought they might be something I could write about in school for the Weekly Reader Food Explorer Club," I rambled, trying to think of a good reason to justify why I had been in the Park.

"Enough of the Food Explorer Club, Mattie Rose," Daddy said impatiently. "You and Annie Lizbeth went down to the Park although you have been told one-hundred times to stay away from down there. Would you say that is a correct statement?"

"Yes, Sir," I replied.

"But, you went anyway, didn't you?"

"Yes, Sir."

I could tell Margaret Holladay was enjoying every minute of Daddy's interrogation, and I was starting to rethink if I was truly sorry I had put the pepper in her sandwich.

The minute Daddy got home and heard Margaret's tale of woe, Annie Lizbeth had snuck back into the living room, doing her best to "disappear" behind the *Highlights Magazine*.

"Annie Lizbeth, I want to see you in the kitchen, right now," Daddy commanded.

"Were you in the Park with Mattie Rose today?" Daddy asked.

"Yes, sir," she replied.

"You know you're not to be down there, right?" he continued.

"Yes, sir," Annie Lizbeth replied.

"Were you involved in picking the pepper and putting it in Margaret's sandwich?"

"No, Daddy," Annie Lizbeth replied.

It was fess up time, so Annie Lizbeth just blurted it all out to Daddy, and to Margaret, who had taken on the appearance of the cat that ate the canary.

"We didn't pick the pepper, Daddy. Tommy House conned Mattie Rose into biting it, and when she did, it burned her mouth real bad, so bad I thought she was going to stop breathing, honest Abe! So, we ran home to get some water, but I didn't know Mattie Rose stuck the other half of the pepper in her shorts, or that she intended to use it until I saw Margaret take apart the cucumber sandwich, and there it was, little pieces of that wicked pepper smashed under the cucumbers and covered in mayonnaise."

Daddy looked dismayed when he said, "Mattie Rose and Annie Lizbeth, I am very disappointed in both of you. You knew better than to go down to the Park and yet you went anyway. Tommy House played a mean trick on you, and what did you do? You turned around and played a mean trick on someone who has never been anything but nice to you. You may have thought playing a practical joke on Margaret was funny at the time, but when someone is hurt, it's never funny.

And, Mattie Rose, what you did was inexcusable! To say that I am appalled by your behavior is an understatement. Well, now you can just go on and call Patti Summerhill and tell her you and Annie Lizbeth will not be able to attend her pajama party on Friday night. Nor will either of you go roller skating with your friends on Saturday. I have plenty of chores to keep both of you busy so you can think about the consequences of your actions. Now, both of you tell Margaret you're sorry right now."

"I'm sorry," Annie Lizbeth said.

"I'm sorry, Margaret," I said. "Will you forgive me?"

"Yes," said Margaret. "As long as you don't offer to make me any more cucumber sandwiches!"

The tension in the room suddenly broke, and we all enjoyed a brief laugh, before Margaret got up, said goodbye, and left for the day.

Annie Lizbeth and I were not laughing when we had to call Patti Summerhill later that evening to tell her why we could not come to her pajama party on Friday night, or go roller skating with her and all our friends on Saturday.

Margaret finished her "tour of duty" with us a week and a half later when Granny returned home from Virginia. As decent as Margaret was, no one could replace Granny, who quickly brought back law and order to our daily lives.

In thinking about my behavior, I realized that had Annie Lizbeth and I stayed away from the forbidden Park like Daddy and Granny had warned, there would have been no jalapeño pepper from Tommy House's garden to burn my mouth *or* Margaret's, and that, instead of staying home all weekend doing various chores for Daddy, we could have gone to Patti's pajama party and roller skating with our friends.

It was a painful lesson to swallow, but swallow it I did as I came to learn that unintended consequences await you at the end of every dark side of enticement.

MARY MURRAY'S VERY WILD RIDE

It was the end of the school year in 1962. As was her custom, our next-door neighbor, whom we affectionately called "Aunt Polly," would send a train ticket to her oversized niece, Mary Murray, to come down and visit for summer vacation.

Mary lived in Rock Hill, Maryland, and both Aunt Polly and her mother thought some country life would be a nice change of pace from the city life she led. To us, Mary was a new playmate, and we looked forward to her summer visits.

Weeks before Mary made the journey to North Carolina, Aunt Polly got busy airing out the smell of mothballs and cedar chips that kept moths, and anything else living, away from the mysterious room at the end of the hall—a room whose door was always closed, a room we were forbidden to enter.

The heavy plastic coverings that encased the dark and heavily ornate furniture were removed; freshly-washed, line-dried sheets were ironed and put on the bed, and the heavy brocade curtains that entombed the room were opened to reveal a window that would provide light by day, and cool summer breezes at night. Once the hardwood floors were hand-scrubbed with Murphy's Oil Soap, Mary's bedroom was ready for summer occupancy.

The big day was finally here! Mary's train was going to arrive at the sad, run-down rail station in Durham, North Carolina.

We accompanied Aunt Polly to the train station to serve as Mary's welcoming committee. Annie Lizbeth and I stood on our tiptoes looking for Mary as people started to exit the train.

Annie Lizbeth and I made a penny candy bet on the ride to the rail station as to the number of people that would precede Mary from train. Annie Lizbeth made me show her my penny, as "proof" before she was willing to bet hers, but we both agreed whoever won would get an Atomic Fire Ball as the grand prize.

Annie Lizbeth meticulously began counting the number of people getting off the train, determined she was going to win the prized Atomic Fire Ball. I bet my penny that Mary would be the tenth person off the train. Annie Lizbeth bet that she would be number thirty. As ten became fifteen, and fifteen became twenty, we started to worry that maybe Mary had not made the journey after all.

As soon as Annie Lizbeth hit twenty, we saw a disheveled, dazed, and exhausted Mary disembark the train. She moved like an old woman, her hands holding a vise-like death grip on the train's side railing as she descended the steps—slow, stiff and shaky.

While Annie Lizbeth and I argued over which of us actually won the Atomic Fire Ball, Aunt Polly gathered the beleaguered Mary's belongings, piled us all in the car, pulled out of the train station and headed home.

On the ride back to Aunt Polly's house, Mary complained bitterly about her seat accommodations.

"The next time I visit by train, Aunt Polly, please buy me a full fare ticket. Those economy seats in the back of the train just about squeezed the life out of me, and I could feel my teeth rattle from the vibrations of those steel wheels pounding the train track for eleven hours. By the time we got to Virginia for a rest stop, my entire body was numb. I was afraid I'd never walk again."

Mary was a city girl and not accustomed to country living. However, once she recovered from the exhausting train ride, and the backs of her calves healed from the basket weave indentions left by the rattan suitcase she pressed under her seat for eleven hours, she seemed happy to be away from the constant din of traffic and city noises that was her daily reality back home.

Mary was grossly overweight, choosing to spend her free time in Rock Hill eating, sleeping, and watching TV. It was an established fact that there were no overweight kids on Peale Road. Maybe Annie Lizbeth was right about the secret meetings of the mothers' or, in our case, Granny, when school ended each year. She figured they all met and devised ways to keep us out of the house, and out of their hair, during summer vacation.

On any given summer day, we ate an early breakfast and were ordered outside to play until lunch. After lunch, we were ordered back outside to play until supper. After supper, we were sent back outside until Granny came out on the front porch and yelled for us to come home. We would take our baths, put on our pajamas, and have a few vanilla wafers and a glass of milk before bed. It was pretty much the same routine for all the kids on Peale Road, so it was no wonder we were all pencil-thin with oomph to spare. Aunt Polly figured we would be the perfect energizers for Mary's lack of get-up-and-go.

Mary Murray was the original plus-sized girl. Growing up in the early 60s, there were no large women clothing stores, so Mary's summer wardrobe consisted of homemade, knee-length culottes that cut into her inner thighs and eventually found their way bunched up in the crack of her rear end. She wore oversized tunic tops in large prints, which only brought attention to her sizable girth. Mary preferred to wear slip-on, open-toed, pink terry cloth bedroom slippers most of the time. She complained that if she wore regular shoes, her feet would swell to twice their natural size by day's end.

Annie Lizbeth, who logistically and systematically analyzed anything someone like Mary said, stated there was no medical way her feet could swell like that since she spent most of the day lying on the couch, watching TV, drinking Coke, and raiding Aunt Polly's icebox. Annie Lizbeth further concluded that, in order for Mary's feet to swell to twice their natural size in a given day, she would first have to stand on them so that the soda would have a place to go.

Mary had a facial tic, and so, one day, out of curiosity, I asked Granny why Mary's eyes blinked all the time giving her such a startled look. Granny told me it was rude to point out other people's physical misfortunes. She then lectured me for several minutes about Mary's other medical problems. She told me Mary suffered from a glandular condition, a condition even the doctors did not understand. She said her glands produced too much of everything, and that was why she was overweight, nervous, irritable, and had excess blond facial hair lightly covering her cheeks and chin. She then looked me straight in the eye and said that if she so much as heard a whisper that Annie Lizbeth or I had said a word about any of this to Mary, we would spend the rest of the summer in our room.

I knew I could not trust Annie Lizbeth with such powerful information, because the minute she saw the summer bookmobile coming down Peale Road, she would hail it down and look up all things associated with "glands." I promised myself to keep Mary's over productive glands a secret, or at least, until she went back home to Rock Hill.

As the days passed and June turned into July, we were all growing frustrated with Mary. After all, Aunt Polly wanted her to get off the couch and out of the house. She wanted Mary to go outside, breathe fresh southern air, and spend her days playing with us. We tried to teach Mary to jump rope, but she could never get her footing or sense of timing right. Inevitably, she would be tangled in the rope and fall to the ground. It would take all three of us to get her up and back on her feet, and then she would stomp off to Aunt Polly's house where she complained of rope burns as an excuse to lie on the couch and watch TV for the rest of the day.

We tried to teach her to play hopscotch, but her weight interfered with her balance, inevitably causing her to stumble, her puffy feet, encased in summer sandals, landing outside the official hopscotch lines drawn by Annie Lizbeth. Stepping outside the lines meant an immediate dismissal from the game by Annie Lizbeth. Annie Lizbeth took on the role of referee for every game that involved a rule. No one knew how she got to know all the rules, but she was adamant about her hopscotch expertise, and the one person you did not want to challenge on Peale Road was Annie Lizbeth.

She was a wiry, wisp of a girl, but she was fast, agile, and quick-tempered.

If you felt lucky and wanted to challenge Annie Lizbeth, you would find her on your back before the count of three as she knocked you to the ground, and pummeled you until you cried "Uncle." I saw Annie Lizbeth in many a fight, and I never saw one she did not win. So Annie Lizbeth ruled as Her Royal Referee of Hopscotch, at least in the summer of 1962.

Poor Mary simply did not have the physical stamina to keep up with us, and that would prove to be her ultimate downfall.

One hot July afternoon, bored, with nothing better to do, I wandered over to Aunt Polly's house where I found Mary engaged in her favorite pastime, lying on the couch. She complained that Aunt Polly's TV was on the blink, and that she was tired of re-reading the same old Hollywood glamour magazines Aunt Polly kept stashed by her bed. She said she had memorized all the beauty and glamour tips her brain could hold, and that when she got home she was going to try some of them out.

I listened patiently for over an hour as she described, detail by detail, the plan of her beauty transformation. She told me she was going to bleach her short, coarse, wavy, red hair blond and style it like Doris Day. She said she was going to have the excess hair removed from her face and chin by a method called electrolysis, if her mama could afford it. She blathered on that if her mama could not afford electrolysis, she promised Mary she could wear makeup when she turned thirteen to camouflage the problem.

As she opened another bottle of Coke and helped herself to a handful of sugar cookies Aunt Polly thought she had hidden on the back shelf of her pantry, she reminded me that the minute summer vacation was over, and she returned to Rock Hill, she was going to try the famous boiled egg and grapefruit diet. She said she would be so thin by next summer's vacation I would not recognize her.

I had grown weary listening to Mary to talk about herself. I asked if she wanted to walk across the street with me to see the new whirligig that Sears had just delivered to the Fuller kids as a present from their grandparents. I told her no one had seen anything of its kind in our neighborhood, and that we could be the first! Since Mary was never the first at anything, she got off the couch, shoved her puffy feet into her summer sandals, and trudged across the street to see the whirligig.

I had already given Annie Lizbeth and Patti Summerhill their marching orders to run across the street and wait for Mary and me to arrive in the Fuller's backyard. Annie Lizbeth rang Mrs. Fuller's doorbell to ask if she could play with the boys. I figured if she would let the boys come out and play, maybe we could convince them to let us take turns riding the whirligig.

Marie Fuller was a quiet, simple, Midwestern woman, married to Dan Fuller who was pursuing his Ph.D. in philosophy at Duke University. They could not live in married housing because they had three children, which was one too many to qualify for university-married housing, so he received a monthly stipend from the university to rent the small brick house across the street from ours.

They were a quiet couple who kept to themselves. They had three sons: Hal, five; Hershel, six; and Henri, seven. Granny called them "stair-step kids," because one followed the other in age. Mrs. Fuller told Annie Lizbeth that if she wanted to play with the boys, she would have to come back later in the afternoon because they were getting ready to leave and take a picnic lunch over to Mr. Fuller at the university.

It was as if the window of opportunity had opened its sash and flung itself wide open for us. With the Fuller boys out of the picture, Annie Lizbeth, Patti Summerhill, and I were not only going to be the first to see the whirligig, but the first to ride it as well! We had one small obstacle standing in our way. We needed a fourth rider, and lo and behold, she was standing right beside me.

The Fuller's whirligig had a chrome stationery base on whose frame rested four fire-engine red seats. To achieve maximum speed and balance, it required four riders. Mary's first reaction to the whirligig was skeptical, but with our encouragement about how we were going to be the first ones in the neighborhood to ride this marvelous piece of modern machinery, she gradually warmed up to the idea.

"You know I suffer from motion sickness, don't you, Mattie Rose?" said Mary.

"Of course I do," I replied. "We're going to go slow, and we are only going to go round a time or two, so you will be fine," I said reassuringly. Mary nervously took her seat, but I could see her eyes twitching and small beads of sweat already forming around her lips.

When Mary took her seat, the sheer weight of her bloated body tilted the whirligig backwards, her seat resting a few inches above the ground. Annie Lizbeth, Patti Summerhill, and I were pitched higher, which meant we would have to pump harder to get the thing to move, but we were undaunted. Our desire to be first overcame any mechanical obstacles that stood in our way.

Operating a whirligig is very much like operating a modern day row machine. You push down on the pedals and pull back on the handlebars. If you want to increase your speed, you push harder and pull faster. Poor Mary huffed and puffed as she pushed the pedals down and pulled back on the handlebar. By now, her face was bright pink, and the sweat that had formed a ring around her lips had extended upwards to her forehead and bangs.

As we made our first full rotation, Mary looked across the whirligig at me and asked once again, "Now Mattie Rose, if I start to feel sick, are you going to stop this thing and let me off?"

"Of course I will. What kind of a person do you think I am?" I replied indignantly.

As Annie Lizbeth, Patti Summerhill, and I mastered the mechanics of the playground marvel, we began to make it go faster and faster. Delighted with our accomplishment, we screamed with glee at the top of our lungs as we picked up more and more speed and transformed ourselves into whirling dervishes.

Around and around we went. I loved the feel of the wind in my face and hair as we went faster and faster. Annie Lizbeth, Patti Summerhill and I were on top of the world, when suddenly, Mary started to whimper, "Mattie Rose, I don't feel good, I'm dizzy, and I want to get off this thing right now!" I pretended not to hear her and continued pushing and pulling to see how fast we could really go.

We went a couple of more turns when Mary started crying, demanding that we stop the ride and let her off. She was leaning a little more to the right than the rest of us, but I figured it was because her weight had shifted during the ride.

"I am begging you to let me off this ride, Mattie Rose!" Mary sobbed. "If you don't let me off this ride this instant, I am going to tell Mrs. Fuller, Aunt Polly, and your granny on you!"

I was furious that Mary was trying to spoil our fun after I had listened to all her mindless talk about Doris Day, bleaching her hair blond, electrolysis—whatever that was—wearing makeup, and how skinny she would be next summer after going on the famous boiled egg and grapefruit diet! My egg was boiling at the thought that she was going to be a tattletale and tell Mrs. Fuller, Aunt Polly, and worst of all, Granny on us! I looked at Patti Summerhill and Annie Lizbeth and yelled, "Push!" knowing that if Mary got off the whirligig, we would all have to get off because we would be minus our fourth rider.

Our little toothpick legs and arms went into overtime. By now, the whirligig was going full steam, around and around, with everyone screaming at the top of their lungs, including Mary. From that moment forward what started out as an adventure turned into our worst possible nightmare.

I watched in horror as Mary's seat finally succumbed to her weight. It was twisted sideways, her massive body almost horizontal to the ground below her. She was sweating profusely, her hair matted to her head, a look of sheer terror frozen on her pasty, white face.

We were trying to slow the revolving whirligig down by dragging our feet on the ground, but that only made the situation worse. The ride came to an uneven halt, which was most unfortunate, because the jolt loosened Mary's final grip on the handlebar.

Mary shot out of that seat like a rocket on the Fourth of July! "Oh no!," Annie Lizbeth exclaimed right before Mary's brief orbit in space ended, and she hit the ground with a thunderous PLOP! Our fourth rider had involuntarily exited the ride after all.

Annie Lizbeth, Patti Summerhill, and I jumped backwards off the still moving whirligig to see if Mary was dead. Patti Summerhill was convinced that we had killed Mary, and to be honest, I wondered if we had as well. Annie Lizbeth went over and put her fingers under Mary's nose to see if she was breathing. She was, but it was several moments before she started moaning and groaning. We tried to get her up, but even the three of us pulling together could not budge her dead weight from the ground. Annie Lizbeth was about to run home and get some Clorox to use as smelling salts, but it was too late.

Suddenly, Mrs. Fuller drove up and saw us huddled over Mary. She hurried the children into the house and ran outside to see what was causing all the commotion.

Her eyes suddenly focused on her children's brand new whirligig, in ruin, its base tipped on one side, three fire-engine red seats suspended in the air, and one fire-engine red seat bent and crushed on the ground, along with a twisted handlebar bearing Mary's sweaty fingerprints.

Mary was starting to come to, and with Mrs. Fuller's help, we were able to get her to her feet. She had a big knot on her head, multiple scratches on her arms and legs, and that same dazed looked she had when she disembarked the train earlier that summer.

Annie Lizbeth and I each took an arm and slowly walked her back across the street, moaning and groaning, towards Aunt Polly's house. When we arrived at Aunt Polly's back door, it was all we could do to keep Mary propped up. Her massive weight was beginning to take its toll on us, and we struggled to keep her from totally collapsing.

Standing beside Aunt Polly was Granny who looked with disbelief at Mary's injuries, and then at us, the ones responsible for them. She helped Aunt Polly get Mary into the house. They cleaned her up, painted all her scratches bright purple with iodine, and took her to Dr. Steiner, who stayed late after his office closed to make sure she had not sustained a head injury from the big knot on her forehead.

Aunt Polly was furious with us for our treatment of Mary. She told

Granny she was humiliated that she had to call her sister and tell her of Mary's unfortunate accident while in her care.

Three days after the unpleasant incident, Mary Murray boarded a train back to Rock Hill, Maryland, and we never saw her again. I would never know if she dyed her red hair blond, styled it like Doris Day, had the excess hair removed from her face and chin, or achieved her ideal weight from the famous boiled egg and grapefruit diet she so anxiously wanted to try.

Aunt Polly stripped the bed of its linens, put the plastic coverings back on the furniture, closed the drapes, and shut the door to the mysterious back room at the end of the hall. I would be a grown woman before I ever saw that room again.

As Annie Lizbeth and I waited for Granny to hand down our punishment, I thought about poor Mary boarding that train, a big red knot on her head, scratches and bruises everywhere. However, going home would be different this time. Granny and Daddy came up with enough money to purchase Mary two seats, side by side, in the front of the railcar. Although her body was bruised, scratched up, and sore, at least she would not have to serve solitary confinement in a cramped economy seat, at the back of the train.

She held not a paper bag of three yellow cheese sandwiches, but a picnic basket Aunt Polly had stuffed full of Mary's favorite foods, along with three thick slices of Granny's pecan pie. I guess Aunt Polly felt the food was a small consolation for the injuries and indignation she had suffered at our hands.

My daddy's brother Clay, a mechanic, came over and worked an entire sweltering July weekend to repair the whirligig. Though Clay worked free of charge, Granny and Daddy had to pay for all the supplies he purchased in order to restore the ride back to working condition. The money spent to repair the whirligig and pay for the two extra seats purchased for Mary's trip back to Rock Hill cost Granny a new winter coat and Daddy some much-needed shoes.

It cost us, too. Annie Lizbeth, Patti Summerhill, and I were designated as free labor for Dan and Mary Fuller the remaining summer and fall of 1962. We weeded, fertilized, watered, and harvested all the vegetables from her summer garden. In August, we spent hours planting seedlings for her cool season vegetables. In early fall, we raked and bagged leaves every Saturday. When the first snow fell in early December, we shoveled it off the walkway that led to the house. Our "sentence" ended at the end of December 1962. As we sat shivering over hot chocolate after one of Dan Fuller's "snow removal" projects, Granny looked at us and said, "I hope you girls have learned your lesson."

I did learn a lesson, and it has remained with me to this very day. My selfishness in wanting to be first in anything taught me something important. To win at any cost isn't really winning at all. When you selfishly sacrifice anything and anybody to get what you want, the person you ultimately sacrifice is yourself.

HAY AND LEMONADE

"Hey girls, I have a riddle for you," Daddy enthusiastically announced one hot, humid, Friday evening in August over one of Granny's beanie-weenie casserole suppers.

"Oh boy, it's corny joke time," moaned Annie Lizbeth, who was already preoccupied with separating the beans from the weenies so they wouldn't touch.

"Okay, girls. What fish in the sea is the most musical?" Daddy asked, his blue eyes sparkling and his dimples deepening as he tried to suppress a laugh.

Since I never tried to solve one of Daddy's silly riddles, I simply shrugged my shoulders, while Annie Lizbeth paused from separating her beanie weenies, looked Daddy straight in the eye, and in her most dead panned voice said, "I don't know. Tell me, Daddy, what fish in the sea is the most musical?"

"A TOO-NA fish!" he replied, as he burst out laughing.

Annie Lizbeth rolled her eyes upward in sheer exasperation and shook her head, while I allowed a little giggle to escape me.

"That was a good one, James," Granny chuckled, as she passed a plate of cornbread around for second servings.

"Speaking of fish, does anyone want to go fishing with me tomorrow?" Daddy inquired. "I have two extra fishing poles and a tackle box full of hooks, lures, and bait. Pete Sims from work is picking me up in his red truck bright and early. I think he's taking his boys, Cody and Timmy, and if you want to go, I'd love to have you come along."

Saturday was usually Daddy's only day to relax, and he liked to spend as much of it as possible with us, since Monday through Friday were work days, and Sunday was reserved for church. On most occasions, Annie Lizbeth and I would tag along and go fishing with Daddy just to be with him, but after we thought about this particular invitation, we respectfully declined.

After all, it was August, and the dog days of summer were upon us. Besides, who wanted to get up at 6:00 on a Saturday morning, sit on a dewy, grassy bank in total silence, swatting away mosquitoes with one hand while holding a fishing rod in the other? Cody and Timmy Murray were seven- and eight-year-old brats who would inevitably spend the day trying to find ways to put worms down our backs or in our hair.

And, if that was not enough to deter two ten-year-old chatterboxes from a sport that encourages silence, if you went fishing, Granny would insist on slathering any exposed body part with her homemade mosquito repellant of half vanilla extract and half water. It worked pretty well, if you didn't mind smelling like a cookie.

Saturday morning, long after Daddy had departed for his fishing outing, Annie Lizbeth and I reluctantly crawled out of bed, rubbing the sleep from our eyes, seduced by the savory aroma of homemade buttermilk biscuits and hickory-smoked country ham making its way into our room from the kitchen.

Our bedroom was small, but cozy. In between our pine twin beds was a one-drawer nightstand with a small lamp on it over which Annie Lizbeth draped a sheer pink scarf. Between our beds lay a rectangular, wool-tufted area carpet covered in red and pink roses.

From the moment Granny laid eyes on that carpet one Saturday morning at a church rummage sale, she knew she had to have it. She and Charlene Andrews actually had words over who was going to buy it, but Granny won out. After she brought it home, she carefully washed and line-dried it before she put it between our two beds. Granny said she could think of no better way to start the day than to wake up and step into a rose garden. We could not have agreed more.

We each had our own narrow four-drawer clothes dresser that Granny bought on sale at the downtown furniture discount store. Granny was as organized a person as I ever knew. I guess the conditions of her life required it. The four drawers were arranged in the manner in which one dresses. Undergarments and socks were in the first drawer, blouses and assorted tops in the second, slacks, culottes, and shorts in the third, and nightgowns, robes and pajamas in the fourth.

At the end of each of our beds was a hope chest that Daddy had built out of red cedar. On the top of each chest he carved our initials. We filled them with little keepsakes, but they were primarily home to sweaters and other woolen clothing items that needed to be protected from moths. They also substituted for bench seats when putting on, or taking off, our shoes.

That morning when we went to our respective dressers, we each pulled out a pair of freshly-washed and ironed pedal pushers—blue striped for me, pink checked for Annie Lizbeth—along with color-coordinated tops. We slid our bare feet into our favorite summer footwear, bright-colored rubber flip flops, and meandered into the bathroom where we robotically went about the morning ritual of washing up before entering the kitchen.

Granny had an unspoken rule; if you were going to sit at her table, you were going to be presentable. Granny said that tables were meant for sharing good food and conversation, and that unkempt people were distractions to both.

When we entered the kitchen, Granny was standing in front of the refrigerator with the door wide open, obviously looking for something she could not find, a puzzled expression on her face.

She was wearing one of her floral housedresses, the kind that snapped down the front. It had little clusters of cheerful red flowers scattered all across the background of its white cotton fabric. On her feet were her favorite, well-worn, Daniel Green, soft leather house shoes. Granny always wore a housedress in the morning. She told us they were comfortable, yet respectable enough in appearance to wear if she had to answer the door.

Most important, she emphasized, they spared her nicer clothes from the battle scars of early morning housecleaning, cooking and baking, which she liked to get done early, especially in summer, to avoid the afternoon heat.

"Well, well," Granny remarked as we wandered into the kitchen and took our places at the kitchen table, distracting her from whatever she was looking for in the refrigerator. "My sleeping beauties are up at last, and I bet you are ready for some breakfast."

"Yes, Ma'am!" we replied eagerly. The smell of biscuits and country ham permeated the kitchen, awakening our taste buds, causing our hungry tummies to rumble.

"Speaking of breakfast, I got up at daybreak with your daddy to prepare him something to eat before he left to go fishing with Pete Sims and his boys. While I was packing up some country ham biscuits for his lunch box, I looked for the last of the deviled eggs I put in the refrigerator after supper last night. I looked and looked for those deviled eggs, and for the life of me, couldn't find them. Would either of you girls know what happened to them?" Granny asked, as she removed two harvest gold Melmac plates from the kitchen cupboard.

Before I could think up an answer, Annie Lizbeth jumped in and said, "Why yes, Granny, I can tell you what happened to the deviled eggs. I got hungry after Mattie Rose fell asleep, so I went out to the kitchen, saw them in the refrigerator, and ate the last of them. But don't worry, I brushed my teeth afterward."

A silent hush came over the room, and I could feel my face flush with color, just like Daddy's whenever he was embarrassed, upset, or feeling ill at ease.

Annie Lizbeth had just told a lie to protect me, because she knew full well it was my idea for us to sneak out of bed and split the last of Granny's creamy, mustardy, deviled eggs filled with chopped green olives, celery seeds, and lightly dusted with paprika for what Granny called "a hint of color." I had given into temptation, even after Granny had specifically told me, as we cleared the supper dishes the night before, that she was going to put them in Daddy's lunch box when he went fishing the next day.

Obviously annoyed by Annie Lizbeth's answer, Granny huffed, "Well, I hope you are proud of yourself, Little Miss Gobbler. Your daddy is out there fishing with Pete Sims and his boys all day with nothing but some country ham biscuits, a couple of packs of nabs, and a thermos of coffee. You better believe Dottie Sims packed her boys more than that for lunch! I'll have to see her at church tomorrow, and after Pete tells her what your daddy's had in his lunch box, she'll probably think I was too lazy to get up and fix the poor man a proper breakfast, much less lunch, and you know what a gossip she can be!"

With her hands planted squarely on her broad hips, Granny's lecture continued. "How would you girls like it if your daddy packed up all the leftover country ham biscuits for himself this morning, leaving the two of you with nothing but cold cereal for breakfast?"

I looked over at the counter near the stove where Granny had been busy preparing our breakfast plates, prior to the lecture about the missing deviled eggs. Each plate contained one of her homemade, oversized, buttermilk biscuits stacked high with thinly-fried slices of country ham that were slightly frizzled at the ends, accompanied by a side of fried apples fragrant with cinnamon, and a generous mound of creamy stone-ground grits, butter oozing down every side like molten lava. My mouth watered at the mere sight of it.

"Granny," Annie Lizbeth piped up and said. "I'm sorry I ate the deviled eggs. I didn't know they were for Daddy's lunch box, because if I had, I would have left them alone."

"Well if you didn't know, you didn't know," Granny replied, her mood lightening a bit. "I said something to Mattie Rose when I was wrapping them up, but I guess she didn't mention it to you before she fell asleep. And, we all know that once your daddy gets to fishing, the last thing on his mind is food, so why don't you girls just eat your breakfast before it gets cold," as she set our plates in front of us.

I sat silently picking at my oversized, overstuffed, homemade country ham biscuit, pushing my buttery grits and fried apples to the side, my empty stomach now over-filled with guilt. If I'd heard Granny say it once, I'd heard it a thousand times, "Tis one thing to be tempted, another thing to fall." I had fallen into the deviled eggs and taken Annie Lizbeth with me.

After we finished eating, Granny set us about our morning chores. After washing and drying our breakfast dishes, wiping off the kitchen table and sweeping the floor, I told Annie Lizbeth we better think of a way to get out of the house early if we wanted to make it up to Bessie Mae Carson's to play.

Bessie Mae told Annie Lizbeth and me that if we wanted to play together on Saturday, it would have to be in the morning because her grandmother was hosting a tea party that afternoon. Mrs. Carson wanted her only granddaughter in attendance so she could show her off to all her lady friends. Since Granny wanted our chores done in the morning, I had to come up with some excuse to get Annie Lizbeth and me out of the house.

Granny was busy stripping sheets off the beds for washing when I approached her.

"Granny, Bessie Mae Carson is having a tea party for all her friends up at her grandmother's house today at noon, and she's invited Annie Lizbeth and me. She said she was going to need extra help, and we volunteered. We've washed and dried the breakfast dishes, put them away, wiped the table and swept the floor. Would it be okay with you if we went on up to Bessie Mae's now to help her? If there's any leftover chores, we'll do them when we get back," I said reassuringly. "Can we go, can we?"

Granny, reluctantly agreed to let us go, but as we ran out the back screen door like two streaks of lightning, she came out on the back porch and yelled, "I want the two of you back here at three o'clock because I have to go to the Cottingham's Meat Market to pick up a fresh fryer for tomorrow's Sunday dinner. If we are later than three-thirty, all the good fryers will be gone. Mattie Rose and Annie Lizbeth Radley, do you hear me? I want you back here by three o'clock, or else!"

"We hear you, we hear you, Granny," we hollered back as we took off up the road, our flip flops snapping against our heels as Granny's voice began to fade off in the distance.

We ran up the road towards the Methodist church, figuring we would be far enough away from Granny's voice so that we could pretend not to hear her in case she had second thoughts about us helping her with chores.

The Methodist church sat about a quarter of a mile up the road from our house.

Though we were members of a Southern Baptist congregation, Annie Lizbeth and I found the church, with its sprawling, shady oak trees and luscious green lawn, an irresistible place to escape the seemingly endless hours of afternoon summer heat. We spent many an hour lying under the canopy of those old oak trees, which seemed to possess a spirituality all their own, our bodies absorbing the coolness of the soil beneath us, as blades of green grass tickled our bare feet.

The church's parsonage was located right next door to the church, and Reverend Hall, a widower for as long as we had known him, lived there with his spinster sister, Miss Maureen. Miss Maureen was a devoutly religious middle-aged woman who tended house for the Reverend, played the church organ on Sunday, and acted as the Reverend's official "church hostess" when the occasion called for one.

Annie Lizbeth and I tried to figure out a way to get Granny and the Reverend Hall together, but we could never get so much as a spark to strike between them. I guess Granny had her hands full with us, and the Reverend Hall had his hands full with his church, so outside of a neighborly, "How-do-you-do," the two of them went about their parallel lives without so much as casting an eye in the other's direction.

Annie Lizbeth went by the theory that there must be a law forbidding a Methodist and Southern Baptist to marry. Even if they could, Miss Maureen would personally see to it that nothing upset the world she had created for her and her brother.

There was a graveyard on the church property. Annie Lizbeth and I often stopped there as we walked up Peale Road toward Bessie Mae Carson's house. Annie Lizbeth said the graveyard reminded her of an outdoor museum with its distinctive and elaborate markers and statues, most weathered by the passage of time.

Some folks felt uncomfortable visiting a graveyard, but not Annie Lizbeth and me. We liked the quiet, respectful atmosphere there that seemed to honor those who had passed on before us. Because the graveyard went back to the Civil War, it was almost as if we were on a walking history tour as we passed by various markers, which Granny called "guardians of the soul."

There were two particular gravesites that held endless fascination for Annie Lizbeth and me, and we never failed to visit them.

The first belonged to a young woman by the name of "Rachel," who died of whooping cough in the early 1920s. Her family had a black and white photograph of her encased in thick glass and embedded in her marble grave marker. She had a lovely face with dark, sultry eyes, but the most memorable thing about Rachel was the curl, which flappers fancied in the 1920s, styled right in the middle of her forehead. She was hauntingly beautiful and mysterious-looking, and Peale Road folklore had it that she wandered around the graveyard late at night in a black gown and veil, though we could not testify to such a sighting since we had to be in bed by 9:00 PM.

The other gravesite belonged to a little four-year-old boy whose name was "Toby." On his white marble marker a pair of hand-carved marble baby shoes lay one on top of the other, with an etching that read, "I put my little shoes away." He, too, had died of whooping cough.

I was much too young to grasp the tremendous amount of grief the child's parents must have felt as they put his little shoes away, but those words, and that marker, have stayed with me all my life.

After our visit to the graveyard, we continued to walk up Peale Road. Funny thing about Peale Road, it was a road divided between the haves, the have-nots, and the never-going to-have people who lived down in the Park.

We lived on the have-not end, but after you passed the church and walked about a half-mile up the road towards the Bennett Place, you came upon the "haves" which belonged to the Carson family. The Carsons were the richest family on Peale Road. The family prospered during Durham's tobacco boom, and they subsequently bought up almost all of the property leading down to the Bennett Place, which was now a historical site.

Situated on ample acreage, the centerpiece of the property was a magnificent old Victorian house belonging to Bessie Mae's father's parents, Mrs. Anna Louise Carson and her husband, Thomas, a gentleman farmer in the truest sense of the word.

On the left side of the property lived Mrs. Carson's widowed sister, Alma, and on the right lived Bessie Mae's family.

I had only been inside the house a few times, but saw more than enough to know that the Carson family lived a lifestyle far removed from my own. While at the time I did not know the origins of their household furnishings, I had enough sense to know they were of great value and that I better keep my hands to myself.

Years later when I learned about the finer things in life, I discovered that the house was filled with period antiques, and that the tables were draped in Damask linen tablecloths. Spode china and Waterford crystal sparkled in the china closet, and sterling silver flatware was kept tarnish-free in silver cloth storage rolls. Everything in the house was kept in pristine condition by housekeepers and maids.

While we were sitting down to Granny's one-course beanie-weenie casserole, in the Carson household, a three-course dinner was being prepared by the family cook.

As was our tradition to gather our family around the kitchen table for supper every night, the Carsons also gathered their family, meaning everyone living on the property, for a formal dinner in the grand dining room in the home of Bessie Mae's grandparents.

Bessie Mae and her three brothers ate at the "children's table" in the side parlor that mirrored the big dining room on the other side of the hall. Their dinner was served at 6:00 PM every evening while the adults enjoyed their cocktail hour.

Like clockwork, at 7:00 PM, Mrs. Carson rang a silver bell that signaled to the kitchen staff that dinner was to commence. The children were shuffled out of their dining room, while the adults were escorted into theirs.

It all seemed a bit more refined than Granny standing on the back porch calling us in for supper, or else!

Annie Lizbeth and I could barely recall a directive from Granny that did not end in her two favorite words: "or else!" We never figured out what the "or else" meant, but knew Granny well enough to know we didn't want to find out!

Bessie Mae's house was the last house on the property, and totally fenced in, since several hundred feet away was a set of railroad tracks not far from the Bennett Place itself.

We were strictly forbidden to go anywhere near the railroad tracks. Granny said if we ever crossed over them, we would be eaten by a bear that lived at the Bennett Place. I guess Granny thought the fear of being eaten by a bear would be incentive enough to keep us away from those backwoods railroad tracks, whose only signal of an approaching train was an air horn blast.

Our granddaddy had been killed when he fell off a train at the age of thirty. Some folks said he was drunk when he fell, and others say he lost his footing while jumping rail cars. However he met his untimely demise, I guess Granny did not want her grandchildren to experience a similar fate. The thought of that bear devouring us was deterrent enough to keep Annie Lizbeth and me far removed from the railroad tracks and the mysteries that lay beyond it at the Bennett Place.

That Saturday morning as we made our way up Peale Road, we found Bessie Mae picking yellow buttercups that had sprouted up in her grandmother's front yard. She stopped briefly and greeted us warmly. Bessie Mae was a lovely girl, a year older than us, but very easygoing and undemanding when it came to choosing games, or on whose side she would play. Since Annie Lizbeth had a tendency to be bossy, they paired together like bread and butter.

"Why are you picking buttercups?" I inquired.

"I'm picking them for my grandmother's tea party this afternoon," replied Bessie Mae. "Lida didn't have time to do it, so she sent me out here to pick as many as I could so she could put them in vases and scatter them around the living room. I do so like buttercups, don't you Mattie Rose? They are such a cheerful flower."

"Well, I prefer lilacs, especially the light purple ones," I replied. "Granny says you always bring lilacs to new mothers because they are a symbol of new love," I continued, doing my best to impress Bessie Mae with my knowledge of flowers.

"Well, I like roses, especially pink ones," chimed in Annie Lizbeth. "They smell so good and they are soooo romantic," she giggled.

After we'd all cast our votes for our favorite flower, Annie Lizbeth and I helped Bessie Mae pick the remaining buttercups she needed for her grandmother's tea party and waited on the back steps while she took them into the house.

While waiting for Bessie Mae to come back outside, Annie Lizbeth and I decided to amuse ourselves by playing a game of JUMP. The purpose of the game is to throw marbles at one another's feet to see if you can dodge them without getting hit. The first one hit while jumping loses.

Annie Lizbeth was never without a handful of marbles, and had stuffed some in the pocket of her pedal pushers earlier that morning.

We were forbidden to play JUMP because Annie Lizbeth once hit Cookie Ketchum on the ankle with one of the marbles, causing her to have a major meltdown. She went home crying, hopping on one foot, which prompted her mama Holly to call Granny, which prompted Granny to tell Daddy, which prompted a living room lecture from him, which resulted in us being grounded for the weekend.

All of a sudden we saw Granny's car in Bessie Mae's driveway. I looked at Annie Lizbeth and said, "Quick, hide the marbles before Granny sees them," as I stood frozen in fear of being caught in the forbidden act again. The gardener hadn't cut the grass in a couple of weeks due to rain, so we threw the marbles on the ground, where they lay scattered in the overgrown grass.

"Look who I have here," Granny announced as she began walking in our direction with Cookie Ketchum, whose lopsided pigtails bounced up and down to the rhythm of her stride.

"What in the world is she wearing?" asked Annie Lizbeth.

Eight-year-old Cookie was dressed in a sleeveless, slightly faded, orange cotton jumper that was at least a size too small. The hem of her jumper brushed the tops of her skinny, knock-kneed little legs. She wore a green scarf around her neck, and to complete her outfit she wore nubby, cotton, yellow-striped socks pulled halfway up her calves with a pair of black, scuffed-up Mary Janes on her feet.

"Cookie wants to help you prepare for Bessie Mae's tea party. It's almost 11:00 AM, so I'm surprised to see you girls out here in the yard. Have you already finished all the preparations?" she asked.

Surprised by Granny's remarks about a tea party, Bessie Mae looked at me and whispered, "What tea party?" It suddenly occurred to me that we had gotten so caught up in the merriment of the morning that Annie Lizbeth and I failed to mention the tea party to Bessie Mae.

"*T-h-e o-n-e y-o-u a-r-e h-a-v-i-n-g a-t n-o-o-n!*" I quickly mumbled through pursed lips, my eyes pleading with Bessie Mae not to tell Granny otherwise.

Bessie Mae's eyes narrowed as she glared at me and whispered, "Well, thanks for telling me!" before saying politely, "Why yes, Mrs. Childers, everything has been done. We were just out here picking buttercups, but how nice of you to ask."

Granny had Cookie by the hand, but Cookie broke free and came running over to where we were standing in the yard. In her zeal to reach us, her shoe slipped on one of the marbles we had thrown on the ground, and she fell down. Cookie was a bit startled at first, and patted the grass around her to see what caused her fall. Her hand landed on something small, hard, round, and smooth, and she knew in an instant it was a marble.

Granny anxiously called out, "Cookie, are you okay?" Cookie knew that Annie Lizbeth and I had previously been grounded on her account for playing Jump, and she was smart enough to know that if Granny found out, we would be hauled home and she would miss out on the tea party.

"Yes, Mrs. Childers, I'm fine," Cookie replied. "I think I slipped on some wet grass, but I ain't hurt or nothing." She got up off the grass and looked for grass stains on her orange jumper.

"All right then, girls. You enjoy your tea party, and remember, Annie Lizbeth and Mattie Rose, I want you home by three o'clock, and make sure you bring Cookie with you. Okay?"

"Okay, Granny," I replied. I breathed a huge sigh of relief as I watched her get in the car, back out of the driveway, and putter on back home.

"Whew, that was a close one, wasn't it!" I said to Bessie Mae and Annie Lizbeth, as Cookie looked on confused.

"Sure was," replied Bessie Mae. "If you girls are going to lie to your granny, the least you can do is let me in on the lie before you tell it! I told you Grandmother is having a tea party, but I never said I was having one, too! What would possess you to make up such a story?"

"Bessie Mae, we were just trying to get out of Saturday chores, so we told Granny we were coming up here to help you prepare a tea party for all your friends," I replied.

I was suddenly aware of Cookie's presence, and I was annoyed that she had conned Granny into bringing her up to Bessie Mae's to intrude on our fun.

"And by the way, Cookie Ketchum, how did you talk my granny into bringing you up here?"

"Well, she told me you and Annie Lizbeth were going to help Bessie Mae with her tea party, and I wanted to help," Cookie replied.

"Well, there's not going to be a tea party today," I said. "It got cancelled. And, if you are so intent on having a tea party, why don't you go back home and throw one for your dolls! We didn't ask you to come up here in the first place!"

Cookie was crushed. Tears welled up in her big brown eyes and began streaming down her face. Sobbing between gulps of air, she whimpered, "Mattie Rose Radley, I didn't want to have a tea party with my dolls, I wanted to have a tea party with you, Annie Lizbeth, and Bessie Mae. Your granny brought me up here because I am not supposed to walk up here alone, but since you don't want me, I'm going to walk home by myself anyway. And if that bear from the Bennett Place eats me, it will be your fault!" She turned on her heels, pigtails bobbing up and down, one bright yellow-striped sock up and the other bunched around her ankle, as she started marching down Bessie Mae's driveway towards Peale Road.

Cookie Ketchum was the only child of her twenty-eight-year-old single mother, Holly Ketchum. She was an eight-year-old ragamuffin—a tag-along, our constant shadow, always popping up out of nowhere, sneaking along behind us, and then acting as if it was just coincidental that she found us, regardless of what we were doing.

Holly and Cookie lived in a rented, four-room cottage that bordered on the have-not/never-going-to-have side of Peale Road near The Park. Holly was a cotton mill worker who worked the day shift.

But Holly, always in need of extra spending money for one of her Saturday nights on the town, would put in as much overtime as she could, which meant that Cookie was a latchkey kid who had to fend for herself. Now, our daddy worked overtime as well at the cigarette factory, but there was one big difference between Daddy working overtime and Holly working overtime. We had Granny. Cookie only had Cookie.

I learned firsthand how neglected Cookie really was when I stopped off at her house one afternoon before going home, and she invited me to come inside. She told me she was getting ready to make a snack, and begged me to join her. I figured we were going to have milk and cookies, like we did at our house after school.

Holly was a ghost mother, nowhere to be seen, but that was not unusual.

We were not allowed to turn on the stove without Granny's strict supervision, so I sat in awe that afternoon as Cookie donned an apron three sizes too big for her, knotted it around her waist like a professional chef, and went straight to the refrigerator where she retrieved two eggs and two slices of bread.

"I call these my 'holey eggs,'" she declared as she set about the task of making our snack.

She pulled a well-worn, small wooden stool over to the kitchen counter, which she stood on. She carefully laid out the two slices of bread on the counter as she took a glass out of the dish rack and pressed a hole out of the middle of each slice of bread. She then pushed the little stool over to the stove, stood on it, where a well-seasoned, cast-iron skillet sat on a back burner.

Cookie turned on the stove, put the skillet on one of the front burners, poured in some bacon drippings Holly kept on the back of the stove, and waited for it to get hot before placing the two pieces of bread with the holes in the middle in the skillet. She let them fry in the hot grease for a minute or two before she cracked an egg in each of the holes. She stood on the little stool patiently waiting for the eggs to cook, telling me all about her day, as if this was what all eight-year-old children do when they're hungry for a snack. She took a spatula, and like a line order cook, flipped the toast over and cooked the other side.

When our snack was ready, Cookie turned off the stove, got a hot pad, and pushed the hot skillet over to one of the cool back burners. She then took the spatula and carefully lifted each piece of toast out of the skillet and onto a plate, each egg with their fried yellow yolks facing upwards. As she handed my plate to me she asked, "Do you want ketchup with yours?"

"No thanks," I replied.

"That's good, 'cause I don't think we have any anyway," Cookie replied.

"But we do have salt and pepper. Want some? I like lots of salt and pepper," she said as she sprinkled the black and white seasoning generously across the surface of her egg before eagerly tearing away the crispy brown edges of the toast to dip into the liquid yellow yolk.

Even at ten years of age, I could see that what Cookie craved most had nothing to do with food. Her real hunger came from inside. She was starved for love and companionship.

I was suddenly whipped backed into reality when Annie Lizbeth looked at me and said, "Mattie Rose, if Granny hears we let Cookie walk home by herself, we are going to be in deep trouble. You have really hurt her feelings, and I don't think you would like it if someone talked to you that way," she said, obviously sympathetic to Cookie's cause.

"It's fine with me if she stays," said Bessie Mae. "Besides, I don't think Cookie should be walking down that road by herself," she concluded. "Mattie Rose, go after her and tell her we all want her to stay. We'll think of something fun to do together, I promise."

Consumed by guilt for the second time that day, I ran after Cookie Ketchum as fast as I could until I caught up with her at the end of Bessie Mae's driveway. She had stopped crying, but her eyes were red and swollen. Her spine, stiffened by pride, walked with the dogged determination of someone who had no intention of staying where she was not wanted, but her eyes were filled with the pain of a wounded spirit.

"Cookie, stop, please stop," I begged. "We want you to stay and play with us. We didn't tell Granny the truth about the tea party. The tea party is for Bessie Mae's grandmother, not for Bessie Mae herself. We told Granny that just to find a reason to get out of doing a bunch of Saturday chores. Please don't leave, Cookie, please. I'm sorry I said all those hateful things to you. I didn't mean them, honest I didn't."

Cookie turned around and just glared at me. "I thought you were my friend, Mattie Rose. All I wanted to do was have someone to play with today. You have lots of friends, and you always have Annie Lizbeth, but I don't have anyone. I just want you to like me and be my friend," she sobbed, as once again her eyes misted and her chin quivered. "Is that too much to ask?"

I walked over to her and put my arm around her shoulder, turned her back in the direction of Annie Lizbeth and Bessie Mae and said gently, "No Cookie, that's not too much to ask."

With the tea party fiasco now out in the open, Bessie Mae, Annie Lizbeth, Cookie, and I set about to decide how to spend the rest of the afternoon together. Bessie Mae said she had to be at her grandmother's by 3:30 PM to attend the tea party, which was fine because we had to be back home by 3:00 to go to Cottingham's with Granny.

Bessie Mae's grandpa, Thomas Carson, owned acres and acres of rich and fertile land on Peale Road with plenty of green pastures for us to roam and explore. He had a goldfish pond he kept fully stocked, along with a hay barn that was located a hundred yards behind the main house that he used to store grain and hay to feed the horses and other farm animals.

We started out playing tag in the meadow, but after a while, we grew tired of it. We then went over to the goldfish pond and watched the fish swim around before we abandoned our shoes and socks and dipped our feet into the cool, clear water. Cookie laughed out loud each time some of the fish swam under her feet and tickled them. Long gone were the tears of hurt and rejection, replaced now by the delicious feeling of belonging.

After playing in the fish pond for a while, we decided to go play in the hay barn. Daddy and Granny forbade us to go into the hay barn without Mr. Carson, fearing that we might accidentally get smothered in the grain silo or crushed by the bales of hay that were stacked as high as the barn itself.

Undaunted, we went in anyway where we engaged in friendly hay fights, tossing mounds of straw into one another's hair, rolling around in it, each of us ingesting the dusty residue until our mouths were so dry we felt as if we had swallowed dust balls.

As we were leaving the hay barn, Cookie asked Bessie Mae for something to drink. She said her throat was so dry she did not have enough spit to swallow. We could all feel the dust balls in the base of our throats, and our growing thirst was becoming intense. Thomas Carson kept water tanks in the hay barn for his animals, and had told us on more than one occasion that those tanks were for animals, not people, so we knew better than to drink from them.

We asked Bessie Mae for some water, but she said she had seen Lida, her grandmother's starchy, old black housekeeper on her hands and knees earlier that morning washing the black and white tile kitchen floor in preparation for the Mrs. Carson's afternoon tea party.

Bessie Mae feared if Lida heard her inside running water, or saw so much as a telltale piece of straw or a footmark on her freshly-washed floors, there would be trouble plenty, so that ruled out going inside for water. Besides, Lida did not allow anyone in the Carson's home without Mrs. Carson's express permission, particularly neighborhood children. If she caught you in Mrs. Carson's house, she would chase after you and swat you with her broom.

Lida was a force to be reckoned with. Standing barely five feet tall, she weighed ninety pounds soaking wet. Lida had not a tooth in her mouth. With no teeth, her ebony face had collapsed around her lips, leaving in its wake little more than a puckered opening for the mean utterances she made at any unwelcome children that appeared at the door looking for Bessie Mae.

No one knew how old Lida was, but Annie Lizbeth once counted the circles around Lida's neck and said that in tree years she had to be at least 104 years old. She ruled the Carson house like a master sergeant, carrying her broom like a rifle slung over her shoulder. Every kid on Peale Road knew that Lida's broom would "sweep to kill," and you did not want to be in her line of sight if you did something to set her off.

The inside of our mouths felt like dry, wadded-up pieces of cotton from all the straw dust we had inhaled.

"Look, Bessie Mae," I said impatiently. "All we want is a glass of water. It's hot, and we walked all the way up here to play with you today. Now we have to walk home, and we are dying of thirst. If Cookie goes to our house crying and begging for water, Granny is going to want to know why. If she finds out we've been in that hay barn, we're going to get it, so can you please just sneak inside and get us some water?"

Bessie Mae suddenly remembered that Lida had made two pitchers of homemade lemonade earlier that morning and stashed them in the refrigerator. They were to be served, along with tea, as the afternoon beverage to the ladies attending her grandmother's tea party later that day.

Bessie Mae said that if Lida heard her in the kitchen running water, and caught her, she would surely get broomed.

They say necessity is the mother of invention, and so we devised a plan to quench our thirst. I told Bessie Mae if she was real quiet, she could probably sneak one pitcher of lemonade out of the refrigerator without anyone knowing it. Later, before her grandmother's tea party, all Bessie Mae would have to do was top off the pitcher with water, put it back in the fridge, and no one would be the wiser. The fantasy of that tart, ice-cold liquid cascading like a waterfall down our dusty and parched throats had overtaken all reasonable thought.

Armed with a newfound confidence that only friends like Annie Lizbeth and I could inspire in a person like Bessie Mae, she decided to sneak into the house and execute our plan. Her fear of being caught evaporated as Annie Lizbeth and I reassured her that we had carefully dusted and picked off the last bits of remaining straw from her clothes. As she turned around for final inspection, we were satisfied that we had removed all evidence that could link us to the hay barn and the missing lemonade.

Bessie Mae cautiously opened the squeaky back screen door just enough to allow her to slip inside the house. She prayed that Lida would be engaged in some activity in another part of the house, and was relieved to hear her humming church hymns upstairs. She tiptoed across the freshly-swept and hand-washed floor, and made her way to the refrigerator, where our liquid, lifesaving lemonade resided. Her heart was pounding so hard she had to stop every few steps to catch her breath. When she opened the refrigerator, there on the top shelf, sitting side by side, were two cranberry-red, Victorian glass pitchers, filled to the brim with homemade lemonade.

She grabbed one of the pitchers of lemonade off the shelf and closed the refrigerator door as quietly as she could. She could still hear Lida upstairs, but in her haste to exit the kitchen, and without knowing, she accidentally splashed some of the sticky sweet beverage out of the pitcher and onto the floor. With each advancing step Bessie Mae took towards the back door, she left behind a trail of evidence that would soon betray her. Before sending Bessie Mae into the house to sneak out the lemonade, Annie Lizbeth and I had failed to inspect what turned out to be the most incriminating piece of evidence: the bottoms of her tennis shoes.

We let Cookie take the first swill of lemonade just to hush her up. Bessie

Mae, Annie Lizbeth, and I were each taking turns, hungrily swilling long gulps of the refreshing cold liquid directly from the cranberry-red, Victorian glass pitcher, when Lida made her way back down from the upstairs and into the kitchen. When she bent down to open the lower kitchen cabinet that contained the Butcher's Boston Paste Wax she needed to polish the living room furniture, she saw a wet trail on her freshly-swept, hand-washed kitchen floor. Lida was livid.

Upon further investigation, she saw bits of lemon pulp in the sticky liquid mess, and a trail of yellow straw leading to the back screen door. She marched over the refrigerator and opened it. There sat only one of the cranberry-red, Victorian glass pitchers she had filled with homemade lemonade earlier in the day.

Following Bessie Mae's sticky little trail of yellow pulp and yellow straw, she tiptoed her way to the back screen door where she saw us sitting at the bottom of the steps, our backs turned to her, passing the pitcher around, giggling as we took turns drinking the lemonade. In our greediness, we failed to calculate how much we had consumed before it was too late. We had emptied the pitcher, and no amount of water would cover up our gluttony. I had fallen into temptation again, first the deviled eggs, then the lie to get out of Saturday morning chores, and now the lemonade.

SLAM went the back screen door! Startled by the noise we all turned around and there on the porch, broom-in-hand, stood Lida. The color drained from Bessie Mae's face as Lida descended the steps, swinging her broom in every direction. I snatched the empty, cranberry-red, Victorian glass pitcher from Cookie Ketchum's greedy little mouth and handed it back as quickly as I could to a helpless Bessie Mae.

Cookie took off running the minute she saw Lida. I grabbed Annie Lizbeth's arm and yelled, "Lida's got the broom. Run!" Lida ran after us, swinging her broom, hollering words we had never heard, but she stopped when our feet hit the pavement on Peale Road running towards home, and turned her attention back to Bessie Mae, who stood frozen in the driveway, clutching the empty cranberry-red, Victorian glass pitcher to her chest. Her accomplices had vacated the crime scene, leaving Bessie Mae to face Lida's broom and her grandmother alone.

I don't think I have ever seen a more forlorn face than that of Bessie Mae Carson's as Annie Lizbeth, Cookie Ketchum, and I took off running down that driveway, Lida and her broom in hot pursuit of the lemonade thieves.

We ran the entire distance home, only to find Granny standing on the front porch waiting for us. I felt as if the air in my lungs had been squeezed out of them as my heart pounded and I gasped for breath. My calf muscles were screaming in pain from the adrenaline that rushed into them when I took off running after seeing Lida coming after us with her broom!

"My, you girls are awfully out of breath," Granny said. "You must have been running, but why?"

"We were running from the bear," Cookie blurted out. By now, both of her socks were bunched around her ankles and her pigtails had come undone, her dark brown hair matted with sweat. I could not believe Cookie would say something so dumb to Granny, but she did, and in doing so, set the stage for one of Granny's famous inquisitions.

"A bear you say? You girls weren't up by the railroad tracks by any chance were you?" Granny asked in her warning voice.

"Oh no, Granny," I replied in earnest, shaking my head back and forth, still heaving and gasping for air. "We were just telling Cookie that she should never cross the railroad tracks because of the bear that lives at the Bennett Place. She must have misheard us and thought we said we saw the bear and she took off running. We were only running after her to make sure she got back safe." I fumbled, trying to come up with some excuse to cover Cookie's stupid bear comment.

"Oh," Granny replied. "Well, that would certainly explain why you are all so out of breath. By the way, how was the tea party?" she inquired, her gray green eyes widening as she asked the question. At that moment, I could have sworn Granny had grown a foot taller than when I last saw her.

"It was great, Granny, just great," I stammered. "We had a really fun time with Bessie Mae, didn't we Annie Lizbeth?"

"Oh yes, a really lovely time," winced Annie Lizbeth, who had lost her flip flops while racing down the driveway to escape Lida's broom. Running down the gravel driveway, and the hot black asphalt road back home had left "hot spots" on her toes and heels that were beginning to form blisters.

"What did Bessie Mae serve you girls at the tea party?" Granny continued.

"Lemonade and tea cakes," we all said in unison. "Well, at least Cookie got that much right," I thought to myself.

"Lemonade and tea cakes, you say. I bet that lemonade tasted very refreshing on a hot day like today, didn't it, Cookie?" Granny said.

"Oh yes, Mrs. Childers. It was very tasty," Cookie replied, smiling ear to ear. Maybe Cookie wasn't so dumb after all, I thought to myself.

Granny's inquisition continued. "Let me ask you girls' a question. By chance, was that lemonade in a cranberry-red pitcher?"

Annie Lizbeth looked at me and I looked at Annie Lizbeth, both of us as cranberry-red as the lemonade pitcher from which we drank. Cookie's face seemed frozen in time.

"Well, yes Ma'am, as a matter of fact it was," I answered sheepishly.

"That's what Mrs. Carson said when she called to tell me how you two talked Bessie Mae into stealing lemonade from the refrigerator that Lida hand-squeezed early this morning for her tea party this afternoon," Granny continued.

Turning her attention to Cookie, Granny said, "Cookie, Mrs. Carson told me you were right in the thick of things, and when Lida caught you guzzling lemonade, you took off running, Annie Lizbeth and Mattie Rose right behind you leaving Bessie Mae to take the blame. Do you think that would be an accurate description of what happened at your so called 'tea party' today?" Granny asked sternly.

Cookie started to cry. Annie Lizbeth finally gave in to her aching feet, and collapsed on the ground, exhaustion and pain taking their toll as tears began to roll down her face.

This time I stepped up and said, "Yes, Granny, that's pretty much what happened." The gig was up, and there was no use continuing the charade.

Mrs. Carson was a pitcher short of lemonade, but I was a quart low on character.

All I could hear inside my head was Granny saying, "Tis one thing to be tempted, another thing to fall." Not only had I fallen once that day, but once I fell, I never got up. Instead I pulled Annie Lizbeth and Cookie down with me in the dark hole of deceit.

Granny stood on the porch just looking at the three of us. Suddenly she said, "Okay everyone, let's get in the car, we are going to Cottingham's."

Granny looked at Cookie and said, "You may as well stop crying because there's no use crying over spilt lemonade, but you can right a wrong. Do you have any pennies saved?

"Yes, Ma'am," Cookie answered between sobs, her head looking down at the ground. "I have five."

"Very well then. I always tell Annie Lizbeth and Mattie Rose that it is good to save for a rainy day, and girls, this is your rainy day. Cookie, I am going to take you home on the way to Cottingham's, and I want you to go inside and get two pennies. If your mama is home, just tell her you are going on an errand with us, I'm sure she won't mind!" Granny's sarcastic tone went right over Cookie's head.

"Annie Lizbeth and Mattie Rose, go inside right now and empty your piggy banks. If there's any money left over after we buy the lemons to replace Mrs. Carson's lemonade, you can split it in half and put it back in your banks."

"But Granny, we were saving our money to go to the movie next Saturday," we protested.

"You should have thought about that before you took something that did not belong to you. Now, go empty your piggy banks."

Granny was steaming mad, so without additional protest, we went inside and emptied our piggy banks.

We made the short trip to Cottingham's where Granny haggled with Artis the butcher over which chicken was the plumpest. Granny got her chicken for Sunday dinner, and we bought two dozen lemons. Cookie chipped in her two pennies, and we chipped in the rest. Our contribution cost us each a ticket to next Saturday's movie.

When we got back home, Granny put away her chicken and sliced a dozen lemons in half, handing each of us eight halves to squeeze into one of her glass, quart-sized Mason canning jars. By the time we were finished squeezing the lemons, the acidity of the juice had turned our fingers into wrinkled prunes.

She then drove us back up to Mrs. Carson's house, where Cookie, Annie Lizbeth, and I delivered the tart and tangy liquid to Mrs. Carson herself, who promptly handed it to Lida, whose puckered mouth looked like she had sucked on a few hundred lemons already as she muttered hateful things under her breath in our direction.

We then had to apologize to Bessie Mae for talking her into stealing the lemonade in the first place, and begged Mrs. Carson not to punish Bessie Mae for our wrongdoings. Bessie Mae accepted our apology, but Mrs. Carson said we would not be allowed back up there until we learned to respect other people's property.

We then got back in the car, and Granny drove Cookie the short distance down the road to her house. When Cookie got out of the car, she looked at Granny and started to cry again. "I'm sorry, Mrs. Childers," she whimpered. "Please don't be mad at me, and please let me come back to your house so I can play with Mattie Rose and Annie Lizbeth. They are the only friends I have, besides you."

Granny got out of the car and Cookie ran straight into her outstretched arms, burying her tear-stained face in Granny's dress. "Cookie, sweetheart," Granny said as she stroked her matted hair, "I was never mad at you; but I was disappointed that you, Annie Lizbeth, and Mattie Rose did the wrong thing. You would not like it if I took something of yours that did not belong to me, and that's what you girls did when you took Mrs. Carson's lemonade. There are consequences for the things we do, and I hope you've learned a lesson today."

"Yes, Ma'am," Cookie said, her head still buried in Granny's dress.

"Well then," Granny said as she lifted up Cookie's face and looked in her eyes, "Dry your tears before your mama wants to know why you've been crying. And tell her you're going to Sunday School with Annie Lizbeth and Mattie Rose tomorrow morning and back home with us for Sunday dinner. I'm making fried chicken, mashed potatoes, gravy and biscuits, and strawberry shortcake for dessert!"

"Oh boy," Cookie exclaimed, as she ran towards the back door of her house. "I'm going to go pick out my clothes for church right now!"

"That's what I was afraid of," Granny chuckled under her breath.

When we arrived back home, Daddy was already there, grinning from ear to ear, and eager to tell us all about his day of fishing.

"Hey, Girls!" Daddy hollered over at us as he was washing the smell of fish off his hands in a wash basin Granny had set up for him on the back porch. "Do you know why it's so easy to weigh fish?"

"Oh no," I thought. The last thing I wanted to hear was one of Daddy's corny fish jokes. Annie Lizbeth looked at me with dread in her eyes, as I looked at her with dread in mine, as we said in unison, "No, Daddy, why is it so easy to weigh fish?"

"Because they have scales!" as he burst out laughing. "Pete Sims told me that one today, and I couldn't wait to get back home and tell you girls," he chuckled.

"By the way Ruby Mae, I caught a mess of catfish today. Do you want me to fry some up for supper tonight? I know you don't like the smell of fish in the house, but I can set up the electric fryer out here if you're in the mood for some."

"That sounds good to me, James. Do you mind frying some hushpuppies too? I'll make some coleslaw, and slice some of those ripe tomatoes I picked from the garden today." Granny replied.

"And Ruby," Daddy asked, "if you don't mind, could we have some lemonade? It was awful hot out there fishing, and I think some lemonade would really hit the spot!"

"Sure thing, James," Granny replied. "I'll get Annie Lizbeth and Mattie Rose to do it. Those girls are mighty good at squeezing lemons, and we bought a couple of dozen when we went to Cottingham's this afternoon."

As we set about getting supper together, Daddy outside frying fish and hushpuppies, Granny inside making coleslaw and slicing fresh tomatoes, she handed Annie Lizbeth and me the bowl of leftover lemons.

"I'll slice them in half for you, but you girls can do the rest."

"But, Granny," I whined, "My fingers are still wrinkled up from the last batch."

"Mattie Rose," Granny said, "I don't want to hear another word about this from you. I think your time would best be spent remembering: 'Oh, the lemons I must squeeze when first I practice to deceive.'"

When we picked up Cookie Ketchum for church the next morning, she came bounding out of the house in her "Sunday best." She wore a wrinkled purple flowered blouse underneath a black plaid jumper, both of which looked as thought they had been at the bottom of a clothes basket for quite some time. She had on pink socks, and her well-worn, black Mary Janes. She had a straw bonnet on her head with a pink ribbon tied in the back. Annie Lizbeth and I giggled briefly before both Daddy and Granny turned around in the front seat and gave us a stern look.

Granny said, "Cookie adores the two of you, and the fact that her mama could care less how that child looks is not her fault. Now, we're all going to church to hear Pastor Lewis's sermon, and then we're going home for Sunday dinner. Today, Cookie is as much a part of our family as you. Do I make myself clear?"

"Yes, Ma'am," we replied.

Holly was at the front door, still in her robe, her eyes squinting against the glaring light of the morning sun. "Just send her home when you're tired of her. I told her to pack some play clothes for later. Cookie Clarice Ketchum, did you pack some play clothes for later?" Holly hollered.

"Yes, Mama, I sure did. They're right here in this paper bag," Cookie declared as she held up a grocery bag for her mama to see.

"Well, don't get your good stuff dirty, 'cause I ain't washing until the end of the week," Holly shouted in Cookie's direction before she shut the front door. The Ghost Mother had disappeared just as quickly as she had appeared.

We went to church, where Cookie, still as a mouse, sat beside Granny as she listened intently to Pastor Lewis's sermon. When church services were over, we all piled in the car and headed back home to prepare Sunday lunch.

Granny told us to change into our play clothes and meet her back in the kitchen. "I'm going to need helpers to get Sunday lunch on the table," she said, chuckling.

We changed into our play clothes and went back into the kitchen where we each donned one of Granny's aprons.

She had washed and cut up her chicken the night before and left it sitting in the refrigerator in a bowl of buttermilk. Granny said the best fried chicken was always soaked in buttermilk the night before you intended to fry it, because it tenderized and moistened the chicken, making for the best fried chicken you ever ate!

After we all washed our hands, she sat us at the table. In front of Cookie was a big bowl of flour, in front of me was the bowl of chicken in buttermilk, and in front of Annie Lizbeth was a big bowl of cornmeal, seasoned generously with salt and pepper.

"Okay, girls. This is how you prepare your chicken," Granny said.

"Mattie Rose, you take a piece of chicken and drain off as much buttermilk as you can before you pass it over to Cookie. Cookie, you are to dip the chicken in the flour and shake off any excess before you hand it back to Mattie Rose. Mattie Rose, you are to dip the floured chicken back into the buttermilk before you hand it to Annie Lizbeth to coat in the cornmeal. Annie Lizbeth, I want you to coat that chicken real good in the cornmeal. Does everyone have their marching orders?" Granny laughed as she set about peeling potatoes.

We all worked together preparing Sunday lunch that day, and though we always helped Granny prepare Sunday lunch, this Sunday was different, and the difference was Cookie.

What Annie Lizbeth and I saw as chores, Cookie saw as an opportunity to be a part of something we took for granted: a family.

When the last of the cornmeal-crusted, buttermilk chicken was fried, the potatoes mashed into velvety smoothness, the pan gravy glistening in its gravy boat, the pungent stewed collards steaming in their serving bowl and Granny's golden brown, flaky biscuits were on the table, it was time to give thanks.

As we all bowed our heads, Cookie suddenly looked up and to everyone's surprise said, "Can I say grace? Mama never does it, but I think I know how."

Daddy winked at Granny, and she looked at Cookie and said, "Well, of course you can say grace, Cookie. You're our guest, and we'd be honored."

We all bowed our heads, and this little snip of a girl began to say:

"God is great, God is good,
And I thank him for our food,
Thank you God for friends like these,
Keep them safe, I ask you please.
Amen."

Granny quickly dabbed a tear away from her eye and announced that it was time to eat! That Sunday at our kitchen table, Cookie received more than nourishment for her body, she received nourishment for her soul. Cookie became part of our family, and we all took her under our wing, especially Granny.

By the time Granny passed away many years later, Cookie was a grown woman living in Charlotte. Every year on the anniversary of Granny's passing, a basket of lemons with two pennies glued to an elaborate yellow bow were placed at her headstone with a card that read, "A good friend is like a four-leaf clover—hard to find and lucky to have."

CHICKEN-FRIED STEAK

People often assume that all twins, even fraternal, are reflections of one another. Such was not the case with Annie Lizbeth and me.

We both had dark brown hair, but mine was thick and wavy like Daddy's. During times of high humidity, my hair would swell like a tsunami, wave after wave crashing around my heart-shaped face, while Annie Lizbeth's fine, straight hair lay flat against the cheekbones of her oval-shaped face.

We both had brown eyes, but I likened Annie Lizbeth's to chocolate tootsie pops: hard on the outside, but tender inside. I had a small upturned nose, which put me in the category of being "cute." Annie Lizbeth's nose was straight and a bit more elongated than mine, giving her a stately appearance despite the smattering of freckles across it. We both had lush, full lips like Daddy's, mine masking the same slight overbite as his.

Our complexions were smooth and milky white with a natural flush of color extending across our cheekbones. Granny said the secret to a fair complexion was lots of milk, fresh air, and sunshine. If there was one thing we got lots of it was milk, fresh air, and sunshine!

And while Annie Lizbeth and I bore a striking resemblance to one another, our personalities bore no resemblance at all. Annie Lizbeth was a wiry little girl who possessed a warrior's spirit. She was a natural-born detective, more serious and contemplative in nature, always looking for clues to put together the pieces of life's puzzle. I, too, was a wispy girl, but

I possessed an impish quality that was combined with contagious energy. I was a ten-year-old whirling dervish, spinning full speed ahead, dodging torpedoes as I went along.

Granny reinforced the notion of our individuality by reminding us that just because we arrived in the same car didn't mean we would eventually go on the same trip. Each of us needed to carry our own luggage, just in case one went one way and one the other.

The first of our separate "trips" began with our taste buds.

I was an enthusiastic member of the Weekly Reader's Food Explorer Club, and the Club's team leader for any fifth-grade student who wanted to participate. Patti Summerhill was my co-team leader. The goal of the club was to encourage students to become Food Explorers by looking at, touching, smelling, and tasting new foods.

Our Food Explorer group consisted of six people; five girls and one boy:

- *Mattie Rose Radley*: Team Leader
- *Patti Summerhill*: Co-Team Leader, and best friend of the Team Leader
- *Miranda Stone*: Miss wanna-be-in-charge of everything, everything that is, except the Food Explorer's Club. Patti and I were in charge of that!
- *Penny Sue Anders*: She lived in the Park, but we figured she was trying to better herself and expand her horizons beyond beans, greens, and crackling cornbread.
- *Bessie Mae Carson*: Though she was technically in sixth grade, she was allowed in the Club because we convinced Miss McGee she was extremely knowledgeable about table manners, three-course meals, and the habits of sophisticated diners.
- *Tommy Jones*: Because his Mother wanted him to be part of a group, any group, just so she could tell the church ladies he was in one.

My job as team leader was to lead discussions on individual members' new food experiences at our monthly meeting, which was held in the school cafeteria on our lunch break. We could not meet before or after school because we all rode the bus, and there was no way Miss McGee was going to give up her valuable classroom time to a special interest group such as ours.

So, once a month, The Food Explorer's Club was relegated to the back of Carver Elementary's cafeteria, a vast open space filled with endless rows of long, gray, Formica-topped tables, and dozens of metal chairs that scraped across concrete floors like fingernails on a blackboard as kids dragged them from table to table.

We were assigned to a table in the back of the room, as far away from the deafening din of noisy students that filled the room as possible. Once the meeting got started, and we became absorbed in our food topic of the month, the din in the cavernous room evolved into a harmonious hum to which we were oblivious.

This month's topic focused on respecting other people's tastes and food preferences. Miss McGee instructed us to write a one-page report citing a personal example for discussion at our next meeting.

As the meeting concluded, I asked anyone if they had a questions regarding next month's assignment. The first question came from, who else? Tommy Jones.

"I don't know why we have to write a one-page report," Tommy whined. "I already know my father hates Brussels sprouts."

"You have to write a report so Miss McGee can verify our meetings," I replied indignantly.

"What if you don't know nobody with a food preference?" Penny Sue asked looking bewildered.

"First of all, Penny Sue, it's, what if I don't know 'anyone,'" I said self-righteously, displaying my command of the English language. "Your family is the size of a small army; surely you can choose from one of them."

"How can you find someone with a food preference when you all eat the same things?" she further queried, looking more confused than ever.

Patti Summerhill, already exasperated at Penny Sue replied, "Listen, Penny Sue, you either do as we say or you're out of the group. There has to be someone in your family of four boys and two girls that doesn't like something your mama puts on the table! You can't tell me that all of you love those liver pudding sandwiches your mama puts in your lunch bag almost every day!"

A light bulb suddenly went on in Penny Sue's head. "You're right, Patti. Not everyone does like a plain liver pudding sandwich. Daddy likes a big slice of raw onion and lots of mayonnaise on his. Maybe I can write my report on that!"

"Yuck," Patti replied as she rolled her big blue eyes and shook her head from side to side, surrendering to Penny Sue's simple-mindedness.

"I'm going to have my mother type my report for Miss McGee," a snooty Miranda Stone chimed in.

"Well, I'm going to see if my grandmother will loan me a piece of her linen stationery on which to write mine," Bessie Mae countered.

"Well, now that everyone is clear on next month's assignment, I declare this meeting to be over," I stated emphatically.

"And, as co-team leader, I second Mattie's declaration," Pattie announced smugly to remind everyone, especially Miranda Stone, that she was in charge as well.

The lunch bell sounded that signaled we were to return to our classrooms for the rest of the afternoon.

I couldn't wait to get home to start my latest Food Explorer's assignment. Little did I know it would not take long before the assignment would come to me.

Annie Lizbeth was a very finicky eater. I think she could have lived her entire childhood on butter and sugar sandwiches had Granny allowed her to do so. She had an obsession about one food touching another; her theory being that anything touching something else contaminated it, therefore creating a rich and fertile environment for cooties to grow.

Where Annie Lizbeth developed her "cootie phobia" I do not know. Perhaps she never got over being fed baby food out of separate jars, but for whatever reason, as passionate as I was about seeing, touching, smelling, and tasting new foods, Annie Lizbeth remained equally as passionate about seeking out, identifying, and eliminating cooties from everything she put in her mouth.

Granny, having lived through The Great Depression, had a waste not-want not mentality, and so, every Friday night you could count on seeing Granny's 13" x 9" glass Pyrex dish sitting on top of the stove, shrouded in shiny, silver aluminum foil, its mysterious contents hidden from the world until she unveiled it, like an original work of art. She called it her "Poor Man's Casserole" because every unfortunate leftover that got relegated to "refrigerator row," Monday through Thursday, would eventually be reincarnated into some kind of casserole on Friday night.

I likened those leftovers to the outcast kids at my school, the ones with no athletic ability or social skills, the ones who were never selected to be first for any schoolyard games. Like the leftovers in our refrigerator, they were pushed to the back of the playing field and forgotten, until some teacher, using Granny's, "Poor Man's casserole" method, finally decided she could do something useful with them.

Annie Lizbeth complained that just because Granny lived through The Great Depression didn't mean she had to drag us through one every Friday night.

Granny planned our weekly meals with military precision, knowing that on Friday, any accumulated leftovers would go into her "Poor Man's casserole," leaving her "a clean plate" on which to plan next week's meals.

Every Saturday morning after breakfast, if Daddy had not planned a special outing for us, we would tag along with Granny to the A&P grocery store. Like an Army general who had been given marching orders, Granny would enter the store, where she scoured aisle after aisle of goods holding in her hand a white mailing envelope that was filled with coupons for weekly specials she had neatly clipped from Thursday's newspaper flyer and organized according to dry, canned, or household goods.

As she located the items on her check list, she would remove the designated coupon from the white mailing envelope and slip it in the back zipper pocket of her purse. When it came time to check out and pay for what she had purchased, Granny would unzip the pocket, remove the coupons, and present them to the cashier for credit.

At the end of our shopping excursion, Granny was rewarded with sheet after sheet of S&H Green Stamps which she later meticulously licked and pasted into her S&H booklet until she accumulated enough to redeem them for something she had her eye on in the S&H catalog, or at their redemption center. Granny once saved enough stamps to trade them in for an electric toaster so we could make toast without having to turn on the oven. Annie Lizbeth loved that toaster, because it transformed her butter and sugar sandwiches into warm and toasty delights.

It got to the point where I dreaded supper on Friday night, because inevitably, it would dissolve into the war of the casserole between Annie Lizbeth and Granny.

The tension over Friday's Poor Man's casserole had been building for quite some time, but on this particularly warm, humid, summer evening, things reached their final boiling point. Granny was determined that Annie Lizbeth was going to eat and appreciate the food that was placed in front of her. Annie Lizbeth was equally determined that she would never eat anything that touched something else for fear of a widespread cootie epidemic.

Tonight's special was what I called The Princess and the Pea Casserole. I called it that because it reminded me of the many layers of mattresses the poor princess had to sleep on to avoid the irritating pea. I wondered how many layers I would have to dig through before I discovered the irritating peas in tonight's casserole.

Green peas from a can were my least favorite vegetable because they were mushy and bland-tasting. As I looked through the glass Pyrex dish sitting on the table, I started counting the mattresses.

The bottom mattress was Monday night's mashed potatoes spread thinly across the bottom of the dish.

Mattress number two was home to the green peas that Granny served on Tuesday, sprinkled like confetti on top of the mashed potatoes.

Mattress number three provided bedding to Wednesday's yellow corn.

Mattress number four held the last remains of Thursday's shaved ham.

The fifth, and top, mattress of this culinary wonder was the last of the shredded yellow cheese sprinkled on top of sliced biscuits, leftover from our morning breakfast.

Tonight the princess need only look under three of the five mattresses to discover her green pea nemesis.

After Daddy said grace, Granny took one of her big wooden spoons and began to dish up the casserole, setting our plates in front of us as she went around table. When Granny asked Annie Lizbeth for her plate, she refused to give it to her. "Annie Lizbeth, what's gotten into you? I want you to give me your plate right now so I serve this casserole while it's hot," Granny demanded.

Again, Annie Lizbeth refused to hand her plate over to Granny, and responded by saying, "If this is a Poor Man's casserole, why not give it to a poor man?"

At first, Granny was taken back by Annie Lizbeth's impertinence. Granny was a no-nonsense kind of person, so after gaining her composure, she looked straight into Annie Lizbeth's big brown tootsie pop eyes, which had visibly hardened, and said, "You know what Miss Annie Lizbeth Radley, you're right. Perhaps we should think of someone who might appreciate tonight's casserole, and guess what Miss Fire and Vinegar, I know just the very people to give it to."

Bewildered by Granny's rapid fire response, Annie Lizbeth looked at her and said defiantly, "I can't think of anyone that would want it?"

"Well, I can," Granny responded. "How about the Brickle family? I'm sure this casserole would be a welcome change from the cans of potted meat sitting on their table every Friday night? And I'm sure the Brickle family would love the chocolate icebox pie I made for dessert tonight, the one with the whipped cream on top."

"No!" Annie Lizbeth hollered, shaking her head violently back and forth, her straight brown hair switching the sides of her face. I never said I wanted to give my dessert away, just this horrid casserole. I hate it when my food touches, and everything in here is touching something else!"

"Annie Lizbeth, just because something is touching doesn't mean you can't eat it." Granny was growing increasingly impatient with Annie Lizbeth's stubbornness. "The whipped cream is touching the pie, and you don't seem to have a problem with that,"

Granny said trying to reason with Annie Lizbeth.

"That's because whipped cream is sweet," Annie Lizbeth huffed. "Cooties don't grow in sugar, only in Poor Man's casseroles," she replied adamantly.

Daddy could see that Annie Lizbeth was visibly upset, and that tonight's casserole was turning into a tug-of-war between Annie Lizbeth and Granny.

Granny looked over at Daddy with an exasperated look on her face. "James, will you please tell Annie Lizbeth to give me her plate? These temper tantrums of hers have got to stop. In all my days, I have never seen such foolishness over one thing touching another!"

Annie Lizbeth was hunkered down, ready for battle, so Daddy decided to referee the situation using a more subtle technique.

"Annie Lizbeth?" he asked. "Have you heard about this new food detective game that all the kids are playing? I heard about it at lunch from one of the fellows at work. He said his kids play it all the time."

"No, I haven't heard about it, Daddy," Annie Lizbeth replied. "How do you play it?"

"Well, in order to play, I'm going to need your plate. Would you mind handing it over to me?"

Annie Lizbeth eyed Daddy suspiciously and, with great trepidation, slowly handed over her plate. Annie Lizbeth's eyes widened, and she had a look of horror on her face when Daddy took her plate and scooped onto it a small dollop of the steaming hot casserole.

"Eewhhhhh, it's touching!" Annie Lizbeth protested, a scowl on her face as Daddy sat the plate with the small scoop of Granny's Poor Man's casserole in front of her.

"Now hold on a second, Annie Lizbeth. We're playing a detective game here, and when you're a detective you cannot get all emotional about things. That's one of the rules, and if you're not willing to follow the rules we'll just have to stop," he said, waiting for Annie Lizbeth to make the next move.

Looking at Daddy and the plate sitting before her, Annie Lizbeth's curiosity got the best of her, so she sucked in her cheeks, gave Daddy her most serious look and said, "Okay, I'll follow the rules. What's next?"

"Well, to begin with, I want you to take a good look at what's on your plate and see if you can figure out the first clue. If you're going to solve a mystery, you have to be able to identify clues," Daddy replied.

"See what clue?" Annie Lizbeth asked as she lowered her head, pressing her face as close to her plate as possible, squinting her eyes tightly to examine its contents. "It would be easier if I had a magnifying glass," she told Daddy when she finally lifted her head, blinking her eyes to refocus her vision.

"Well, since we don't have a magnifying glass, I'll give you the first clue, but after that I want you to solve the rest of this mystery on your own so I can tell the fellows at work what a good detective you are!"

And so the game continued, Granny and I looked on, waiting to see the next trick up Daddy's sleeve.

"Okay, Annie Lizbeth, correct me if I am wrong, but do you see any gravy crossing into enemy territory?" Daddy asked.

"No, Daddy, I don't see any gravy."

"Well then, that's a good thing, don't you think?" Daddy continued.

"I don't know, what do you mean?" asked Annie Lizbeth, casting a skeptical eye at Daddy.

"Well, Annie Lizbeth. When I think of gravy, I think of it as some kind of glue that holds things together, don't you?"

"I guess so," Annie Lizbeth replied.

"Well then, since Granny did not put any gravy in the casserole, that must mean these layers are nothing more than blankets, one stacked on top of the other. So why don't you and I take this little investigation a step further and dissect this little scoop of casserole layer by layer so that we can report our findings to Mattie Rose and Granny. What do you say?"

Once Annie Lizbeth got grasp of the first clue, her inner detective suddenly emerged, her eyes sparkling at the prospect of having a little mystery to solve on her plate, even if it was in the form of Granny's Poor Man's Casserole.

"Okay!" she replied enthusiastically.

"Well then, let the investigation begins! What do you say if I do the first layer and you take over after that?" Daddy asked.

"Hummm," murmured Annie Lizbeth as she sat contemplating Daddy's proposal. After a minute or so, she looked at Daddy and said, "Okay."

Daddy, using a spatula, slowly and carefully lifted one of the biscuits covered in melted cheddar cheese off the top of the casserole and said, "Now look at that, Annie Lizbeth. This is nothing more than one of your favorite things in the whole wide world, a cheese biscuit. I bet you can eat that can't you?"

"Un hum," Annie Lizbeth replied, looking sideways at Daddy as he put the cheese biscuit on one side of her plate.

"Okay, now it's your turn," Daddy said, looking at some exposed ham peeking up from underneath where the cheese biscuit had been removed. "You like ham, and it's just sitting there all by itself, bothering no one. Why don't you scoop a little bit of that up and put it next to your cheese biscuit." Annie Lizbeth took the spatula and carefully lifted some of the shaved ham off the casserole and put it on her plate.

"You're right, Daddy," Annie Lizbeth exclaimed! "If there's no gravy glue, these are just blankets lying on top of one another, just like in our closet."

"That's right, Annie Lizbeth, and when you need an extra blanket at night, it doesn't stick to the others just because it happens to be laying on top, does it?" Daddy asked.

"No," she replied.

"Well, Annie Lizbeth, since Granny doesn't put gravy in her casseroles, these layers are just resting on top of one another, just like the blankets in your closet."

Annie Lizbeth toyed with the cheese biscuit and ham on her plate while Granny and I looked on, curious as to what Daddy would do next.

"But hold on just a minute, Little Miss Detective. We haven't finished our project. Have you taken a look at what's under that ham?"

"Corn, Daddy…it's yellow corn!" Annie Lizbeth exclaimed with delight.

By now Daddy did not need to encourage Annie Lizbeth to explore the layers of the casserole any further. She eagerly scooped up some of the yellow corn and put it on her plate alongside her cheese biscuit and shaved ham, taking extra care to keep them from touching one another.

Daddy could see the green peas had sunk into the mashed potatoes from the weight of the other layers, and knew better than to press his luck with Annie Lizbeth.

"Well," Daddy announced. "I would say from the looks of things on Annie Lizbeth's plate, this game is over and Annie Lizbeth has solved the mystery of the casserole. Without gravy glue, all those layers are nothing more than a stack of blankets which can be removed one at a time without fear of them sticking together."

Annie Lizbeth, always happy to be the winner of any game, picked up her cheese biscuit and began to gnaw away at it.

The following Friday night, I noticed that the glass Pyrex casserole dish containing one of Granny's Poor Man's casseroles was not sitting on top of the stove, covered in foil.

"Oh well, maybe she stuck it in the oven to keep it away from the prying eyes of Annie Lizbeth," I thought to myself.

As we took our seats around the kitchen table, I also noticed that Granny had replaced our regular oilcloth tablecloth, the one covered in green ivy, with one of her Sunday, hand-pressed, pale blue cotton ones with white lace around the edges.

"Are we having company tonight?" I asked.

"Is your name Sergeant Joe Friday?" Granny asked, looking me straight in the eye.

"No, Ma'am," I replied sheepishly, while Annie Lizbeth let out a giggle.

"Why can't someone do something different around here without going through the third degree? Granny huffed.

"Okay, Mattie Rose. That's enough," Daddy interjected into the conversation. "Maybe Granny needed to wash the other tablecloth and decided to use this one. You know, she's right. If you girls spent as much time listening as you do questioning everything and everybody, you might be surprised at how much you might learn. Now, everyone bow their heads and let's say grace."

"James," Granny interrupted, "tonight I would like to say grace. Do you mind?"

"Well, of course not, Ruby Mae. I'd be honored," Daddy replied, a slight look of surprise on his face. After all, saying grace was a job that had been relegated to him for as long as I could remember.

The last time Daddy asked one of us to say the grace, Annie Lizbeth bowed her head and simply said the word, "Grace." I had put her up to it, but neither Granny nor Daddy was amused. As I recall, we both lost one of our favorite desserts, banana pudding, which was punishment enough, but to make sure we got the point, we spent the afternoon in our rooms writing "I shall not be disrespectful at the table" twenty times. We never repeated the infraction.

Granny lowered her head and began, "Dear Lord, we want to thank you for allowing us the chance to gather around the table once again to share in the fellowship of this meal and one another's company. We want to thank you for the many blessings that you have bestowed upon us as a family. As we share in this special meal tonight, we do so in the spirit of gratitude…gratitude for the job that allows James to put food on our table—food that is meant to sustain and nourish our bodies. We are also grateful for the promotion that James received last week as supervisor of the purchasing department."

"This prayer of thanks and recognition comes a week later, but not a minute too soon as we rejoice in James' accomplishments. May we all be reminded that hard work and a good attitude seldom go unrecognized. In your name we pray, Amen."

When we lifted our heads, I could see that Annie Lizbeth had heard Granny's prayer loud and clear, and I guess that's why Granny wanted to say it. Daddy had received his promotion last Friday, but had put it on the back burner in order to deal with Annie Lizbeth's meltdown over Granny's Poor Man's casserole.

Granny had taken her own suggestion from the week before and converted this week's leftovers in "refrigerator row" into a casserole for the Brickle family that she delivered in person earlier in the afternoon.

"Why Mrs. Childers, what's this?" asked a surprised Thelma Brickle when she answered the door, three young children huddled around her, peeking up occasionally to see who the stranger was at their door.

"Well, my girls know your boys from school and they said you were traveling back and forth to Alamance County to help out your sister with the broken foot. I figured you could use a night off from cooking so I made your family supper tonight," Granny said, taking extra care not to make her visit seem like a charity call.

"Well, that's mighty neighborly of you, Mrs. Childers," a grateful Thelma Brickle replied. I was just sitting here thinking of what to make for supper, and now you have solved my problem.

This will be quite a treat for my family, I assure you. There haven't been many hot meals for my family since I've been gone. If there's ever anything my boys or I can do to return the favor, don't hesitate to ask."

"Well, thank you, Mrs. Brickle. I'll keep that in mind. Now I best be getting back home before my family puts out a missing person's report?" Granny said with a laugh as she turned and started her walk away from the Road to Nowhere, towards the Road to Somewhere that she called home.

Granny got up from the table and walked over to the stove. Much to our surprise, when she opened the oven door she didn't bring out the 13" by 9" glass Pyrex casserole dish, but the big cast-iron skillet she used for frying chicken.

Fried chicken on Friday? No way. Fried Chicken was reserved for Sunday lunch and I knew that was one tradition Granny would break for no one.

When she lifted the heavy, black, cast-iron lid Annie Lizbeth and I opened our mouths in awe. Granny had made a family favorite—chicken-fried steak, a true Southern delicacy of tenderized top-round beef cutlets, battered and deep-fried—to celebrate Daddy's promotion. Most chicken-fried steak is covered with cream gravy, but Granny had made hers separately and put it in a gravy boat.

When she served Annie Lizbeth's plate, she placed in separate corners, a plain, deep-fried, tenderized beef cutlet, a scoop of mashed potatoes, and a biscuit, taking great care to keep them from touching one another. Into a separate little bowl she dished up some pole beans fresh from her garden that had been simmering all afternoon, and placed it beside her plate.

"Annie Lizbeth, do you want some gravy?" Granny asked. "I could put it in its own little bowl if you'd like?"

"Would you please, Granny?" Annie Lizbeth replied, her formerly-hardened tootsie pop eyes now softened with gratitude. "I really love your gravy Granny; I just prefer to use it as a blanket and not as glue."

"I know, Sweetheart, I know," replied Granny, who got up and retrieved a small saucer from the cupboard and handed it to Annie Lizbeth, who promptly filled it with gravy and then dipped each individual bite she took into the thick, creamy-white, peppery sauce.

When Granny served my plate, all you could see was a milky sea of gravy under which chicken-fried steak and mashed potatoes were hidden, like buried treasure. I split my biscuit in half—one for sopping up gravy, and the other for the molasses and butter spread Granny had put on the table as an extra treat.

I learned a lot from my Daddy and the Annie Lizbeth casserole incident. It was with great pride that I read aloud my one-page report the following month to the Food Explorer's Club, recounting the ingenious way Daddy handled the persnickety Annie Lizbeth, and how our family came to understand and respect her food preferences.

Daddy understood Annie Lizbeth's need to deconstruct the casserole, but he also understood the need not to deconstruct Granny's waste not/want not sense of values.

Daddy also understood that differences can be seen as positives, not negatives, and can become a source of richness when one person does not seek to change another. Daddy encouraged our individuality and used it not to separate us, but to help us establish common ground, and by doing so, taught us that the casserole of life was more than the sum of its parts.

GROWING AND BECOMING
Epilogue: 1 April 2004

It was the hardest phone call I ever had to make. My fingers were trembling as I dialed Annie Lizbeth's phone number in Georgia, my chin quivering as I struggled to fight back tears, my mind trying to assemble the right combination of words to deliver what I knew would be devastating news to her.

Bur-ring, bur-ring went her phone.

"Come on, Annie Lizbeth, answer the phone," I pleaded impatiently inside myself as I paced the hardwood floors in my kitchen, taking note of some scratches and marks I had never noticed before.

At fifty-one years of age, Annie Lizbeth and I had long since moved away from the small, white frame house on Peale Road.

Annie Lizbeth now lived in Georgia with her husband of thirty-one years, Sean. She was a professor of psychology at the local university, the mother of two daughters, and the grandmother of four grandchildren. She and Sean had moved from South Carolina to Georgia after he retired from active Navy duty in the early 80s to assume a position as the CFO of a large banking organization. Annie Lizbeth lived an active, happy, and productive life.

I had remained in Durham, where I married Sheldon, my husband of thirty-two years.

We had one son who was busy pursuing a career in sports media. I was educated as a teacher, and later returned to school for a nursing degree. After seventeen years as vice-president of a local manufacturing business,

Sheldon wanted to explore his entrepreneurial side, and so in 1988, we started the first of two businesses—one that we later sold, and one in which we are still actively involved today.

Over the years, the home place on Peale Road had some minor improvements made, but basically remained the same. After we left for college, married, and started families of our own, Daddy and Granny continued to live there until Granny passed away from cancer in 1982 at the age of 78.

When Granny was diagnosed, Daddy tended to her with the same compassion and devotion with which she had tended to all of us during her lifetime. Granny lived one year after her diagnosis and, as difficult as it was to see her slowly decline, we cherished every second with her. When she died, we did not mourn her death, we celebrated a life well-lived.

After Granny passed, Annie Lizbeth and I begged Daddy to split his time between Georgia and North Carolina, but he would not hear of it. The house on Peale Road had been his home for almost fifty years, and it was Granny's express wish that it remain his home for as long as he chose to live there. Daddy's independence was important to him, and his happiness was important to us, so we respected his wishes to remain there.

I was lost in my memories about our house on Peale Road when someone picked up the phone. It was then I heard the sweet and familiar voice of Annie Lizbeth say, "Hello?"

I took a deep breath and said as calmly as I could, "Annie Lizbeth, this is Mattie Rose."

Annie Lizbeth could sense something was amiss by my somber tone.

"What's wrong Mattie Rose, are you okay?"

"I'm fine," I responded, "but Annie Lizbeth, I want you to sit down because I have something I need to tell you."

"Mattie Rose, you're scaring me. What's wrong? Has something happened?"

"Yes," I replied. "Something has happened...to Daddy."

I could hear Annie's breath quicken as she said anxiously, "What's happened to Daddy?"

Annie Lizbeth had always been a give-it-to-me straight kind of person, so I gathered up the last ounce of courage I could muster up and said, "Annie Lizbeth, Daddy passed away in his sleep last night."

At first, I heard her gasp in disbelief, and then there was complete and utter silence on the other end of the phone.

"Annie Lizbeth, are you still there?" I asked nervously, my temporary sense of composure starting to crumble.

Annie Lizbeth simply started to sob. She did not wail, she did not scream, she just sat on the other end of the phone sobbing as if her heart had shattered into a million pieces.

When she finally came up for a breath, her first question to me was, "Mattie, what happened? I just spoke to Daddy the other day, and he sounded fine. He said he was a little tired, but I didn't think much of it. Mattie, what happened to him?" I could hear the mounting tension in her voice, so I regained my composure and spoke in short, brief sentences to conceal my own devastation.

"Annie, all I know is that I was supposed to pick him up for a doctor's appointment this morning, and when I knocked on the door, he didn't answer. Sheldon and I were exchanging house and car keys over the weekend, and I accidentally put Daddy's house key on Sheldon's key ring so I couldn't get into the house. I went around to all the windows knocking as hard as I could, but there was still no answer. I called Sheldon who called 911.

"When the paramedics and firemen arrived, they had to break into the house, and that's when they found him lying in that old double bed. Annie, when I saw him he looked as if he were sleeping, at total peace with the world. It was just like something Daddy would do—make an exit without making a fuss.

"The doctors that examined him at the hospital said as best as they could determine, Daddy's heart just gave out. He's gone, Annie Lizbeth. Daddy's gone." I could no longer hold back the grief that engulfed me, and so the dam of tears that had welled in my eyes broke free and cascaded down my face.

"Mattie Rose," Annie Lizbeth suddenly said, "Sean and I are catching the first flight up tomorrow to help you with the funeral arrangements. Do you think you can hold on until I get there?"

"Yes," I replied, "but please hurry."

"Oh, Annie Lizbeth," I sobbed. "Now that Daddy and Granny are gone, we're all we have."

"No, we're not," she replied, choking back more tears of her own.

"Mattie Rose, don't you remember what Granny said right before she died?"

My mind drew a blank, but Annie Lizbeth quickly filled in the picture.

"Granny said that every time God calls one of his children to heaven, he puts another star in the sky so that it can shine down and light the way for those they loved and left behind. We have two stars, Mattie Rose; Daddy and Granny, and I can guarantee they will be the brightest stars in the universe and they will forever light our way."

I found Annie Lizbeth's words to be of great comfort, and I thought of them that night when I walked out on our front porch and looked up at the sky. I looked for the brightest stars I could find, and when I located them, I knew Annie Lizbeth was right. Granny and Daddy were shining down on us, and I knew their light would shine eternally in our hearts and sustain us until it came our time to join them.

Annie Lizbeth and I buried Daddy right beside Granny, which is where he wanted to be. The outpouring of love and affection for Daddy was overwhelming.

Patti Summerhill's family moved back to California when we entered tenth grade, but she and I remained lifelong friends. Patti, always plucky and spunky, became one of the leading female entrepreneurs in San Francisco, but the minute I called and told her of Daddy's passing, she caught the next flight out to attend Daddy's funeral and lend support to Annie Lizbeth and me.

Cookie Ketchum now lived in Charlotte. Her desire to befriend those in need took on new meaning when she became a special needs teacher. She, too, drove up to attend Daddy's funeral. It had been a while since I had seen Cookie, but after Daddy's graveside services were over, she walked over to

Granny's grave and placed two yellow roses on it before walking over to us to convey her condolences.

"Annie Lizbeth and Mattie Rose, I want you to know your Granny will forever hold a special place in my heart. She was never too busy for me, she encouraged me, she nurtured me, and I will never forget her. I am deeply sorry over the loss of your father. He, too, was a special man. You were fortunate to have both of them in your lives," she concluded as a tear rolled down her cheek before she turned and walked away.

Bessie Mae Carson remained in Durham and married a successful business executive. The minute she heard that Daddy had passed, she stepped in and handled all the minute details that seemed overwhelming to Annie Lizbeth and me. It seemed as if all the "social graces" her grandmother had instilled in her had not gone to waste.

Annie Lizbeth and I received visitors at the house on Peale Road. Bessie Mae took complete charge of food and flower offerings, greeted guests, and made sure our time was spent visiting and reminiscing with those whose lives Daddy had touched. Our front door was a non-stop turnstile as folks came to pay their final respects to Daddy, a man respected, loved, and admired by many.

While going through his things several days after the funeral, Annie and I came upon an old jewelry box he had stashed away on the top shelf of his closet. It was dusty, and it was obvious that it had not been opened for years.

Inside the red velvet-lined box we found a handwritten letter from Daddy stating that it was his expressed desire that his life insurance policy, the deed to the house and the remainder of his estate were to be divided equally between his two beloved daughters. We found faded black and white school pictures taken of us through the years. Daddy had marked the dates in pencil on the back of each picture.

And then we found a woman's plain gold wedding ring. It was the ring Elizabeth Rose left on the nightstand beside the bed they shared as she went looking for greener pastures with a truck driver from Arkansas.

Elizabeth Rose Childers Radley broke our daddy's heart, but not his will to do right by his children. At nineteen years of age, with two infant daughters to rear, Daddy could not afford to look back; he could only look forward, taking life one day at a time. With Granny by his side, they forged a family whose bonds would stand the test of time, even after they were gone.

Annie Lizbeth and I share a deep sisterly love that exists to this very day. Though separated by miles, we are forever bonded by the rich tapestry on which our lives were molded. No longer do we run through the woods, fearful of something chasing us. We now stand in the clearing, knowing the light of Daddy and Granny is shining down on us, showing us the way.

The rich emotional legacy left by Daddy and Granny fortified Annie Lizbeth and me to weather life's storms with courage, humility, humor, and grace. And in their memory, it is our hope that we will pass those qualities on to our children, and they to theirs, for future generations to come.

ABOUT THE STORYTELLER

Lynda Schultz was born and raised in Durham, North Carolina.

Educated as a teacher, she later attended nursing school where she obtained her BSN.

During the 80s, Lynda attended culinary school and took her passion for food and cooking to a new level; she opened her own successful catering business.

She later teamed up with her husband, and together they ran one of the top producing franchise offices in the temporary staffing industry.

In 1994, she and her husband designed and implemented a new business model for corporate training. Their model is a stand-alone in the industry today. They have been featured in numerous newspaper articles and business magazines, including *Fortune Small Business*.

Lynda is a true entrepreneur and Southern lady. Her stories reflect her love of the South, family, and the ties that bind them together.

Lynda has entertained people with her unique style of storytelling for years.

Lynda has one son, and she and her husband reside in Chapel Hill, North Carolina.